Praise for Dena

The Probability of...

"So much fun!...What a great emotional ... and purely amazing connection between two fantastic women. If you've read other books of Dena's there are a few lovely surprises throughout this great story too, which were an absolute treat and made me smile!"—*LESBIreviewed*

Love by Proxy

"Brilliantly funny and sweet!...This was such an amazing story! Gripping, exciting, full of twists and turns, unexpected events, and most importantly a little touch of comedy. It really was the perfect rom-com. Packed with drama and lots of conflict, nothing was more exhilarating than being on this roller coaster of emotions with Tess and Sophie."—*LESBIreviewed*

Next Exit Home

"I enjoy Dena Blake's writing, and I enjoyed this book a lot...I especially liked this book because the two single mums who have become mums for very different reasons/experiences are strong women. Proving they are super capable to solo parent and raise rockstar kids. There is something very sexy about a single mum grabbing parenthood by the horns and making it work. I really enjoyed that aspect!...Great small-town romance that packs a punch in the enemies to lovers trope! I'll definitely be rereading this one again soon."—*Les Rêveur*

Kiss Me Every Day

"This book was SUCH a fun read!!...This was such a fun, interesting book to read and I thoroughly enjoyed it; the characters were super easy to like, the romance was super cute and I loved seeing each little thing that Wynn changed every day!"—*Sasha & Amber Read*

"Such a fun and an exciting book filled with so much love! This book is just packed with fun and memorable moments I was thinking about for days after reading it. This is one hundred per cent my new favourite Dena Blake book. The pace of the book was excellent, and I felt I was along for the fantastic ride."—*Les Rêveur*

"The sweetest moment in the book is when the titular phrase is uttered...This well written book is an interesting read because of the

whole premise of getting repeated opportunities to right wrongs."—
Best Lesfic Reviews

"Wynn's journey of self-discovery is wonderful to witness. She develops compassion, love and finds happiness. Her character development is phenomenal...If you're looking for a stunning romance book with a female/female romance, then this is definitely the one for you. I highly recommend."—*Literatureaesthetic*

Perfect Timing

"The chemistry between Lynn and Maggie is fantastic...the writing is totally engrossing."—*Best Lesfic Reviews*

"This book is the kind of book you sit down to on a Sunday morning with a cup of tea and the sun shining in your bedroom only to realise at 5 pm you've not left your bed because it was too good to stop reading."
—*Les Rêveur*

"The relationship between Lynn and Maggie developed at an organic pace. I loved all the flirting going on between Maggie and Lynn. I love a good flirty conversation!...I haven't read this author before but I look forward to trying more of her titles."—*Marcia Hull, Librarian (Ponca City Library, Oklahoma)*

Racing Hearts

"I particularly liked Drew with her sexy rough exterior and soft heart... Sex scenes are definitely getting hotter and I think this might be the hottest by Dena Blake to date."—*Les Rêveur*

Just One Moment

"One of the things I liked is that the story is set after the glorious days of falling in love, after the time when everything is exciting. It shows how sometimes, trying to make life better really makes it more complicated...It's also, and mainly, a reminder of how important communication is between partners, and that as solid as trust seems between two lovers, misunderstandings happen very easily."—*Jude in the Stars*

"Blake does angst particularly well and she's wrung every possible ounce out of this one...I found myself getting sucked right into the story—I do love a good bit of angst and enjoy the copious amounts of drama on occasion."—*C-Spot Reviews*

Friends Without Benefits

"This is the book when the Friends to Lovers trope doesn't work out. When you tell your best friend you are in love with her and she doesn't return your feelings. This book is real life and I think I loved it more for that."—*Les Rêveur*

A Country Girl's Heart

"Literally couldn't put this book down, and can't give enough praise for how good this was!!! One of my favourite reads, and I highly recommend to anyone who loves a fantastically clever, intriguing, and exciting romance."—*LESBIreviewed*

Unchained Memories

"There is a lot of angst and the book covers some difficult topics but it does that well. The writing is gripping and the plot flows."—*Melina Bickard, Librarian, Waterloo Library (UK)*

"This story had me cycling between lovely romantic scenes to white-knuckle gripping, on the edge of the seat (or in my case, the bed) scenarios. This story had me rooting for a sequel and I can certainly place my stamp of approval on this novel as a must read book." —*Lesbian Review*

"The pace and character development was perfect for such an involved story line, I couldn't help but turn each page. This book has so many wonderful plot twists that you will be in suspense with every chapter that follows."—*Les Rêveur*

Where the Light Glows

"From first-time author Dena Blake, *Where the Light Glows* is a sure winner."—*A Bookworm's Loft*

"[T]he vivid descriptions of the Pacific Northwest will make readers hungry for food and travel. The chemistry between Mel and Izzy is palpable."—*RT Book Reviews*

"I'm still shocked this was Dena Blake's first novel…It was fantastic… It was written extremely well and more than once I wondered if this was a true account of someone close to the author because it was really raw and realistic. It seemed to flow very naturally and I am truly surprised that this is the author's first novel as it reads like a seasoned writer." —*Les Rêveur*

By the Author

Where the Light Glows

Unchained Memories

A Country Girl's Heart

Racing Hearts

Friends Without Benefits

Just One Moment

Perfect Timing

Kiss Me Every Day

Next Exit Home

Love By Proxy

The Probability of Love

A Spark In the Air

Visit us at www.boldstrokesbooks.com

A Spark
in the Air

by

Dena Blake

2022

A SPARK IN THE AIR

© 2022 By Dena Blake. All Rights Reserved.

ISBN 13: 978-1-63679-293-4

This Trade Paperback Original Is Published By
Bold Strokes Books, Inc.
P.O. Box 249
Valley Falls, NY 12185

First Edition: December 2022

CREDITS
Editor: Shelley Thrasher
Production Design: Stacia Seaman
Cover Design by Jeanine Henning

Acknowledgments

I've loved the holiday season since I was a child. It's a magical time that brings my family together to eat, drink, and reminisce. From the first moment the air becomes crisp, I'm in heaven. Once Thanksgiving slides into Christmas I'm in holiday mode for the duration. Spending time during the season in a quaint Vermont town is the perfect way to enjoy the magic. After reading this book, I hope you agree.

All you readers out there, I know your schedules are busier than ever these days. Thank you for making time to read and write reviews. I appreciate you all very much. Your positive feedback keeps me writing.

Rad and Sandy—there's no one I trust my work with more than Bold Strokes Books. The support and care provided by the production crew is stellar, from when my first word hits the page until the book is released in print. Thanks to Shelley Thrasher, my editor extraordinaire, for being patient and persistent in teaching me how to be a better writer.

Kate, Wes, and Haley, you'll never know just how much I appreciate you. When I'm down you always bring me up. For a writer, that's so important—for a partner and mom it's an absolute necessity. You'll always be my base camp.

For the holiday lovers.

Chapter One

Crystal glanced at her boss's assistant as she went to the door. "He's expecting me." She straightened her navy suit jacket and smoothed the matching skirt before she tugged open the door and entered the room. The executive suite was lined with floor-to-ceiling windows looking out onto the Dallas skyline. She planned to have this view someday.

Her boss stood, the salt in his hair glistening in the sun, and held his fingers up, leaving a one-inch gap between his forefinger and thumb. "I'm this close to getting the Pine Grove town council on board with the new tower."

"That's great. Congratulations." Nothing like bulldozing hundred-year-old trees in Vermont to put up a cell-phone tower to ring in the new year, Crystal thought.

"We have just a couple of holdouts." He squinted, making the lines fanning out to his temples appear more distinct. The man spent entirely too much time in the sun. "Neither the head of the town council, who runs a bakery in town, nor the ridiculously old-school owner of a small internet café wants to bring the town into the twenty-first century."

"Well, I'm sure you can change their minds."

"Not me." His voice rose. He was about to give marching orders. "I need someone I can depend on to go, and that person's you."

"Seriously?" A shiver of confidence filled Crystal until she realized what her boss wanted her to do. This assignment was going to ruin all of her holiday plans. "I was looking forward to the sunshine in the tropics." She'd planned to spend the days leading up to Christmas on the beach in St. Croix, and Christmas Day at her parents' home in California after that. Not in some cold winter town battling the local government.

"You can get plenty of sunshine on the ski slopes." He raised an eyebrow as much as anyone who received regular Botox injections could. "Maybe I should send Jack Ramsey instead."

"Absolutely not." She refused to give up one more thing to that vulture, even if it meant cold hands and feet for the next week or two.

"Good, because this assignment could lock in that director's seat you've been wanting. You do ski, don't you?" He acted like the sport was a natural part of everyone's education.

"Yes." She hadn't skied in years, but she would figure it out if she needed to hit the slopes. It would come back to her just like riding a bike, wouldn't it?

"Great." He smiled widely. "You leave in the morning. I'll check in with you midweek."

"Okay." That didn't give her much time to clear her desk before going home to pack. Her heart raced as all the things she needed to do today whirled in her head. She turned and walked out of his office and down the hallway to her own. She'd just sat down at her desk when Marie appeared in the doorway. Crystal glanced up to see her smiling face, which would change as soon as Crystal told her the news. "I have to go to Vermont this week."

"When will you be back?" Marie closed the door before she crossed the room, her dark, curly hair bouncing as she moved. She didn't seem upset—yet.

"A week, maybe ten days." Crystal hoped it didn't take that long, but this town had been a challenge since the company had first set out to bring it in.

"What? Why?" Marie bolted closer to her desk. The stack of files she'd been carrying thudded when she dropped them onto the desk. "We're supposed to go to St. Croix next week...and you're supposed to meet my family this weekend."

This was going to be harder than she'd expected. "I have to convince the planning commission to let us put up a tower." Not on her list of fun things to do, but she would close the deal—just like she was going to close this one between her and Marie. Crystal hadn't planned it, but this was the perfect opportunity to cool whatever had been developing between them. The strings were getting denser by the day.

"Can't you just tell him no? For once?" Marie's lips flattened the way they always did when she didn't agree with Crystal's choices. "He's going to shut down whatever internet business is already in town and ruin the holidays for the whole town. Can't that at least wait until after Christmas?"

"Apparently not." Crystal didn't like Marie's insinuation. Crystal didn't always say yes to her boss. She could give the two holdouts her pitch and then fly home and still meet Marie's family, but she wasn't looking forward to that either. Meeting family meant commitment, and she wasn't sure what that meant or whether she wanted that with Marie. She was *absolutely* saying no to that. This hadn't been the smoothest relationship.

Marie held up her hands. "Give them your pitch, and fly back before Friday. Then everything will work out, and we can go ahead with our plans."

"I'm sorry. I can't go. You'll have to take your sister or someone else on the trip." She rifled through the files Marie had dropped on her desk, plucked a few from the stack, and tossed them into her black leather Kate Spade tote. "This is an opportunity to create a whole new hub of wireless services. I can't let an opportunity like this go to Jack."

"Sounds more like you *won't* go." Marie planted a hand on her hip, tilted her head, and pressed her lips together. "You know what? I'm kind of tired of not being a priority in your life." She spun, headed to the door, and glanced over her shoulder as she gripped the doorknob. "I think I *will* take someone else. Whatever we're doing here"—she circled her finger in the air—"isn't working for me. We're done." She pulled open the door. "Merry fucking Christmas, Crystal. I hope you freeze your ass off in Vermont." The bookshelf on the wall rattled when she yanked the door closed.

Crystal flopped back in her chair and let out a sigh. Marie's threat didn't faze her in the slightest. Maybe that was a sign that moving on was best for both of them. She hadn't expected anything serious to come out of her relationship with Marie. Sure, she was fun and great company, but at this point in her career, she didn't have time to worry about someone else's feelings all the time. That just meant more disappointment and pressure when she forgot a special occasion or canceled an event, which was evident by the current situation and seemed to be happening more and more since she'd started seeing Marie.

Chapter Two

Janie picked up the receiver and punched in the number for Cyber Shack. "Hey. I'm running late. Can you fire up the coffeepots in case I don't get there before we open?" Janie had planned to get to the café early, as she did every Wednesday, but that didn't seem to be in the cards this morning. The lukewarm shower her water heater had delivered had not only startled her out of her skin but had also thrown her schedule off. Even the extra body fat she'd accumulated over the year hadn't helped reduce the frigid shock. So far, the second half of her week wasn't all smooth sailing, as it usually was.

"Making it now." Beka to the rescue again. "How's tomato soup sound for the seniors today?"

"Sounds great to me. I love it." Janie took her down jacket from the coat rack by the door and slipped it over her arms as she held the phone between her ear and shoulder.

"You're a lifesaver, Bek." Rebekah Smiley, Beka for short, was Janie's cook at the café. More importantly, Beka was Janie's best friend and was always helping her out with something either at work or at home.

"What would you do without me?"

"I'd never survive." Janie switched ears as she slid her other arm into the jacket. "Do you think Ben can come by the house later and take a look at my water heater?" She shivered as she remembered the shock of the ice-cold water as she'd stepped into the shower.

"I'll check, but I'm sure he can."

"Great. Tell him the key's under the same rock in front. I have to drive by and pick up Grandpa really quick, but that shouldn't take long."

"Sue called." Something clanged in the background. "The bakery is slammed and they're shorthanded this morning, so you'll need to run by there and pick up the pastries."

Janie sighed. *What more can happen today?* "Okay. I'll be there as soon as I can." Janie dropped the receiver into the cradle hanging on the wall, locked the door as she left, and checked to make sure the spare key was still under the rock. The holiday season was always busy, with droves of visitors coming to Vermont to spend their obligatory time in the perfect winter setting. She shouldn't complain. The additional town traffic always gave her business a boost.

She drove the five miles outside of town and up the dirt road to her grandfather's place. It wasn't much of a house, more like a one-room cabin. Life would be so much easier if he'd just move into the retirement community with her grandmother. He spent most of his time there anyway after she'd relocated to be closer to her circle of friends.

He was standing out front waiting for her, as usual. Grandpa was about six feet tall and slim. The man was still strong and youthful due to his active schedule. His short white hair glistened in the sun as he stood majestically in front of the cabin.

He pulled open the car door. "Give me a lift to see your grandma, will you?"

"Absolutely." She waited for him to get buckled in and put the Jeep in gear. "What's on your agenda today?"

"Poker with the boys at the PGR." Janie didn't know if he always referred to Pine Grove Retirement Community as the PGR because it was easier to remember or if he just didn't like the name. They should really change it to something more youthful, like Eagle Mountain or Moonlight Pines. When her grandmother had chosen to live there last spring and he remained at the cabin, it was clear he didn't like the idea of retirement.

"Why don't you just move in there with Grandma?"

"There's too much noise. I need my own space." He grabbed the oh-shit handle as she took a quick curve. "Need my own tools." Grandpa used to build furniture, beautiful furniture. Now he mostly whittled and made small decorative tabletop pieces for special orders he received.

"They have separate cabins there. You and Grandma could get one of those and set up your shop in the garage. Then you could have your tools and a space to work and be within walking distance of the main house to play poker."

"What's the matter?" He reared back in his seat and glared at her. "You don't like picking me up?"

"No, Grandpa. That's not it at all. I love spending time with you. I just think it would be easier on you and Grandma if you were there together."

"Hmph." He crossed his arms and stared out the window. "I'll think about it." He gave her the same answer as he always did. He'd been thinking about it for the better part of the year.

She pulled in front of the Pine Grove Retirement Community and put the Jeep in park. "Are you okay from here?"

The crease between his eyebrows deepened. "Of course. What do you think I am? Some old man like George Mooney?"

"God, no. You're so much younger than him." At seventy-five, George was only two years older than her grandfather, but he showed his age much more. Her grandfather didn't like to be put into the same demographic as anyone who appeared old.

She hit the bakery next to pick up the usual order for the café. Beka was an awesome cook, but she didn't do baked goods. Didn't have time for baking, really. She pulled into a space in front. Sue's place seemed extra busy today, probably because Janie was running late. She rushed inside.

Sue waved her over to the end of the bakery case. "Here you go." She handed her the box of pastries and then swept her dark hair out of her face with the side of her hand. "I'll bring more over later once the rush lulls. We need to catch up on a few things." That meant Sue had something to tell her. She was married to Mason, the head of the town council, also the baker of the establishment.

"Okay. I'll be there all day."

"Get those Christmas lights up." Mason's voice grew loud as he carried a tray of pastries through the swinging door from the kitchen.

"Working on it tomorrow." Janie took the box and hurried out the door to her Jeep. She was almost home free when she heard Ann's voice behind her.

"I'm headed over to your place to pick up some movies for the week. You mind giving me a lift?"

"Not at all. Climb in."

Ann owned the Vintage Mall at the end of Main Street. She'd had to fight for the space since it wasn't the sort associated with the small-town feel the council wanted. She'd taken it over not long after the cornerstone retail store had closed. The prime real estate was larger than any other business wanted to tackle, so Ann promised the council to keep it uncluttered and decorated with the hometown feel the same as the other businesses in town did. Ann had kept her word and had grown the Vintage Mall into a successful business over the years. She didn't take people's trash either, accepting only certain types of merchandise and in good condition. People tended to change out furniture and clothing more often nowadays than in the past.

Ann grabbed hold of the handle on the front of the doorjamb and heaved herself into the passenger seat. "Your brother sure is nice to let you use his Jeep."

"It's mine now. He bought a new one."

"Oh yeah? Which one?"

"The fancy one with the truck bed." Her brother liked shiny and new. Janie, on the other hand, just needed wheels to get her from place to place.

"For hauling firewood?"

"I doubt it. He uses the big truck and trailer for that."

"Oh, right." Ann grinned. "Probably bought it to impress the girls. It doesn't take much around here."

Janie pulled into one of the parking spaces near Cyber Shack and killed the engine. "Who knows? He gave me a great deal on this one, so I'm happy."

"Good for you." Ann climbed out of the Jeep and headed into the café while Janie retrieved the baked goods from the back.

Once inside, Janie shed her jacket immediately, then took the pastries out of the box and arranged them on the rectangular covered dish on the food counter before she crossed the room to check the various cyber areas of the café to make sure all the computers were booted up and running. She wiggled mice and tapped keyboards to bring them to life.

Ann was standing in the small alcove where Janie kept a selection of new and popular DVDs. Demand for them had lessened since purchase prices had dropped, but she still kept a few for people like Ann who didn't want to buy something she'd watch only once.

"Did you hear the news?" Ann dropped a few DVD cases onto the counter.

"News about what?" Janie didn't have to pry information out of Ann, but she did have to fish a bit.

"They're sending someone out to talk to the council about wireless again." She peeled a ten from a wad of bills and set it on the counter. "Mason told me."

"I hadn't heard that." Janie feared the rumors might be true this time. Since she'd been ignoring all communications from Spark Wireless Broadband, she'd suspected they'd be sending someone soon to convince the town council to bring in wireless broadband internet. The gentle nudge the town had received was soon going to turn into a shove. She put the DVDs into a bag and pushed it across the counter. "You want those for a week?"

Ann shook her head. "Probably just a few days. Business is slow, tourists are spending more time doing the outdoorsy stuff, but I expect it to pick up since next week's storm was forecasted. The cold will bring them inside." She slid the bag from the counter. "Sure would be nice to have internet at home if we get snowed in." Ann had always been on the fence during talks of broadband internet. She seemed to have toppled off to one side now.

"Let's hope the snow isn't that bad." Janie put the ten in the register, counted out the change, and handed it to Ann.

"I'm always hoping." Ann gave her a backhanded wave as she left the cyber café.

Janie had been instrumental in leading the PR campaign against the project the last time an attempt was made, while local politicians sought to minimize the city's involvement in the project. She wasn't at all sure they would be successful in preventing it this time—wasn't at all sure she wanted them to be.

Chapter Three

S ir." Crystal waved her hand in the air at the baggage attendant. "Sir. My bag didn't come through the return." She glanced around the tiny terminal. Not what she was expecting at all. Aside from the seven other people on the plane, the place was practically deserted.

"Give me a minute." He walked through a door.

She rubbed the back of her neck. The flights had been long, and the last one had been bumpy. She just wanted to get into a nice hot bath and soak for an hour.

The man returned from the back. "That's all the bags. You'll have to fill out a form, and we'll get yours to you as soon as it arrives." He led her to a counter, reached behind it, and took out a form.

"Do you have a pen?" She was in no mood for this. She should've taken the bus instead of the little puddle-jumper airplane. That way, she'd have her bag, and her stomach wouldn't be in her throat right now.

He went behind the counter, found one, and handed it to her.

"Does this place have a cab stand? I need transportation to Pine Grove." She filled out the details of her luggage, along with her name and cell number, and handed him the completed form.

"Not too many cabs this way. Best bet is to call an Uber or Lyft." He pointed to the sign on the wall displaying both numbers that hung above a ridiculously old-fashioned phone.

"Great." She took out her phone and opened the Uber app to

put in the request. She'd had to take the smallest plane to get here from Boston, and now she was going to have to ride in an Uber to the bed and breakfast in whatever car arrived.

"That cell phone isn't going to work here." The baggage attendant picked up the phone behind the counter and punched in a number. "Got a fare for you." He dropped the receiver into the cradle. "He'll be here soon." He scrutinized the form. "Where are you staying?" He clicked the ballpoint of the pen in and out rapidly.

She froze, unsure whether to divulge that information to a stranger.

"So I can deliver your bag when it arrives." He held the form up in front of her. "You left that part blank."

"Oh. I'm staying at the Pine Grove Inn." She'd forgotten that her cell number wouldn't be reachable there either. She spotted a soda machine near the exit; a soda would help settle her stomach. She fished a few dollars out of her purse and fed them into the machine. She had to hit three different buttons for drinks she wasn't familiar with before a can clattered to the bottom of the machine. She plucked it from the basin, opened it, and took a swig. Thankfully it was rather plain except for a slight taste of something sweet that she didn't recognize. She looked at the label, maple seltzer, then took another swig. Yep. Definitely maple.

The Uber arrived, and she headed out the sliding doors to it. She glanced through the window at the driver then back inside the terminal. "You again?" It was the same guy who'd taken her lost-luggage information, only now wearing a jacket and skullcap.

"Not me, my brother." The baggage attendant appeared quickly and opened the door for her.

The driver got out of the car. "No food or drink in the car."

"I either bring the drink or throw up in your back seat." She wasn't kidding either. Her stomach was still roiling.

"You might give her a break. Pilot forgot her bag too."

"Fine." He slid back into the driver's seat. "But if you spill, you pay extra."

"Got it." She slid into the car and chugged a drink of soda.

"Where to?"

"Pine Grove Inn." The last part of her sentence was accompanied with a loud burp, and she covered her mouth. "Excuse me."

"Stomach better?"

"Much. Flight felt like a roller coaster."

"They can be pretty turbulent. I usually take the bus." He fastened his seat belt.

"Good choice." If she couldn't get a car to drive this far to pick her up, she would definitely take it on the way out of town next week.

He put the car into gear. "They have a nice restaurant at the inn. Been there a few times for brunch." He glanced at her through the rearview mirror. "Also have a nice shop. You'll probably want to pick up some warmer clothes. It's supposed to snow later this week. We should have a white Christmas."

She glanced out the window. Quite a bit of snow covered the ground outside of the road. "Hopefully they'll find my bag soon." Not that she'd packed anything for heavy snow and had only her essentials along with a change of undergarments in her shoulder bag. She'd traveled enough to know to bring spares. "I won't be here that long anyway." She hoped to wrap her business up in a couple of days and then travel to someplace warm for Christmas.

"That's too bad. Pine Grove has lots of holiday events happening this time of year."

The drive was short, only about fifteen minutes. The inn looked majestic from the front as they came closer—much larger than Crystal had expected. She wondered what kind of amenities it had. The online rating had been good, but she didn't want to set her expectations too high. A big bathtub and hot water would work for her right now.

"Here we are." The driver looked over his shoulder. "Just let Dana know when you need a ride to the airport, and I'll come get you."

"Thanks." Crystal handed him a twenty and got out of the car. She slung her smaller bag over her shoulder and carried her purse in her hand as she entered the inn. The lobby was absolutely inviting, with columns and a staircase decorated in evergreen garland and bows, and a large, decorated Christmas tree placed strategically in the corner for guests to view as they arrived. Much more than she'd expected.

The lobby was empty except for the woman at the reception desk, but she could hear people from the restaurant that branched out from it.

"Welcome to Pine Grove Inn." The woman smiled cheerfully. "Checking in?" She flipped her shoulder-length, salt-and-pepper hair from her face.

"Yes. I have a reservation under Crystal Tucker."

The woman tapped at the keyboard furiously. "I have it right here. I'll need to see your driver's license and a credit card, please."

Crystal retrieved them from her wallet and slid them across the counter.

The woman clicked a few buttons on her keyboard and slid the card into the slot in the reader. "It will just be a minute until the approval comes back."

Since it was taking so long, Crystal assumed the woman was using a dial-up connection for the approval. The perfect opportunity to get a bit of PR in. "If you wouldn't mind writing down the Wi-Fi password for me, I'd appreciate it. I have some work to do this evening."

"Sorry. We don't have Wi-Fi. I wish we did. You can plug into the landline hub on the desk. Do you need a cable for that?"

"Yes. I guess I do." She wondered how many of those she handed out regularly. "Is there a coffee shop somewhere that has it?"

"You're not going to find Wi-Fi anywhere in town. The council's dead set against it." The woman reached under the counter, retrieved a blue Ethernet cable, and slid it across the counter.

"Why is that?"

"For some ridiculous reason they think it's going to spoil the hometown feel of the area." She pointed to the cable. "Don't worry about bringing that back. You can leave it in your room when your stay is over."

Seemed this woman could be an advocate for her. Crystal

leaned on the counter and lowered her voice. "What if I told you I'm here to try to change that?"

The clerk immediately glanced up from her small computer screen. "I'd say that's awesome."

"I work for Spark Wireless Broadband, and I'm hoping to show the town council the benefits of wireless technology." She glanced around the lobby. "It would increase your business, wouldn't it?"

"Absolutely. The inn located in the next town over has Wi-Fi, and they're booked solid all the time."

At least Crystal had one ally. "So, who do you think is the biggest roadblock?"

"Oh, that would definitely be Mason Smiley, the head of the town council. He and his wife, Sue, own Sue's Sweets." Her forehead crinkled. "Janie Elliott could be an obstacle too. Her family owns Cyber Shack, the only cyber café in town. She has a lot of influence with Mason. He's been a friend of her brother's since they were kids. They're pretty close. I think they might have had a thing once before Sue came along. I've known Janie since high school, but we don't see eye to eye on everything."

This woman was a fountain of information that was flowing rapidly. Crystal held out her hand. "It's nice to meet you…"

"Dana—Dana Banks." Dana shook her hand. "It's nice to meet you too." She released her grip and then slid a plastic keycard across the counter. "Room two-sixteen. It's a corner suite with a great view of Main Street. It's beautiful all decorated for the holidays."

"As long as it has a bathtub, I'll be happy." She took the key and slid it into her pocket. How could a town be so advanced in some ways and so backward in others?

"Yep. A big soaker tub."

"Great. Thank you so much."

She'd just left the desk and was headed to her room when the front door flew open and a woman rushed through it. She wore jeans, boots, and a navy puffer jacket. Her dirty-blond hair bounced on her shoulders as she moved across the floor and halted at the desk.

Crystal couldn't help but stop to see what was so urgent. She moved away from the stairway and stood behind a thick wooden column in the lobby.

"They're sending another person out to try to sell the town council on internet. Has anyone new checked in?" The ball on the woman's yellow knit cap bounced as she spoke.

"Well…" Dana looked over the woman's shoulder at Crystal for direction. Crystal shook her head, indicating for her not to say anything. "I haven't seen anyone yet." Dana stared back at the woman without giving her a clue.

"Let me know if you hear anything." The woman patted the counter with her hand and took off out the door.

Phew. That would buy her some time. She was unsure if Dana would keep her secret. Crystal raced to the counter.

"That was Janie," Dana said before Crystal could ask.

"Thanks for keeping my secret. I'd like to keep my project quiet for now. At least until I get the lay of the land." Crystal hadn't expected Janie to be so young. What person in their thirties didn't see the benefits of wireless? What person that age didn't own a cell phone?

"Sure. Let me know if you need any help."

"Will do." She turned and headed up the staircase to the second floor. She hoped she could make it to her room before anyone else appeared in the lobby. She was more than ready for that bath.

Chapter Four

Janie glanced over her shoulder as she left the inn. Dana was certainly acting funny today. Maybe she was having second thoughts about allowing Wi-Fi in town. Janie had weighed the pros and cons many times herself, and it was always a close finish. The pros usually outweighed the cons, but Cyber Shack was doing well, and she wasn't ready to upset the tranquility of the town just to satisfy her own needs. She had customers who had been around since her grandfather owned the business. She couldn't just randomly take away their place to socialize and thrive without being afraid they'd lose their online privacy. Could she? It sure would be nice to have wireless access throughout town, though. She'd have to set up a whole new set of internet safety classes for the seniors. She headed up the street and stepped into Rod's Liquor Barrel.

"How's Miss Janie today?" Rod smiled, and his red cheeks shone. He was an avid skier and never used as much sunblock as he should.

"I'm good, Rod. How are you?"

"Not so bad, myself." He rounded the counter. "You here to pick up your grandpa's bottle?" Janie's grandpa had a standing order for a pint of rye whiskey.

"Sure." She wasn't, but she might as well get it now.

He turned around and took the small bottle of Woodford Reserve from the shelf that contained all the smaller bottles of liquor. Rod kept it in stock just for Grandpa, but anyone who had a sip of it with Grandpa seemed to take a liking to it. The flavor was a bit strong for

Janie, so she usually stuck to beer unless she was drinking eggnog or a hot toddy.

"You going to the marshmallow roast Saturday night?"

"Wouldn't miss it." She reached into her pocket for some cash and handed Rod a twenty. "They're still having it, right? I was just at the inn, and Dana didn't mention it." That was odd. Dana was a huge supporter of the high school hockey team, and the marshmallow roast was one of Dana's bigger fund-raising events of the season. They always held it at the beginning of the winter festival. She used to have it at the inn until the attendance became too large. It was one of Janie's favorite nights during the holidays.

"As far as I know." The cash register clanged as he clipped the bill under the spring, fished out the change, and handed it to her.

"Have you seen anyone poking around asking about broadband lately?"

"Nope. No one's been asking about it here." He stared at her cautiously. "You know it might not be all that bad for the business community."

"You don't think it would spoil the tranquility of this beautiful small town?"

He raised an eyebrow. "People once thought a liquor store would corrupt the people here."

"And why not just put a gambling hall next door?" She shook her head and laughed. "You're a *bad* influence, Rod. Don't try to convince me otherwise." She headed to the door and turned and winked at him as she left the store. Seemed she wasn't the only one weighing the pros and cons of Wi-Fi.

She stopped and put the whiskey in her car before she went inside Cyber Shack. She checked the Letters to Santa mailbox located in the front of the café as she entered. She'd seen several kids milling around it yesterday afternoon and was sure there'd been more additions today. Usually, all the letters were related to games they wanted her to bring into the store for the gamers to play in the fishbowl, a section of the café surrounded by glass walls. Except for the year she'd had to use some of her funds to create the glass enclosures for the room, she was usually able to provide whatever they asked for unless it wasn't available for sale yet. Even with the headphones provided, that was necessary due to gamers yelling as they played. It wasn't any quieter when the seniors got in the fishbowl with them or when they had their scheduled time alone.

She emptied the box and took the letters to the counter with her. She shed her jacket and cap, then tucked them under the counter before she opened the first letter. Maya asked for *Jumanji*. Janie could always count on her to want an adventure game. Oliver, as usual, requested one of the most popular games, *Mario Party Superstars*, which might be difficult to get this close to Christmas, but Janie might be able to find one through her wholesale contacts. She'd been able to come through on his wish last year. Harley wished for *Halo*. She was almost seventeen, and her parents had given permission for her to play whichever games she wanted. Her little sister, Aria, on the other hand, was a lot younger and had asked for *Call of Duty*. That wasn't happening, even if Janie brought it into the store. Aria was way too young for that. Who was she trying to kid? Aria would end up playing *Halo* with Harley anyway. Janie would do her best to find a tamer game that would also keep Harley's interest. Something like *Fortnite* or *Minecraft*. She sighed. Whatever happened to playing *Paperboy* and *Aladdin*? Those were the good old days. Maybe *The Legend of Zelda* would interest her. It had sword-slashing and adventure.

Her heart broke at the next letter she pulled out. Noah had asked for a game console for home so he could play games with his mom at night before bedtime. Janie didn't know the full story behind Noah's dad's disappearance, but he'd been out of the picture since Noah was a baby. His mom cleaned rooms at the Pine Grove Inn during the day and then most evenings waited tables at the restaurant. Noah spent a lot of time at Cyber Shack helping out when he wasn't playing games. Janie would move him to the top of her list. She'd try to find an older game deck and a few games on eBay for him to share with his mom in the evenings.

Chapter Five

After her bath, Crystal changed into the clothing she'd brought in her shoulder bag. In her suitcase, she'd included some jeans and a light turtleneck or two, but she'd been packed for the tropics. In her haste to get ready for the trip to Vermont, she hadn't switched out much of her clothing. Plus, the sweatshirt she'd included had the Dallas Cowboys trademark star plastered across the front, a clear sign she was from out of town. Whatever clothing was in her bag when it arrived wouldn't protect her from the cold very well. The only thing she had that would provide any real warmth was the knee-length brown wool coat she'd carried on the plane with her. At least she'd had the foresight to realize it would be cold when she arrived, but it was made of a lighter wool blend intended for Dallas winters, not Vermont. She had to find a place to buy some local clothing.

She glanced at her watch. It was still early afternoon, and shopping would be a good way to scope out the town. After unpacking the rest of the minimal clothing from her shoulder bag, she headed downstairs to the front desk to talk to Dana, her newest ally.

"I need your help."

"Sure. What can I do?" Dana was very accommodating.

"They lost my bag at the airport, so I need to get some warmer clothes until they find and deliver it." Crystal pinched at her thin turtleneck. "I don't have anything much thicker than this." She needed clothes that wouldn't make her look out of place.

"That's a shame." Dana looked her up and down. "They're usually pretty quick about getting luggage delivered. You're not really accessorized appropriately for the snow we're expecting if they don't. We have some lovely scarf and mitten sets, and even some nice sweaters, in the gift shop, but I'm afraid we don't carry much outdoor gear." She handed Crystal a small map of the area. "Pine Grove Sports is just a few blocks away if you need to pick up a heavier coat. You can find some nice undergarments at the boutique on Main Street if you need them."

"Thanks. I'm hoping my bag will be here soon, but I want to blend in as well. Is there a thrift store in town?" She also didn't want to buy an expensive coat that would sit in her closet in Dallas unused after this trip, not that she couldn't afford it. She wouldn't mind seeing what kind of lingerie was available at the boutique if she had time, though. She always had room in her drawer for more of that.

"There's Ann's Vintage Mall on Main Street. I think a couple of booths in there sell clothing." Dana assessed her again. "Should have some things in your size. I suggest buying in layers. Just ask Ann for help. She runs the place and should be at the counter near the entrance."

"Great. Can I ask one more thing of you?"

"Sure."

She'd noticed that Dana was about the same size as her, with similar features, but somewhat older. "Do you think, while I'm here, we could pretend I'm your cousin?"

"Well, that would make me a good fifteen years younger. Not sure anyone would believe that." Maybe Dana wasn't as willing to help as she'd let on. "How about you become my sister from California's girl? No one's met her before."

"That's perfect, Aunt Dana." Crystal grinned. "Now, which way to the Vintage Mall?"

"Straight ahead when you leave here and then to the right. It's about four blocks that way." Dana pointed her arms forward and then toward the wall like she was a traffic cop.

Crystal slipped on her sunglasses and tugged the lapel of her coat close to her neck as she walked the sidewalk to the nearby mall. It wasn't far at all, and luckily not too many people were out shopping at this time. Sporadic mounds of snow appeared along the edges of the street, and the windows of all the stores had been painted with Christmas themes, which made the atmosphere more magical than she'd expected. It was a lovely town, indeed. Bringing wireless wouldn't change that fact. It would only make the outside world easier to access and, in Dana's case, make the inn more attractive to visitors. Maybe that was what the town council was trying to avoid, but tourist traffic probably kept this little town alive.

She pulled open the door of the Vintage Mall, propped her sunglasses on her head, and walked to the counter. The place seemed empty, not a soul in sight, not even at the counter. A small bell with a note beside it said *Ring for Help*. She tapped the plunger lightly, and the ping rang through the place with a ridiculous echo. She quickly put her hand over the bell to quiet the sound.

A dark-haired woman wearing jeans and a pink tie-dye hoodie appeared from the open door behind the counter. "How can I help you?"

"Are you Ann?"

She nodded. "The one and only."

"Dana, from the inn, said you might have some winter clothing or coats for sale. I don't have much in the way of clothing and wasn't expecting it to be quite so cold." She hoped Ann didn't question that statement. She didn't want to tell everyone in town why she was here until she got a feel for who was for or against wireless internet.

"I'm sure we have some somewhere." Ann came around the counter. "Follow me." She led her to the other side of the store, and Crystal found herself at the beginning of a maze of booths containing everything from furniture and kitchenware to jewelry and clothing. "Someone in town must have a tropical vacation planned. That never fails to bring heaps of snow our way."

The photos of the beach from the travel website flashed through Crystal's head. There was so much truth in that statement, but she wasn't one to believe in Murphy's Law.

Ann glanced at her head. "Fancy pair of sunglasses you got there."

Crystal had forgotten that they were DiorSignature, a birthday gift from Marie. She took them from her head. "Oh, these? A friend gave them to me."

Ann plucked them from Crystal's hand and assessed the nude lenses. "You should get something a little more sporting with a darker lens if you plan on doing any skiing, or the snow will blind you."

She'd noticed that fact on her walk here. The sun seemed to be much brighter than back home. "Do you have any here that might work?"

Ann shook her head. "We get a pair or two every once in a while, but they're a hot commodity. It'll cost you, but they should have some at Pine Grove Sports."

"Thanks. I'll head that way after I finish up here." She perused the various clothing racks in the small square booth and found a jacket, a couple of sweaters she could switch out with her jeans, and a pair of winter boots that miraculously fit her perfectly. She carried them all up to the counter, where Ann was watching something on a small, portable TV.

"Looks like you did well."

"I did. Seems that someone cleaned out their closet recently."

"Happens a lot. A pound or five one way or the other makes people reassess their wardrobes." She held up the boots as she keyed in the price. "You'll need to pick up some wool socks to go with these."

"I suppose I can get those at the sporting-goods store as well?" Crystal handed Ann her credit card.

"You can probably find those anywhere." Ann slid her card through the reader. "I usually have them here on the counter, but they're on order. Just sold my last pair yesterday." She slipped all the items into a bag. "Should have them by tomorrow if you don't find any."

Crystal waited patiently as Ann processed the transaction. "Is there a problem with my card?" She'd let the bank know she was traveling before she left town via the app on the phone. She took hers out to make sure. No signal. Surviving here would be harder than she'd thought.

Ann shook her head. "Dial-up's slower than usual today."

Crystal glanced at the foil wrapped around the tips of the TV antenna. "You don't have cable or wireless?"

"Nah. Don't have much use for that here. Not in any rush." The machine spit out a strip of paper. "There it is." Ann ripped it free and laid it, along with the receipt, on the counter for Crystal to sign.

Crystal scribbled her first initial and last name in the usual manner before she slid the bag from the counter. "I'll be sure to come back if I have trouble finding socks." She held up the bag. "Thanks for your help, Ann."

"My pleasure."

While she was at Pine Grove Sports, she picked up a yellow Wolverines beanie with a navy puff ball on top, like she'd seen Janie wearing earlier, and a navy-blue team sweatshirt, along with a nice pair of Ray-Ban sunglasses. She'd seen several people wearing the Wolverine shirts and spotted a schedule for the high school team taped to the door as she'd entered. It appeared the town was big on high school hockey. She remembered all the school sweatshirts she'd packed away when she'd moved to California from Lake Placid, New York, and then to Dallas, Texas. She didn't have much need for them there. Her parents probably still had them squirreled away on the top shelf of one of their closets.

❖

Janie let the water run through the espresso machine as she scrubbed the base of the screen with the small brush. She inserted the backflush basket into the portafilter before she attached it to the machine and slid the water lever. The machine whirred as she let it run for about five seconds. She flipped the water off, removed the portafilter, and dumped out the dirty water. She repeated the step nine more times before wiggling the portafilter around to clean the edges of the group head on the last round. At the end of the night, she would run the cleaning solution through the machine and backflush it again to finish the cleaning process. Maintaining the machines at Cyber Shack was a never-ending task.

After switching back to the regular portafilter basket, she filled it with fresh ground coffee, tamped it down, fastened it to the machine, and slid the water lever one last time. She listened to the machine whir as it spit espresso into the shot glass below. The area filled with the aroma of fresh coffee, a scent she would always adore. Her fingers burned as she picked up the glass of hot liquid and tasted the brew. Perfect. She'd just finished wiping down the area when Sue burst through the door.

"I thought I'd never get away from the bakery today." Sue set a box on the counter. "I brought you some treats."

"Ooh, Sue." Janie widened her eyes in excitement. "I love treats." She opened the box and took out a chocolate cupcake. "You know exactly what I like." She dove in and took a big bite.

"It's not like you change your order much."

"What can I say? I'm a creature of habit." She licked the buttercream frosting from her lips. "What brings you here in the middle of the day?" It was unusual for Sue to come over before mid-afternoon.

"Mason heard a rumor that the internet company has sent another person out."

"Ann mentioned that this morning. Where does Mason hear these things?"

"I don't know. The man has ears everywhere. But we need to get a plan together on how we're going to deal with the company this time." Sue glanced over her shoulder at the woman behind her. Janie hadn't seen her before. "I'll have him set up a meeting."

"Okay. Just let me know when."

"Will do." Sue grinned, then turned around, giving the new woman the once-over as she scurried out the door.

"What was that about?" the woman asked.

"Nothing. The people in this town get a little paranoid when they think someone's going to take away their anonymity."

"How would someone do that?" The stranger didn't seem to be familiar with the town.

Darlene, a longtime customer and vendor, appeared beside the woman at the counter. She must've entered as Sue left. "It's the internet. They listen to everything." She set a basket of candles on the counter and lowered her voice. "They're watching us right now with their satellites, and now they want to tap into our internet and steal our ideas through Wi-Fi."

"No one wants your candle or soap-making secrets." Janie picked up a candle, screwed off the lid from the wide-mouth pint jar, and sniffed the scent. "You need to stop listening to Earl so much."

Darlene emptied the basket. "He says the government is keeping an eye on us with all that new technology they're putting in cars. Computer chips and such."

Janie didn't like the fact that Earl filled Darlene's head with stories of government plans to spy on the town and everyone who used any type of technology. He probably wouldn't let her frequent the shack if she didn't have to sell candles to support him. She took another candle and opened it. "This one is new." It had the scent of vanilla, and something else Janie couldn't quite place. "What scent is it?"

"Vanilla and Grandpa's pipe. You know that cherry tobacco he always smoked?" Darlene stacked the soaps in the counter display.

Janie chuckled. "It smells exactly like that." She arranged the candles on the counter in front of the soaps. "Okay. We'll try these six and the usual soaps. Same price?"

Darlene nodded. "Let me know if you run out, and I'll bring more when I come for *Grand Theft Auto* night."

Janie would see Darlene before then. She'd be in here practicing to beat the others. She was more competitive than most of the women in town—most of the men as well.

The other woman watched Darlene walk out the door. "Why would anyone want to do any of that spying she was talking about?" Definitely new in town.

"They wouldn't. Her husband's full of conspiracy theories."

Janie straightened the items on the counter, making room for the additional candles. "I think he just wants to make sure she doesn't leave him. Men can be kind of proprietary about their women here."

"It wouldn't be the first time a man lost a woman to someone else on the internet." The woman's brown eyes sparkled with flecks of amber as she stared across the counter. "What about your husband? What does he think about wireless?"

"I'm not married. Wouldn't matter if I was. I form my own opinions."

"And what would your opinion be on the matter?" The woman tilted her head. "Do you think people are listening? Should I be careful what I say?"

"Only in front of Sue and Darlene." Janie assessed the stranger. She wore jeans and a cream turtleneck under a long, brown wool coat. "You're new in town."

"Yes. I'm Crystal, Dana's niece." She held her hand out. "I'm staying at the inn for the holidays." The woman's smile could light up a room.

"Oh. She didn't mention that." Janie gripped her hand—held it a bit longer than she should have. It was like the softest rose petal. "I'm Janie."

"It was kind of last minute." Crystal released Janie's hand, picked up the vanilla-and-tobacco candle, screwed off the lid, and smelled it. "How much are these?"

"Twenty-five."

"I think Aunt Dana will like this one." Crystal slid it across the counter.

"I'm sure she will." Janie screwed the lid on the candle, wrapped it in some tissue, and put it in a bag. "Can I get you anything else?"

Crystal took some cash from her pocket and dug out a couple of twenties. "Yes. Can I get a latte with two shots of espresso, a splash of nonfat milk, and a big squirt of caramel?"

"Coming right up." Janie smiled and turned to the espresso machine, which whirred as Janie ground the beans to prepare the latte. She dumped the shots into the cup and pumped the caramel plunger a couple of times. She added the milk to a small metal pitcher and then hit it with the steamer. She poured it slowly into the cup before she snapped on the lid and handed it to Crystal. "There you go." She collected the cash and slid it into the register. "Thank you."

Crystal took a sip. "Thank *you*, Janie. This latte is perfect." She held up the cup and then the bag. "And I've been looking for the right Christmas present for Dana." Crystal turned and headed to the door.

Janie noted the shiny highlights in Crystal's blond hair as it bounced on her shoulders. "You're welcome to come back if you get bored at the inn." The invitation flew from her thoughts and out of her mouth without notice.

"I might just take you up on that offer." Crystal swung around and smiled. "Oh, and you have a button missing on your flannel."

Janie glanced at her faded red buffalo plaid shirt briefly as it hung open more than usual over her black thermal. She looked up and stared at the door as it closed behind Crystal, then watched her through the window until she was out of view.

She'd invited her back. What was she thinking? Her stomach swirled a tiny bit. She was going to have to dig out something new—up her wardrobe game over the holidays just in case Crystal took her up on it.

Chapter Six

Crystal sat on the bed, closed her eyes, and tried to concentrate on what she'd seen in Cyber Shack. The first image that came into her head was a pair of beautiful blue eyes mounted above a slight nose and plump red lips—Janie. She opened her eyes, jumped to her feet, shook out her arms, and tried to wash the image from her thoughts. "Business, Crystal. This is a business trip." She took in a few deep breaths and sat on the bed. Janie's voice flew through her thoughts. *I'm not married.* She stood again and paced the room to the window, counted the storefronts to where Cyber Shack was located before she turned and let her gaze skitter across the room as the details of the store flooded in.

She dropped to the bed again, took out a pad, and began to sketch the space. "When I walked in, there was a bar to the right that lined the window." She scrunched her forehead. "Four—maybe five stations at the bar with internet ports and power." She closed her eyes again. "Immediately to my left was another area where customers could plug in, with a couch and several comfortable chairs to relax in." The area was really quite inviting. Farther in on that same side were a couple of tables that included partitions between each station. She tried to remember what the sign hanging above them said. "Fiber...station...spot...Fiber *Zone.* That's it." She labeled the area on her sketch. "Straight ahead and to the left was a glassed-in gaming area with a big flatscreen TV. Top Net Zone." She remembered that name clearly because it was printed on the glass. She hadn't seen a game deck, so there must be an interchangeable hub. "Outside of that were several square tables," she muttered to herself, squinting. "For eating, maybe?" She rolled her lips in. It was a café, after all. "And directly across was another room with a large sliding-glass door." She remembered the name printed on the door. "Collaboration Station." She had seen the end of what looked like a conference table from the door but hadn't ventured inside, as it was occupied. "What kind of businesses would use that?" She flipped the page and scribbled her question on a separate piece of paper.

Crystal closed her eyes and walked herself through the space back to the door. "Coffee bar and retail to the left. Multiple types of coffee and specialty drinks." Janie's beautiful blue eyes entered her thoughts again—the moment when she'd gotten distracted. Everything was a blur after that.

She stood and paced the room, then went to the window and spotted Janie crossing the street to the hardware store. Her stomach jumped as she recalled the zap that had coursed through her when Janie had shaken her hand earlier. She pressed her hand to her stomach to calm the reaction. When she'd arrived in Pine Grove, she hadn't expected anything like this to happen—not even close. She'd honestly expected the cyber-café owner to be much older and cynical. Janie seemed nothing like that—so far.

She returned to the bed and studied her diagram. "For an area this size, with this many ports, Janie would have to have multiple servers and switches," she murmured to herself. The business had to have a temperature-controlled closet somewhere inside to maintain a temperature between fifty and eighty-two degrees. She flopped back onto a pillow and stared at the ceiling. She hadn't noticed a door for that either. Clearly she'd have to make another trip over to the Cyber Shack for more coffee. She took her jacket from the chair where she'd hung it and slipped it on. Hopefully she'd be able to keep her mind on the task at hand rather than on the beautiful store owner.

Dana was at the desk as usual when she got downstairs.

"Where are you off to?" Dana was taking the role of playing her aunt more seriously than Crystal expected.

"Just thought I'd head back over to Cyber Shack to see what kind of business it draws."

"If you really want to get a feel for the town, you should go to the high school hockey game tomorrow night."

"Oh. Okay. Is it close by?"

"Not too far. Janie always picks me up. You can ride with us."

"Sounds great. Thanks. It's been a while since I've been to a hockey game." Not since she'd moved from upstate New York. "Do you need me to pick up anything while I'm out?"

"Bring me back a vanilla latte, full strength, none of that sugar-free, nonfat stuff. Janie knows how I like it."

"Will do. It might be an hour or so before I get back. Is that okay?"

Dana nodded. "Appreciate your thoughtfulness."

"I'm happy to do it." Politeness seemed to run through this town like a simple-syrup river.

❖

Janie picked up a box and moved it to another stack. She needed to organize the storage closet after the holidays. She didn't have time right now, though, because she was already late putting the Christmas lights up in the window. If she didn't get it done today, Mason would be all over her—might even fine her for not conforming to the Christmas Spirit ordinance he'd put in place a few years ago. She moved another box and opened the one that had been beneath it. "Yes." The word hissed out of her mouth. She took a Sharpie from her back pocket, dropped to a squat, and wrote *Christmas Lights* in huge letters across the side and on one of the top flaps of the box. She slid it onto the portable dolly she kept in the closet and wheeled it out into the main part of the café.

"Beka, can you help me with these lights?"

Beka wiped her hands on a towel as she came from the kitchen. "Why don't you get some of the kids to help you?" She glanced at the counter. "Or Tara? Didn't she do it for you last year?"

"Tara's busy cleaning the rest of the coffee machines, and a couple of weeks ago, I planned for the kids to help, but here we are a week away from Christmas, and I haven't even started. I'd just like to get them done while I can."

"I can help you." Crystal's voice came from across the café.

Janie glanced over her shoulder at Dana's niece. "Oh, no. I couldn't ask you to do that." She hadn't even known she was there. Must've come back while she was getting the lights out of the storage closet.

"Of course you can. I'm here, ready to help." Crystal smiled widely. "What do you need me to do?"

Janie took a ball of mini-lights out of the box. "You can start by untangling these." That should keep her busy for a few minutes while she figured out how she usually hung them.

Crystal sat cross-legged in the middle of the floor next to the pathway that ran through the store. "Do you have a diagram or something to work from?"

"I usually wing it." Janie lifted each of the chairs at the window bar and moved them away from the bar.

"Oh." Crystal looked up at her as she worked with the lights.

"You say that like it's a bad thing." Janie took hold of the center of the bar and pulled it away from the window.

"I'm just used to working with a plan." Crystal laid the lights out from end to end. "Keeps me on task."

Janie walked to the other side of the door and moved the furniture away from the window there too. "With the contest and all, I like to create a new design every year."

"Contest?" Crystal's voice lilted.

"Storefront-decorating contest. The town council puts it on every year."

"Who does the judging?" She worked a couple of tangles free on another string of lights.

"Usually random volunteers who don't have any affiliation with the businesses in town."

"Makes sense." She leaned back on the palms of her hands, giving Janie a hint of the wondrous features hidden under her jacket.

Janie hesitated, losing her train of thought for a moment. "You'd probably be a good one."

"Not after I help you with your display. People would think I'm biased." Crystal bent forward and slipped her jacket off before she continued working on the lights.

"Around here, they probably would." Janie laughed. "It's pretty competitive."

"Do you have any duct tape?" Seemed Crystal might have an interest in the competition.

Janie turned slowly. "Planning to kidnap the judges?"

Crystal let out a laugh that sent a jolt right to Janie's midsection. "That's an option, but let's not go there yet. I thought we could create some lines on the window to make the scene look more rustic." She stood, hung her jacket on one of the bar chairs, and glanced around the room. "Electrical tape will work better, if you have any."

"I think I have some." Janie headed to the storage area. "Be right back." She went inside, closed the door, and leaned up against it. *What was that?* She contemplated the jolt. She hadn't had that feeling in a long time. She took in a deep breath to settle herself before she pushed off the door and found the electrical tape.

"Do you have a tree and maybe a reindeer or two?" Crystal entered the small, cluttered space.

Janie was frozen—stuck—mesmerized by beautiful brown eyes that had widened, adjusting to the dim lighting.

Crystal glanced around the area. "You do." Excitement filled her voice as she brushed past Janie to grab the two small reindeer. "You have a Santa as well." She wrestled with the reindeer to get them out of the boxes. "We can do a lot with all of these." She positioned a reindeer under each arm, and took the tape from Janie's hand. "Can you bring Santa and the tree?"

"Sure." Janie took in a breath as Crystal squeezed by her, and musky amber with a slight hint of caramel filled her nose. She didn't know what it was, but it smelled wonderful.

By the time Janie had brought the rest of the decorations to the front of the store, Crystal had already started sectioning the window with the electrical tape.

"Wow. That looks really cool." It really did look like a vintage paned window.

"Right? And you can just peel it off after the holidays." Crystal backed up and assessed her work. "We'll need to get some of that fake snow spray to make it look more authentic."

"They should have some of that at the hardware store." Janie glanced at her watch. "I'll run over now. It's going to close soon."

"We can pick that up tomorrow." Crystal went to the counter. "Do you have any paper and pen I can use to sketch out a design?"

"Sure. Should be some right behind the counter." Janie stopped unpacking the tree and moved toward it.

Crystal put up her hand. "I'll get it. You keep doing what you're doing."

Janie watched Crystal walk to the counter. Seemed she was in charge of the decorating, and Janie kind of liked it. Once Janie had finished setting up Santa and the reindeer, she went to the counter to see that Crystal had mapped out a plan that included the blow-mold figures, a sign for the North Pole, and mounds of snow.

"How did you do that so quickly?"

"I've always been able to envision layouts in my head." Crystal scrunched her nose. "I know it's kind of weird."

"Not at all. It's kind of impressive." Janie went back to the window area and hoisted the tree onto its stand. "I could've used your eye when I changed the layout of this place last year."

Crystal glanced around the café. "Looks like you did a good job."

"It took several tries to get it arranged this way, and sometimes I still think it could use some tweaking." Janie straightened some of the branches. "Can you steady this while I stabilize it in the stand?"

"Sure." Crystal came Janie's way. "There's nothing wrong with tweaking on occasion to make it look fresh." Crystal held the tree as Janie tightened the screws.

Janie had never thought about it that way. "I guess that's true."

Crystal went back to her drawing. "We should probably put some lights around the window before we place the tree too close, don't you think?"

"Good idea. I'll get the ladder." Janie headed back to the storage closet. She despised decorating the store, but doing it with Crystal's help was making it a whole lot more enjoyable.

Janie set up the ladder before she retrieved the first string of lights from the floor. "Where should I start?" She went to the counter and glanced at the sketch Crystal had drawn. It was a perfectly drawn likeness of the front of the store. "Wow. You could be an artist."

"Not really. I just do it for fun." Crystal tapped the sketch with her finger. "I see you already have plastic hooks around the window." She climbed up the ladder. "Let's start in this corner." She held her hand out for the lights. "The clear, medium-sized lights will be good here. They'll give the window a nice glow at night."

Janie handed Crystal the lights and steadied the ladder as she hung them. This proximity was only making the swirl in Janie's belly stronger. Crystal climbed down from the ladder, and Janie moved it under the next hook. They did that several more times until they reached the last one. Just then, Crystal caught her foot on the lower rung of the ladder and fell into Janie. The swirl in Janie's stomach turned into a full-on tornado as Crystal grabbed hold of her to keep herself from falling.

"Oh, my." Crystal let her go. "I'm sorry about that." She smiled. "Thank you for catching me."

"Of course." Heat rose in Janie's cheeks. "Where do you want the tree?" She looked at the sketch, avoiding eye contact with Crystal.

Crystal seemed to leave a little sparkle wherever she went, and Janie wanted more of it. How she was going to get it was still to be determined.

❖

After they finished putting up the decorations, Crystal sat at the coffee bar and watched Janie as she helped the barista handle a small rush of people wanting coffee. She was glad she'd come back to the café this afternoon because it gave her the opportunity to get to know Janie. Working together, they had quickly put the lights on the tree and set up Santa and the reindeer, and she had to admit the display looked pretty good.

The rush finally dissipated, and people went to different areas of the café. Janie came from behind the counter to the coffee bar. "You up for a cup of coffee, or do you need to get back to the inn?"

"I'd love one." She had nowhere else to be right now—nowhere else she wanted to be.

"Great." Janie grinned as she returned to the counter.

Crystal followed her. "You get people in here just for coffee, huh?" Crystal glanced at a couple drinking coffee and eating muffins at one of the square tables.

"Yeah. When I upgraded the equipment, I had to hire the barista to keep up." Janie pointed to the young woman behind the counter. "We also get some lunch and afternoon business. Sue from the bakery drops off another batch of sweets after it closes at three."

"I heard you talking to her when I was here earlier."

"Right," Janie said.

"The croissants look delicious."

"You'll have to find out if they taste as good as they look." Janie took a couple of croissants out of the case, put them into a pastry bag, and set it on the counter. "You want coffee or a latte?"

"A latte, please. Two shots of espresso, a splash of nonfat milk, and big squirt of caramel."

"I remember. That's a pretty specific order."

"Yeah. I'm not sure how I landed on that mixture, but it's my favorite." Crystal had actually dated a barista once. The latte turned out to be the best part of the relationship.

Janie made the latte and then poured herself a mug of coffee. "Can you grab the croissants?" She carried the drinks to one of the square tables.

"I didn't know cyber cafés served lunch."

"Most don't. Food service gets complicated with health inspections and all." Janie held her mug between her hands. "It wasn't something I wanted to branch out into, but some of the seniors from the retirement home, my grandmother included, come in to become more tech savvy." Janie took a sip of coffee. "Grandma mentioned on more than one occasion that it would be nice if we served lunch while they were here." She tore a piece from her croissant. "So now we do. It's nothing big, just soup of the day, sandwiches, and salads. We're not a full-blown restaurant."

"Seems Grandma has a lot of pull in this establishment." Crystal knew some of the history behind the café from what Dana had told her, but she wanted to hear what Janie had to say about it.

"Don't all grandmothers have that?" Janie laughed. "My grandparents established the shack long ago. I'm just the newest general manager."

"Oh, so you don't own it?" That was a good tidbit to know.

"I own a piece of it. Grandpa passed it down to my dad, and I'm planning to take it over from him." Janie stared into her coffee before she glanced at the front of the store. "Thank you for your help with the display. It looks better than it ever has when I've done it alone." She sipped her coffee. "Cyber Shack is definitely going to be a contender in the contest this year."

Crystal noted the shift in conversation. Maybe ownership of the café wasn't as clear as it seemed.

The door to the kitchen opened, and a woman came their way talking as she walked. "Ben worked his magic on your water heater again. No more cold showers for now, but he said you should budget for a new one." Once she got to the table, she stood like she was waiting for something.

"Tell Ben thanks for me, Beka." Janie held up her cup. "He still gets free coffee for life."

"Will do." She glanced at Crystal and then at Janie. "Who's this?"

Crystal wiped her hand on her napkin and then reached out her hand. "I'm Crystal."

Beka shook her hand. "Nice to meet you, Crystal. I'm Beka. I do all the cooking around here."

"Crystal is Dana's niece. She's in from out of town for the holidays." Janie gave her a smile, and Crystal couldn't believe how good it made her feel.

"Oh." Beka slid into the chair across from Crystal. "Whereabouts are you from?"

Crystal hesitated. "California."

"Northern or Southern?"

"Northern. San Francisco Bay Area." Her parents had moved there from Lake Placid when she was in middle school.

"Nice weather out there."

"Yes. Very nice. A lot warmer than here, but it can be a little rainy during the winter when we're not experiencing a drought." Crystal remembered the climate well. She'd spent a fair amount of her adolescence and young adult life in San Francisco before moving to Dallas in her mid-twenties.

"When you get back there, if I come out, will you show me the sights?" Beka's forehead crinkled.

Janie blurted out a laugh. "Beka, you just met the woman, and you want to use her house as a hotel?"

"Once we get to know each other a little better." Beka shrugged. "I'm not a serial killer or anything like that." She popped Janie on the shoulder. "You can vouch for that."

"She's harmless, but I'm not sure I'd invite her into my home." Janie winked.

Beka's mouth dropped open. "That's not a nice thing to say about your best friend."

"True." Janie grinned. "You can invite her in, but lock the fridge, or she'll be cooking all kinds of fabulous meals that will go straight to your thighs." She slapped her hand against her leg.

Crystal smiled. "My kind of houseguest."

"Then it's a plan." Beka stood. "We'll talk about this again, soon." She twirled around and headed back to the kitchen.

"Don't mind her. She'll never take you up on it. She rarely travels."

"How about you?" Crystal planted her elbow on the table and rested her face in her palm. "Do you ever get out of this town?"

Janie shook her head. "No. Not really. Never had the opportunity—never really wanted to leave."

Crystal dropped her hand to the table. "Really? Not even for a vacation?"

Janie shook her head. "Running this place doesn't allow for that."

"Can't your dad run it while you take a week?" Surely, she had some sort of backup for when she needed to take time off.

"He's been retired for a while." Janie scrunched her eyebrows together. "Have you met my dad?"

"No. You just mentioned that Cyber Shack is a family business and that you'd taken it over from your dad. Dana mentioned it also." *Whoops. Stay in your lane, Crys.* Dana hadn't really. She'd found that out through research as well.

"What else did Dana tell you about me?"

"Not much." She was going to have to backpedal a bit. "Just some tidbits about the town, and you came up as one of them."

"Tidbits, eh?" Janie raised an eyebrow. "Never been referred to as one of those before."

"You are a very sweet tidbit." Crystal tingled as she stared into Janie's eyes. That was unexpected. She cleared her throat before she took the last bit of her croissant and held it in front of her mouth. "Thank you for this. It hit the spot."

"Thank you for helping me with the window. The design you created looks awesome." Janie's cheeks were red. It seemed she was feeling the tingle as well.

"Now you have a plan to work off of next year. That will make it much easier to put them up again."

"I guess I do." Janie laughed. "I've never been one to plan things out." She sipped her coffee. "Or you can just come back and help me again."

"Or that." Crystal grinned as the tingle spread throughout her again.

Chapter Seven

The phone on the nightstand jolted Crystal out of her sleep. She flew up and then flopped back against the bed. Her dream was just getting to the good part. She picked up the receiver. "Janie?"

"Only when I cross-dress." Bob's deep laugh came through the phone. His humor was so inappropriate. "Made any progress?"

"I've barely been here a day, Bob. I can't make wine from water." She glanced at the clock next to the phone—close to eight a.m., which meant it was earlier than seven in Dallas. "Why are you calling this early?"

"Jack."

"What about Jack?"

"He's itching to come your way."

She bolted up again. "Absolutely not. These people need more of a soft touch—they need to be eased into it."

"Jack knows how to be subtle."

"No. He doesn't. He's never been subtle about anything. Remember that little town outside of Pennsylvania? They were ready to negotiate until he showed up."

"Right." Bob drew the word out.

"Took me an extra week to get them back to where they were before he blew everything up."

"Okay. I'll hold him off for now, but keep me updated."

"I'll call you tomorrow."

"Tonight. Call me tonight." Bob was a ridiculous micro-manager.

"Fine. I'll call you later." She dropped the receiver into the cradle. She'd said she'd call him, but whether it happened was up in the air. She flopped onto the pillow. Now back to a perfectly good dream that contained a beautiful girl with dirty-blond hair and gorgeous blue eyes. It wasn't long before she drifted back to sleep.

When Crystal awoke again a few hours later, she didn't want to move. She'd thought she'd hit the gym this morning, but her arms felt heavy, and her head was pounding. She lay there for a few minutes before rolling out of bed and getting into the shower. She hadn't eaten much yesterday besides the croissant at Cyber Shack and probably just needed some food.

When she came down the stairs, the scent of pancakes filled her nose, but she didn't see anything to eat. She crossed the small lobby area to spot Dana at the front desk. "Am I too late for the continental breakfast?"

Dana nodded. "Wraps up at nine." She pointed to another area that Crystal recalled hearing voices from the day before. "But the restaurant has breakfast until eleven."

"Oh. I was hoping for something light." She needed something now, or she was going to pass out.

"Sue's bakery is right down the street. She has a variety of pastries and croissants. That's where we get ours." Just like Cyber Shack. It must be the only bakery in town.

"Thanks." Crystal's head throbbed, and she grabbed the counter to steady herself.

Dana rushed around the counter to her. "You all right?"

"I have a little headache. I need something to eat." Traveling always gave her a headache, especially when she didn't eat much after she arrived at her destination. Days on the road were always hectic and filled with anxiety for her. You wouldn't know it by the amount she traveled for her job. Burying that kind of anxiety was common in her line of work. Only so much could be done over the phone. Face-to-face meetings were a must.

Dana wrapped her arm around her. "Let's get some food into you." She set a bell in the middle of the counter and led her into the small restaurant. They walked through it, past a few people who were having breakfast, to a table by the window. "I'll be right back."

Crystal watched Dana walk across the room and into the kitchen before she veered her gaze to look through the window. The view of Main Street was spectacular from this particular spot. From here she could drink it all in. Pine Grove was indeed the perfect picture of a Norman Rockwell winter town, almost exactly like the Christmas-house collection her mother displayed during the holidays every year. As a child she'd always wanted to be one of the small ceramic people milling about in the perfect snowy scene it portrayed. Warmth filled her. She hadn't realized how much she'd missed the holiday atmosphere—hadn't realized she'd missed it at all until she'd arrived here in Pine Grove.

"I put in an order of steak and eggs for you. That should get rid of that headache." She set two mugs on the table, poured coffee into them, and placed an insulated decanter on the table.

"I thought I'd just have some fruit."

"You need protein, girl, and maybe a pancake or two." Dana took a sip of coffee and relaxed into her chair.

"Thanks, Dana." She didn't usually eat a large breakfast, but it did sound good—all of it. "Any chance you might be able to provide me with a little information on Janie Elliott?"

"Depends on what kind of information you're looking for."

"I'm just wondering why she's so adamant against broadband. It would certainly help her business."

"That's a long story." Dana sighed. "Way back in the day, Janie's grandfather preferred to live off the grid, and by creating Cyber Shack, he made it easy for others in town to do so as well while also giving them a connection to the outside world, mostly through ham radios." She glanced up when the server arrived at the table with the food, took it, and slid it in front of Janie. "Eat."

"Thank you." Janie picked up the knife and fork and sliced off a small chunk of steak. "How long has it been in business?" She put the piece into her mouth and chewed.

"Since Janie was just a kid. Back in the day, it started out with the radios. Then, when people lost interest in that, he made it into a video store, but when that became outdated, it changed into the Cyber Shack. Her dad was running it by then, and Janie worked there in the afternoons after school. Once Janie took over, she upgraded the equipment and added the food and snacks."

"So, why not add broadband and Wi-Fi?" She scooped up a forkful of eggs.

"The business has built a long-standing reputation in the community. Trust in those you know, and know those you trust. They take only the information necessary to find people and retrieve their merchandise. Lots of people prefer to rent movies rather than pay the cost of cable or streaming." Dana took a cup of coffee. "I've checked the prices. That stuff is expensive."

"It can be, but there are packages for places like the inn, and if you want broadband in the town, others here are bound to want it as well. I'm sure Ann could use it at the Vintage Mall. She was struggling with dial-up when I was in there." Crystal shoveled in another bite of steak, along with some eggs, before she washed them down with some coffee. She was feeling better already.

"True. There aren't many people living off the grid in the area anymore either. The argument has become more about preserving the small-town atmosphere." Dana picked up the decanter and filled their cups. "And it would probably put Janie out of business."

"I guess that's a possibility." Crystal didn't see that happening if Janie promoted the new services right. "If Janie changed her business model to add newer technology, the shack would thrive." Crystal had put so many ideas into play with previous customers to accomplish that goal.

"The town supports Janie because it's what they did for her father, and her grandfather."

Crystal glanced out the window. In all its beauty, this town was still more primitive than Crystal had imagined. "Sounds like Janie is the key to getting the town broadband."

"Her and Mason. He's the head of the town council."

"What's his motivation to keep it away?" She ate another bite.

"He'll tell you it's because he wants to keep Pine Grove's quaintness, but I really think it's about his kids. His wife, Sue, says their nieces and nephews in Burlington are always on their phones and have the attention span of a squirrel."

"Just because the town has broadband doesn't mean everyone will buy their kids phones." They would eventually, though. It was bound to happen everywhere. "Sue seems nice. I saw her yesterday at Cyber Shack." Crystal made a mental note in her head to gather more information on Mason and his family.

"She's very nice but follows Mason's lead in that respect."

"Understood. Is there anyone else in town I should worry about?" The fork clinked against the plate as she swept the last of her eggs against a piece of toast.

Dana shook her head. "Those two usually head up the opposition." She relaxed into her chair. "You're not the first one to come to town selling technology, but let's hope you'll be the last."

"I really need to get acquainted with the town and the people in it."

"There's the high school hockey game tonight that I told you about. Usually have a big crowd if you want to come along."

"I'd love that." She pushed away her plate and wiped her mouth with the linen napkin. She couldn't eat another bite.

"Game starts at seven. Janie usually picks me up around six thirty." The bell at the front desk rang. "How's that headache?" Dana stood.

"Better." The food had done the trick. "Thank you, again."

"Good. Let me know if you need anything else." Dana sped out the door of the restaurant.

Looked like Crystal had her work cut out for her. She could handle Mason and his worries about his children, but changing life-long traditions was going to take some effort. Today would be filled with more research on Pine Grove and the people that made it come alive.

❖

Janie parked in the circle drive of the Pine Grove Inn and went inside. Dana was usually ready early for the hockey game, but sometimes she got caught in something last minute that she had to deal with before leaving. She was behind the check-in counter as usual.

"Ready?"

Dana handed the clerk a piece of paper. "Don't call me unless it's an emergency." Her usual instruction before she headed to a Wolverines game.

Janie glanced around the lobby at the Christmas decorations. "The place looks good. You've really decked it all out for the holidays." Janie felt a little pride at what she and Crystal had accomplished yesterday. "Your niece helped me with the window at Cyber Shack."

"Who?" Dana tugged on her jacket.

"Crystal, your niece." Janie glanced at the steps and saw Crystal coming down them. "Speak of the devil."

"Oh, right." Dana came around the counter. "I invited her to come along tonight."

"Great." Janie had hoped for an opportunity to see more of Crystal. She'd been disappointed when Crystal hadn't come to the shack for coffee or anything else today.

"I hope you don't mind." Crystal smiled, and Janie's legs turned to jelly.

"No. Not at all. I was hoping we'd get to spend more time together while you're in town."

"Me too." Crystal grinned.

"Come on, you two. I want to get a good seat." Dana rushed to the door. "Someone might steal my usual spot."

"I thought that's why you painted your name on it." Janie laughed. On the occasion that someone did take her place, they didn't stay there for long once Dana set them straight.

"We've got an extra tonight." She flipped her hand toward Crystal before she pulled open the door and sped outside.

Janie held the door for Crystal as Dana rushed to the Jeep and climbed into the front seat. There was no question about who rode shotgun when Dana was in the car either. Janie opened the back door for Crystal before she rounded the Jeep, climbed into the driver's seat, and fired the engine.

"Buckle up." Dana turned and glanced at Crystal.

"Always do, Auntie." Crystal pulled the belt across herself and clicked it.

Dana frowned. "Cut the auntie crap. Makes me sound old."

"You? Old?" Janie laughed. "You're more active than I am." Dana was involved in just about every activity in town. Janie guessed that came with running the inn and keeping her customers happy.

The drive was short, as usual. Janie dropped Dana at the door so she could run in ahead and grab their seats. Luck was in her favor tonight, because she found a parking space fairly close to the entrance. "You ready for some hometown hockey?"

Crystal nodded. "Absolutely."

"Just let me know if you want to step outside. The crowd can get pretty rowdy. Especially when the players fight."

"I love a good brawl on the ice."

The ice hockey arena was packed, as always. With the season running from mid-November to late February, high school hockey was in full swing. It was really the only form of entertainment most people in town agreed on. Something to cheer for as a community.

Janie took Crystal's hand and led her up the stairs, an unplanned, instinctual action that Crystal seemed to embrace as she laced their fingers together. She spotted Dana and Sue in the usual spot and gave them a wave. She tugged Crystal toward them and then waited as Crystal entered the row before her, taking the seat next to Dana.

"I really like your sweater." Sue reached around Dana and plucked at Crystal's sleeve.

"It was a gift…an early Christmas present from Aunt Dana." Crystal glanced at Dana.

"I've had my eye on it at the vintage mall for a couple of weeks." Sue frowned. "Been working a lot at the bakery and hadn't had time to get back there and buy it."

Janie grinned and looked at Dana. "Well, we all know where Dana does her shopping."

"You've gotten some pretty good gifts from there, haven't you?" Dana didn't miss a beat. She pulled an oversized team jersey from her bag and handed it to Crystal. "Put this on so everyone knows which side you're on."

Crystal took the jersey and slipped it over her head.

"And here's the roster." Dana handed her a sheet of paper. "Learn those names and numbers."

"Got it." Crystal studied the sheet in front of her.

Crystal's interest in attending the hockey game had been unexpected, as had Janie's own reaction to the news that Crystal was coming along tonight.

Dana squeezed Crystal's forearm. "The first rule in hockey fandom is that if you think you're too loud, yell louder."

"Got it. My brother played hockey in high school, remember?" Crystal nudged Dana.

"In California?" Janie was surprised they would play a winter sport in high school there.

Dana interjected. "They lived in upstate New York before they moved to the West Coast. Right after her brother graduated. Crystal was still in middle school then."

"Football games just aren't the same." Janie watched as each player skated to the goalie and tapped him on the pads for good luck and to signal that the goalie was ready for action.

Crystal settled into her seat. "That's for sure." She immediately jumped up and screamed as the player raced across the ice. "Go—go—go!"

The puck flew into the air, past the goalie into the goal. Immediately the red light went off, and the goal horn sounded. The crowd cheered between each blast, and the sound of the wolf howl filled the arena.

"It must be hard to eat when you got no hands," Dana shouted at the goalie.

"Was that Mike?" Crystal glanced at the roster, then squinted as she stared at the ice.

"No. That's Joey. He's taller." Dana knew each player's characteristics.

Janie leaned into Crystal. "She can tell by their skating technique." She pointed to Joey. "He looks slightly awkward because of his height." She pointed to another player. "Others who are shorter move smoothly, like figure skaters."

"Right. I'd forgotten those details."

"Well, that kind of obsessive observance tends not to come into play unless the player's number is blocked from view so even the announcer isn't sure who it is." Janie glanced at Dana, who was focused on the game. "Dana knows everything about the players, stats as well as when Coach will put each player into the game. She could easily be the backup coach for the team."

"That's pretty obsessive." Crystal gave her a clenched-teeth grin, then flinched when the horn went off.

The teams left the ice for the locker rooms for the first twenty-minute intermission. Music blared as the Zamboni came out to clean the ice.

"Yep." Janie stood. "You want to get some hot chocolate?" She ignored the urge to put her hand out, avoiding the unintentional overreach she'd done earlier.

"Absolutely."

They made their way across the row, down the stairs, and through the opening to the small area containing the snack bar.

Crystal glanced around the area. "This place could really use a makeover."

"Yeah. Seems like there's something new to fix every week. It's kind of falling apart." Janie held her fingers up. "Two hot chocolates."

"Doesn't the school district fund the repairs?"

"Nah. Mason's grandmother, who loved hockey, donated it. She died about five years ago, and now the town has to handle the upkeep."

"Mason didn't take that on?"

Janie shook her head. "He donates what he can, just like the rest of us, but the maintenance expense is huge."

After the person running the concession set their drinks on the counter, they retrieved them and headed up the steps and to their seats.

The goalie stepped onto the ice, and the rest of the team followed. As they circled the ice, Dana was ready to go again. "Goalies are warm. Shoot to score."

They lined up for the face-off, and the crowd stilled. They battled for the puck, and Joey took possession and did a breakaway across the ice. Once in range of the goal, he hit the puck, and it sailed past the goalie. The noise from the crowd was deafening. All players on the team raised their sticks in triumph. One of the players on the opposing team checked another and sent him hard into the boards.

"Oh, man. The gloves are gonna drop. I can see it in his eyes." Dana jumped to her feet. "Protect your face, honey."

Sure enough, another player threw off his gloves as he used the tips of his skates to gain speed across the ice. Everyone leapt to their feet as punches started to fly.

The horn went off again, and the last intermission was upon them. Dana shot out of her seat. "I'm going down to play." She scanned them all. "Anyone coming with me?"

Janie put her hand on Crystal's leg as she started to move, then looked at her and shook her head. "It's better to watch this part—for your own safety."

"Okay." Crystal grinned. "Now I'm intrigued."

They watched the crew set up four inflatable chairs in the middle of the ice, two navy and two yellow. After a few minutes, four people—including Dana, two kids, and another adult—and the Wolverines' mascot slid onto the ice. All were dressed in helmets along with knee and elbow pads. The announcer skated out, made sure everyone was the appropriate distance away from the chairs, and explained the game. The music played, and they all circled the chairs until the music stopped and they all scrambled for one, with Dana fighting for the one with the other adult. Dana was the victor, as usual. She danced around the chairs until the music stopped again and she aced out one of the kids. Her competitive streak was strong. She didn't just let kids win.

Janie turned her attention to Crystal, watching as she danced and cheered for Dana. She usually loved coming to these games, but tonight the entertainment was sitting right next to her. She'd enjoyed watching Crystal react more than anything.

"Go, Dana," Crystal shouted and pulled Janie into a hug when Dana aced out the mascot for the win.

Once intermission was over, Dana returned to her seat, waving her gift certificate to Pine Grove Sporting Goods. "New snow boots for me."

From that point on, the rest of the game was a blur. All Janie could think about was the soft body pressed against her when Crystal had thrown her arms around her and squeezed. It was clear it had been too long since she'd had close contact with a woman she found attractive.

It was near the end of the game, which had been neck and neck, and the score was now tied. All they needed was one last goal to wrap it up, but the refs weren't calling for them. They'd had at least one man in the penalty box since the third quarter began.

"Put the ref in the box," Crystal chanted with the rest of the crowd.

Dana bolted to her feet again. "Hey, stripes. The whistle ain't a dick. Get it out of your mouth."

"Wow. Dana really gets into this." Crystal's eyes widened.

"Right now, I'd say you two are running neck and neck."

"What?" Crystal raised her hands palms up, glanced at the ice, and then shot up. "They're already taking him out. He's just like a tampon. Only good for one period. Come on, boys. This isn't pond hockey."

Janie grinned. She was amusingly surprised at how vocal Crystal was. She hadn't gotten an inkling of this side of her yesterday at the café. Janie sprang up as well. "We may suck, but we know how to plan a mean parade."

"We don't suck anymore." Dana jumped to her feet as the puck flew across the ice and into the goal. "Score."

The crowd screamed in victory. Their team had won, which set the mood for the whole town.

They funneled out of the arena with the rest of the crowd. Janie wasn't done for the night and was hoping that Crystal wasn't either. "Anyone up for a nightcap?"

"That's a hard no." Dana shook her head. "The bar will be filled with obnoxious assholes, and I've had enough noise for one night."

Janie had hoped Dana would come along. She wasn't ready to be left alone with Crystal. "Come on. Just one drink? We can have it at the inn."

"Yeah. Come on." Sue chimed in as she looped her arm with Dana's. "Let's celebrate."

"Okay. One drink but that's it. Then I have to get my beauty sleep."

"Nah. You're already beautiful." Crystal grinned as she took Dana's other arm.

They all piled into Janie's Jeep and headed over to the bar. Janie was beginning to like Crystal more with each moment she spent with her. She was like a sweet and sour candy. Her sweetness provided a warm, fuzzy feeling, and when the sour kicked in it brought all your senses to life with a little jolt.

❖

Crystal had enjoyed the hockey game. It had been fun and a bit eye-opening about the town and about Dana. She was a die-hard fan of the Wolverines for sure. Janie, not so much. The arena had been full. The community was much larger than Crystal had imagined. She had no idea how she was going to convince everyone in there that installing broadband would benefit them. The arena wasn't in the best shape, but the community clearly supported the team. She took a couple of mental notes on things Spark Wireless could do to persuade them. *Funding for hockey team—skates, pads, helmets, sticks, jerseys? Funding for stadium—could use a major renovation.*

As they entered the Pine Grove Inn, Dana immediately headed to the reception desk, which had customers waiting but no clerk to help them. "I'll be right there. I need to check on these guests." She scanned the area, looking for whoever should've been manning the fort while she was gone.

Crystal followed Janie and Sue into the small sports bar located next to the restaurant. The two were separated by a partition that let customers dine without the noise and distractions of the TV above the bar.

Janie went to the bar. "Whatever porter you have on tap, please." She glanced at Sue. "Rosé, as usual?"

Sue nodded. "I'll grab that table over there." She pointed to a four-top close to the windows.

"Wine for you as well?" Janie patted the bar in front of Crystal.

"I'll have the porter." Crystal drank wine on occasion, but beer went with sports.

"Good choice." Janie smiled and then turned to the bartender. "Two rosés and another porter."

Crystal took a twenty from her pocket and offered it to Janie.

Janie put her hand up. "I'll get this round." She handed Crystal her pint of porter along with one of the glasses of wine before she picked up the other two drinks and carried them to the table.

"I bet they get a crowd here on football game days." If this bar was full, Crystal imagined the other bar in town was as well.

"They do when the local channels show the game."

"Oh, they don't get them all?" Another reason to introduce broadband.

"No. We have limited packages here."

Crystal glanced around the bar. It was time to test the waters. "I noticed there isn't any wireless in town. Has Dana ever considered getting satellite?" Crystal hated to ruin the fun mood from the game, but she had a job to do. Both Janie and Sue stilled. Seemed it was a subject of contempt.

"Most people around here are happy with antennas." Sue sipped her wine.

"With all the entertainment available to stream now, I'd think most people would want more than what they can get with an antenna."

"We aren't most people here in Pine Grove. We like our town the way it is." Sue glanced at Janie, who seemed to be focused on the TV.

"Right." Janie returned her attention to the table. "We're good with what we have. Been that way since I can remember."

"Seems like a silly reason to stay in the dark ages," Crystal said. "I for one love relaxing on the sofa after work and streaming a good comedy show."

Janie raised an eyebrow. "What exactly do you do for a living?"

Shit. Not the way she'd expected the conversation to go. She'd dug this hole for herself, and now she had to think quickly to get out of it. "I'm an interior decorator." A total lie, but she was good at it—always helped her friends find the right styles for their homes.

"After the way you helped me with the window today, I kind of figured you did something like that."

"She helped you with your window?" Sue's eyebrows went up.

"Sure did." Janie's voice lilted. "There isn't a rule against that."

"But she's a professional."

"I'm not a professional Christmas-window decorator, and Janie didn't know I was a decorator at all at the time." She certainly didn't want to get on Janie's bad side by having her be disqualified from the contest.

"Still doesn't seem kosher." Sue frowned as she took another sip of her wine.

It seemed the contest was very competitive, just as Janie had said. Time for a subject change. "I can't believe Dana can move that fast on the ice." Crystal hunkered her arms to her sides into a running position. "And the way she knocked those kids out of the way trying to get into a chair was vicious." She poked an elbow at Sue.

"Yeah." Janie chuckled. "Dana's super sweet until the gloves come off. When it comes to ice games, she's going to win at all costs." She glanced at the door. "I wonder where she is. I'm going to check on her." She stood and walked toward the door.

Crystal watched Janie take long strides, shoulders back and an off-the-charts sexy swagger, a walk that projected confidence with every step. Janie had a quiet certainty about her that made her even more attractive as Crystal got to know her better. She pulled at the top of her sweater.

"Alcohol getting to you?" Sue seemed to have noticed her discomfort. "It does that to me too. Makes my rosacea flare up like a backyard torch." She ran her fingers across her cheek.

"Yeah. That and this wool sweater." Her temperature had catapulted to the extreme and popped the top off her internal thermometer quickly.

"Best thing is to just power through the first glass and move on to the second." Sue took a gulp of wine. "That always does it for me." She switched her empty glass out with the one Janie had bought for Dana. "It was getting warm." She winked. "We'll order her another one when she gets here."

Seemed Sue liked her rosé. Might be a prime time to get some information out of her. "So, how long have you and Mason owned the bakery?"

"We moved back here and opened it right out of college." Sue looked into the air with a dreamy smile. "It's all I've ever wanted." She played with the stem of her glass. "Well. I really want to bake but don't get much time to do that now."

"Oh? Why not?"

"Someone has to run the front of the shop—take the orders and do the bookkeeping. Mason's not good at any of that." She frowned.

"Maybe you could hire someone to run the front, and you two could do the baking together."

"I've thought about that but haven't found anyone who's as passionate about it as we are. I'm hoping one of the kids will want to be part of the family business when they get older."

Janie and Dana crossed the bar to the table and sat.

"What are you two talking about so seriously?" Dana didn't miss a beat.

"The kids working at the bakery."

"Those kids don't want to do anything but mess around with their friends. Can't blame them for that." Dana slid into a chair. "That's all you wanted to do when you were their age. Right, Janie?"

"High school should be a fun time. We all know how hard the world hits us after that, with college and then adulting." Janie glanced at the empty glass on the table and then at Dana. "I'll get you a glass of wine." She looked at Crystal. "You need another beer?"

"I'm good. Thanks."

Janie nodded and headed to the bar.

Crystal noted the bitterness in Janie's voice "What's up with her?"

"Family businesses aren't always the easiest to navigate." Dana glanced at the bar. "Janie and her dad don't see eye to eye on everything. Been that way since high school."

Janie appeared at the table with Dana's glass of wine and took her seat. "Let your kids be kids right now. I'm not sure about Teddy, but I think Stephanie really likes the bakery."

"Really?" Sue leaned forward, waiting for more details from Janie.

"Yeah. Why do you think I got that bakery game at the shack? She asked for it in last year's Santa box." Janie picked up her beer. "Just give her some time."

"What made you want to take over your family's business?" Crystal really wanted to hear that from Janie to understand more about her. This had nothing to do with business.

"I'm not sure. I came back from college, and it just kind of happened." Janie glanced around the bar. "I love this town and the people in it." She smiled softly. "I guess that's what did it. That and Dad had no idea how to update the shack with servers and a local area network." She laughed. "If it were up to him, he'd still be renting games and DVDs."

"You still have a selection of those, though, right?"

"Yeah. For some of the die-hard people still hanging on to their players."

"Seems like you have something for everyone at your place." Crystal took a drink of her beer and let the rich taste linger on her tongue. What would her life be like if she hadn't been able to pick her own career? It was so fast-paced she rarely had time to socialize with anyone or just go out and enjoy herself, like she was doing tonight, but she was okay with that…wasn't she?

"I do my best to please." Janie held up her glass.

"I'll keep that in mind." Crystal gave Janie a sideways smile. The tingle in her belly returned, but tonight she wasn't going to ponder the reason for it. She planned to relax and enjoy the feeling.

Chapter Eight

Janie wiped down the gaming equipment in the Top Net Zone before the Thursday gamer group arrived. She glanced at her watch. They would be here soon, in about fifteen minutes. The group reserved the room from seven to nine and consisted of mostly adult men and a few of their wives. They played *Minecraft*, *Just Dance*, or *Golf With Friends*, depending on whose night it was to choose the game. This group was more about socializing than game play, but Janie still made sure the servers were clean to allow the fastest internet speeds for all the gamers, serious or not.

She'd already prepped and reserved one of the tables for her weekly card game with the girls. Beka, Dana, and Sue had been playing Hearts at this time for as long as she could remember. Cards were a tradition for them from the time before video games were even born, and they'd outlasted many social games throughout the years. She checked the collaboration room. It was ready for the Thursday night book-club group. Tara, her part-time evening barista and counter clerk, must have cleaned it. Thursday nights were busy group nights at Cyber Shack.

Sue came in, went straight to the counter, and held up a few large shopping bags. "Can you put these behind there for me?"

"Sure." Janie tucked them under the side coffee-bar area. "You've got quite a stash. Are you done with all your Christmas shopping?"

Sue nodded as she picked up a couple of mugs and set them near the cash register. "Can you ring these up for me, Tara?" She handed her some cash. "Keep the change and just add them to one of the bags. I need to run to the bakery really quick. Be right back." She grinned at Janie. "Now I'm one hundred percent finished."

"Wish I could say the same." Janie watched Sue rush out the door as Dana entered.

"Say the same about what?" Dana asked as she entered. The woman had the hearing of an elephant.

"Being done with my shopping." Janie took her list from her pocket and waved it in the air. "Been carrying this thing around for weeks but haven't made a dent in it yet."

"You haven't started your shopping?" Dana seemed appalled at the thought. "Mine's been done for over a month."

"I've got too much going on around here."

"You need to give Tara a little more responsibility and get out of the place once in a while." Dana motioned to the merchandise on the counter. "That or everyone on that list is going to get candles, soap, or mugs."

"Then I'd just have to deal with things I need to fix at the house."

"Ben can help with that." Beka flattened her lips. "He fixed your water heater, didn't he?"

"He did, but I hate to keep asking for his help." Ben was sweet and would never tell her no even if he didn't have the time to help her.

"You know that's not an issue." Beka rolled her eyes. "We just need to find you a girl to occupy some of your time." She picked up a candle, screwed off the lid, and sniffed. "You could make do with these for gifts."

"She needs more than that. She needs to get laid," Dana said flatly.

Janie raised an eyebrow. "Why? Aren't you planning to buy me a new vibrator for Christmas?"

Beka moved her eyes from side to side. "That's not a bad idea. I'll check you off my list." She leaned forward. "But finding you a woman would be a better present."

"Stop. I'm fine." She wasn't. Her libido had shifted into high gear since Crystal had come to town. Letting Beka know that would set her into action, and then she wouldn't stop until marriage plans were in place with whomever she set her up with. Not her first walk down that path with these women.

"The new girl in town—what's her name again?" Beka snapped her fingers.

"Crystal." Dana spat it out like it had been sitting on the tip of her tongue.

Janie tried to stifle the shiver that came across her.

Beka's eyes widened. "She could be the one for you. Like in one of those cookie-cutter romances on TV." She grinned. "You know, she comes to town for a few weeks and falls in love with the town, the people, and a man. Only it wouldn't be a man. It would be you." She popped Dana in the shoulder. "That could happen, right?"

Dana rolled her eyes. "I doubt it." She pointed at Janie. "This one takes way too long to see when a woman's interested." Dana hadn't seemed to notice any of the subtle flirting between her and Crystal last night at the hockey game. Maybe Janie's instincts were way off, and it wasn't flirting at all. Was Crystal just being friendly? Had she imagined all of the glances?

Janie flattened her lips and shook her head. "That's not true, but my life is far from cookie-cutter, and I have too much on my plate right now keeping the café running to worry about romance."

"Besides, Crystal's only here until the holidays. Unless you want a short dalliance, it won't work." Dana wiggled her eyebrows.

"Nothing wrong with that." Beka's expression became intense, and Janie could almost see the wheels setting into motion in Beka's head.

"Don't even think about it." Janie stood. "If, and I mean if, anything happens between me and Crystal, it will happen naturally." She glanced at Dana. "Dalliance or whatever."

Sue pushed through the door again and hurried to the table. "What'd I miss?" She slid a pink bakery box onto the table.

Dana immediately opened the box and took out a cherry

turnover. "I was going to be upset if you didn't bring these." Still holding the turnover, she hopped up and grabbed a stack of napkins from the counter.

"We were discussing Janie's love life." Beka reached into the box and took out a pastry.

"More like her lack of one." Dana laughed as she bit into her turnover.

"I'm perfectly happy with my life right now. You all need to stop meddling." Janie brought a decanter of coffee and an additional mug for Sue to the table and sat.

"I thought Dana's niece, Crystal, would make a good match." Beka was never shy about voicing her opinion.

Sue's eyes widened. "That's a great thought." She looked at Dana. "Why didn't you bring her along tonight?"

"Hearts is a four-player game. No one wants to watch. Besides, she said she had some work to do, and maybe she's not into girls." Dana set her pastry on a napkin and picked up her coffee. "Said she might come by later."

With that news, Janie's system lit up from top to bottom like the Christmas lights running sequentially in the window. She didn't know if Crystal was interested in women or not, but she sure wanted to find out.

"Now let's get down to business." Dana picked up the cards and dealt the first hand.

It went quickly, with Beka and Sue winning immediately. The next couple of hands took a bit longer, but they won those as well. Janie was having trouble concentrating on the game since Dana had mentioned that Crystal might come by.

"Score." Beka grinned as everyone counted their pairs. She and Sue had won yet again.

Dana tossed her cards to the middle of the table. "What's wrong with you tonight?"

"Bad luck, I guess." Janie had spent too much time watching the door rather than watching the cards being played. Yet Crystal had been a no-show so far.

Beka stood. "I need a bathroom break."

Sue stood as well. "Me too."

"I'll get some fresh coffee." Janie pushed away from the table.

"You're hoping she'll show up, aren't you?" Dana gave her a sideways glance.

"Who?" Janie played dumb.

"Crystal. You two seemed to hit it off pretty well last night." Dana seemed to be more intuitive than Janie thought. "Staring at the door won't get her here. You want me to call the inn and check on her?"

"Sure. Tell her I suck at Hearts. She can come watch me lose." She went to the counter and filled the decanter with coffee. "That'll impress her, for sure."

Dana followed her around the counter. "Damn, girl. Don't you know. You *are* impressive. Even if you do suck at Hearts." She shook her head as she picked up the receiver and dialed. "Maybe her being here will help your game."

"I doubt that." It would probably only distract her more.

Dana smiled widely as she held the receiver to her ear. "Hey, girl. I'm having a lousy night at cards. Why don't you come over to the Shack and take my hand for the next deal?" Dana nodded a few times. "All right, then. We won't start the next set until you get here." She hung the phone on the receiver. "She'll be right over."

Janie went to the latte machine and began making Crystal's favorite drink.

Dana watched her pump the caramel into the cup. "You drinking a fancy drink tonight?"

Janie shook her head. "This is for Crystal." She continued making the latte.

"You know what she drinks already?"

"I know what everyone drinks." Janie rolled her eyes. "It's my job."

Dana grinned. "You do have it bad for this one." She headed back to the table.

Dana wasn't wrong about that.

❖

Crystal was excited to join the card game. She'd finished her notes from the scouting she'd done today and her to-dos for tomorrow. This was a good opportunity to get even friendlier with Janie and the rest of the women. Besides, what else did she have to do at close to nine o'clock on a Thursday night? It had been a while since she'd played, but Hearts was a common game at family events. When she was a child, her parents had planned game nights on Fridays. She would partner with her dad and her mom with her brother. Once her brother began playing sports in high school, that tradition ended, but they still played on occasion and always at large family holiday gatherings. She was looking forward to that when she arrived at her parents' house for Christmas.

She pushed through the door of Cyber Shack and headed straight to the back tables. It was later than she'd been there before, and she was happy to see that the place was fairly busy with people in the separate rooms. It seemed Janie's business was doing well. When she reached the table, she wasn't expecting the huge greeting of smiles she received. Something weird was happening.

"Dana must really be having a bad night for you to be desperate enough to call an outsider into the game."

Dana popped out of her chair, giving way for Crystal to sit. "You're not an outsider. You're family." Dana was playing her role perfectly.

"Right." Crystal glanced at Dana and smiled. "I guess I am." She hung her jacket on the back of the chair before sitting in the chair across from Janie. Sue was to her left and Beka to her right. "Thank you for inviting me." She glanced at Janie and smiled, felt the wonderful tingle as Janie smiled back at her.

"You want a cup of coffee or a latte?" Janie stood.

"A caramel latte would be great. Can you make it with two shots of espresso, a splash of nonfat milk, and a big squirt of caramel?" Apparently, Janie didn't remember what she liked. That was disappointing. Maybe she was just playing it cool.

"That's right. You like it made precisely that way." Janie laughed as she came back to the table and set the drink in front of her.

"Thank you." Janie *had* remembered. Warmth rushed her as she took a sip. "This is perfect." The cards were already dealt and laying on the table in front of her. "What game are you on?"

"Fifth, so you'll pass to Sue." Dana pulled a chair up behind her, looking over her shoulder.

Crystal smiled as she picked up her cards. The first few were shit, and the rest weren't much better. She had a handful of clubs but no card higher than a jack. The deck was stacked against her for sure. She glanced around the table to see if anyone was looking for a reaction. Everyone was concentrating on their cards. Must be just her bad luck.

"Your bid, Beka," Dana said.

"I'll go with two."

Janie glanced up from her cards at Crystal. "Five." She must have a decent hand.

"Two." Sue bid next.

Crystal glanced at her cards again. She could get two, maybe three tricks comfortably. Someone was underbidding. "I'll bid three." She hoped it was Janie.

Sue tossed out the two of clubs. Everyone went small, and Crystal took the trick with the nine of clubs and led with the jack. Janie sloughed a three of diamonds, which meant she didn't have any clubs. If Crystal won this trick, she'd lead with them next. She did indeed win the trick and led with the ten of diamonds. Sue played a five, and all eyes were on Janie, who took a minute to re-sort her cards. She should've done that at the beginning of the hand.

When Janie played the queen of diamonds, Dana stood and walked around to see Janie's hand. "Oh." Trumping your partner's card meant Janie didn't have anything smaller. Either that or she didn't know how to play the game. She doubted that was the case.

"Hey. Sit down." Beka pointed to Dana and then to her chair. "No table talk."

Seemed these women took their card games seriously.

Janie led the next hand with the five of spades, Beka tossed out the ace, so she threw in her lowest of the suit, and then Sue played a spade as well. Their trick.

On the next round, Janie broke the hearts. She must've not had much of anything else in her hand. Then, bam, Janie took trick after trick as she ran the hearts. Crystal was impressed. Janie hadn't given anyone a clue as to what she'd had in her hand, and she knew how to play it.

"Oh, man. I'm sorry. I didn't mean to do that." Janie glanced up from the cards at Crystal. "I should've bid higher."

Watching Janie run the board sent a chill through Crystal. Janie had such a still confidence that didn't waver but was also full of self-deprecation when she'd realized what she'd done.

"I'm good with underestimating." Crystal pulled her lip to the side and smiled. "That was awesome."

Everything slowed as Janie's eyelids slowly closed and opened again, and their eyes locked. Everyone else in the room seemed to disappear, leaving just the two of them in some sort of timeless moment. This woman was special—more special than anyone Crystal had ever met.

"Looks like Crystal is your good-luck charm." Dana's voice broke the moment.

"Must be." Janie blinked a few times before she stood and rushed to the counter like she was running from a ghost who had just flown into the room. "Anyone up for more coffee?"

"None for me." Sue glanced at the clock on the wall. "It's getting late. I'm going to head home."

Dana stood and moved her chair to another table. "Mind dropping me off at the inn?"

Beka seemed to be reading the room. "Sue's going the other way. I'll drop you."

"I guess I missed most of the game." Crystal helped Janie clear the table. "I should've come over sooner." She glanced around the café. "This place really clears out in a hurry."

"Small-town sidewalks roll up at nine."

"I didn't know that." Crystal lived in a large suburb just outside of Dallas, where a lot of places were open until the wee hours of the morning.

"Dana shouldn't have called you. She's not very subtle." Janie avoided eye contact. "None of my friends are."

"I can see that." Crystal smiled. "But I don't mind. They're just looking out for you."

Janie walked behind the counter and wiped it down before she propped herself up on it with her forearms, lacing her fingers together. "She seems to think we make a good match." She glanced up and gained eye contact, possibly looking for validation.

Crystal contemplated her next words. She should really stop this right here—not mix business with pleasure. "She's not wrong." The pull to explore more with Janie was too strong. She moved to the counter, parallel from Janie, reached across the counter, and cupped Janie's hands between hers. "I like you."

They stared into each other's eyes without even a blink. Crystal had never felt anything like this connection with Janie. The feelings bubbling inside were overwhelming.

"Kitchen's clean." Tara's voice jolted them out of the moment. "I'm heading out."

They jumped and retracted their hands quickly. It was clear that neither of them knew anyone was in the café and were obviously not ready to make any of what was happening between them known.

"I should go." Crystal smiled. "See you tomorrow?" She moved toward the door in a backward step.

"I'd like that." Janie seemed to be inside her head for a moment. "Hey. I'm supposed to help my brother load some trees at the Christmas-tree farm to bring back to the lot tomorrow. You want to come with us?" She stepped from side to side. "I mean it's okay if you don't. It's just really beautiful at the farm."

"I'd love to." With the way Janie made her feel, she'd learn how to make her own lattes if she had to just to be near her.

"Great." Janie grinned. "I'll call you in the morning."

"Sounds good." Crystal turned toward the door and practically hit the glass with her face. She tugged it open and waved at Janie as she passed by the window. *Way to be cool about it, Crys.*

They'd had a moment, Janie and she, and she hoped for many more in the future. Was it too much to ask for some pleasure to come from this trip? Considering she hadn't been truthful with Janie from the get-go, Crystal was probably hoping for too much. Besides, she was here on a mission, and Janie was part of that.

Chapter Nine

Crystal walked to the Christmas-tree lot. Janie had called her mid-morning to let her know they would be heading to the tree farm around eleven, told her to eat a good breakfast, and had offered to pick her up on the way. Crystal had opted to take the short walk to the stand instead. The clean winter air was refreshing.

As she came closer, she could see Janie and her brother shifting trees around the space from down the street. They seemed to be taking inventory. When she reached the curb in front of the crosswalk, before crossing the street, she stood and watched for a few minutes. Janie was dressed in jeans, a navy jacket that hit just below her butt, and a multicolored knit cap. When Crystal had gotten to her room the night before, she'd talked herself out of what was happening between them, but as soon as she caught sight of Janie again, she knew she hadn't been wrong about it.

Janie spun around as though she sensed she was being watched. She smiled widely and waved, and all the butterflies Crystal had released last night swarmed in her stomach again. Definitely something there. She waved and sucked in a breath of cold winter air to calm herself before she crossed the street.

"Good morning."

"Welcome to the Elliott Tree Lot." Janie swung her arm in front of Crystal. "Let me give you a tour."

"Why, thank you." The area wasn't large, just a small corner between two brick buildings with a silver Airstream trailer parked in the middle. It was prime real estate that must cost them a fortune to book for the holidays.

"We have wreaths, holly, garlands, and stands over here."

Janie led her through the first area nearest the trailer, then on to a larger empty area.

"And here is where we keep all the trees that we're going to pick up today."

"You've sold a lot."

Janie nodded as she turned and walked back to the trailer, where a table with a couple of large pump thermoses stood. She picked up a Styrofoam cup and filled it from one of them. "Hot cocoa?" She held the cup out to Crystal.

"Don't mind if I do. Thanks." Crystal took a sip and enjoyed the chocolaty flavor as it warmed her. "Why is this so good here?"

"We make it three times a day with snow."

"Really?" Crystal glanced at the snow that had been plowed in front of the lot.

Janie laughed. "No. Not with snow, but at least three to five times a day." She filled a cup for herself. "We'll hit the road as soon as my dad gets here to watch the place while we're gone."

"How often do you go to the farm to pick up trees?"

"Nate picks up a couple of times a week. The closer we get to Christmas, the busier the lot gets." Janie pinched the needles of a wreath and rubbed them between her fingers. "We'll get a bigger load than usual today." She held her fingers to her nose and sniffed. "As they get older, they lose their scent." She must have realized that action looked weird—and it kinda did.

"Oh, so that's why you invited me." Crystal held up her arm and flexed her bicep, which couldn't be seen under her jacket. "You needed extra muscle."

"Maybe." Janie gave her a half smile as she took a drink of cocoa and swallowed. "This coming week will be busy. We can use all the help we can get. You still in?"

"Absolutely." She wasn't afraid of a little hard work.

"Honestly, though, I really want you to see the farm." Janie's excitement made Crystal's stomach tingle. "With all the snow we've had, it's beautiful." It had been a while since someone wanted anything *for* her rather than *from* her.

As Nate came out of the trailer, he pulled on a black skullcap. Dressed in boots, jeans, and a Carhartt utility jacket, he was the quintessential mountain man, every straight girl's dream.

He glanced up as he pulled the trailer door shut. "Is this the friend you told me about?"

"Yes." Janie stumbled on her words. "She's my…I mean…"

"I'm Crystal." Seemed Janie had already discussed her coming along.

"Nate." He nodded as he checked his pockets for gloves. "Mom should be here in a minute. Then we can go." He walked to the beverage table and filled a thermos with hot cocoa.

"Your mom's coming too?" She hadn't expected to meet her. This could be an opportunity to gain more information about why the town was so against Wi-Fi.

"I thought Dad was manning the lot." Janie leaned closer. "It's a small community, but sometimes people forget to leave a note when they pick up a tree."

Nate shook his head. "He's already up there. Came up last night to help cut trees."

A random woman and child caught her eye as they walked through the lot to the cocoa stand and chatted with Nate for a minute. She filled two cups, then went on her way. No wonder they had to make so much.

A late-model Ford truck pulled up in front of the lot, and Janie touched Crystal's hand. "There she is now."

Her mom stepped out of the truck, went to the back and took out a box, and carried it to where the wreaths and holly were hanging. "Got some more mistletoe."

Janie picked a couple of stems from the box. "We'll wrap these with ribbon when we get back."

"I'll do it while I'm here." Her mom rearranged the chairs closer to the fire pit.

"Do you buy that somewhere?" Crystal had never seen fresh mistletoe before.

"Got it from my trees." Janie's mom squinted. "You're not from around here, are you?"

"Mom. This is Crystal Tucker, Dana's niece. She's in town for the holidays."

"Oh." She nodded. "Sandy Elliott."

"Nice to meet you."

"You staying at the inn for Christmas?"

"Yes. I'm staying there, but I'm afraid I won't be here for Christmas." Crystal glanced at Janie and saw her smile fade just a bit, and oddly, it made her sad. "I'll be going home before then to spend the holiday with my family." A couple of days ago, she'd still planned to take her tropical vacation if she could get this contract signed quickly, but as of right now, she wasn't sure she wanted that anymore. Since she'd arrived in Pine Grove, the thought of spending additional time during the Christmas holiday with her family kept floating through her mind.

"Let's load up." Nate went to the flatbed truck with staked sides parked on the street. "We'll pick up Grandpa on the way."

Front seat only—she hadn't planned on being in such close quarters with Janie so soon, but she was willing to let it happen. Janie climbed in first and slid to the middle. Once Crystal was inside, Janie reached across and tugged the door shut. A whiff of vanilla and tobacco floated to her nose. It smelled just like the candle she'd purchased a few days ago, with a pinch of Janie in the mix—a wonderful scent.

❖

Grandpa was waiting out in front with his hands on his hips as usual when they pulled up in front of his house. He looked almost exactly like Nate, except for the red plaid trapper hat. Nate would age well. Once Nate stopped the truck, Grandpa pulled open the door. He stopped mid-climb when he noticed Crystal. "We've got extra help today, eh?" He slid into the seat and slammed the door. "Whose girlfriend is she?"

"Not mine. She's with Janie," Nate said flatly.

"This is Dana's niece, Crystal. She's visiting for a few days." Janie shifted closer to Nate as Crystal scooched closer to her. "Sorry. It's only about a thirty-minute drive once we get out of town." She hadn't realized Grandpa was coming today, or she might have rethought her invitation to Crystal. It was going to make the ride there and back pretty cozy.

Grandpa nodded as he looked out the windshield. "Nice to meet you." He popped open the glove box and searched inside. "You bring extra gloves for her?"

"Yes, Grandpa." Janie shook her head. "But we're not going to work her too hard."

"Everyone puts in the same effort." He continued to stare out the windshield.

Crystal grinned as she slipped her hand on Janie's knee and squeezed. Uncomfortable just went up a notch. Janie was concentrating so hard on Crystal's hand on her knee that she almost didn't hear her whisper, "I'll be fine."

It wasn't Crystal she was worried about any longer. The heat in the cab was about to make Janie explode. She flipped the temperature to low, took off her knit cap, and unzipped her coat midway. They couldn't get to the farm quick enough so she could get some fresh air.

Crystal smiled as she removed her hand from Janie's knee and unzipped her coat as well. "It's a little warm in here," she whispered into Janie's ear, and it got even hotter.

Janie glanced at Nate, then her dad. Neither one seemed to be paying attention to them. None of this was her imagination. Crystal was flirting with her.

By the time they pulled into the farm, Janie was ready to strip off all her clothes and create snow angels naked in the snow.

Grandpa twisted and gave them a side-eyed glance. "You girls ready to work?"

"Yes." Janie probably said it louder than necessary, but she'd welcome anything that got her out of this truck and let the heat dissipate between her and Crystal.

"It'll take us a minute to get the equipment set up." Nate tossed her the key to the ATV. "Why don't you show Crystal the young trees before we get started? Grab a walkie-talkie from the house, and we'll meet you at the mature section." It seemed Nate was now her wingman. He must've noticed her body heat rise during the ride.

Janie glanced at Crystal and cocked her head toward the ATV. "You want to go for a ride?" If Crystal said yes, her temperature was going to rise a whole lot more. Probably not the best idea if she wanted to cool whatever this was she was feeling.

"I'd love to." Crystal grinned.

"I need to call the café first to make sure everything's okay. I left Tara running the counter."

Crystal pulled a cell phone from her pocket and held it up. "You know, if you had one of these, she could call you if she needs you." She glanced at the screen and then held it up in the air. "Isn't there a cell tower anywhere around here?"

"No. Dad hates cell companies, and I'm not sure if being so accessible would be a blessing or a curse." Janie rushed into the house, picked up the phone, and dialed the café. It rang once before Beka picked up. "Cyber Shack. How can I help you?"

"Hey, Bek. Everything good there?"

"Yeah. I'll call the fire department if Tara sets the place on fire."

"Thanks." She dropped the receiver into the cradle, then grabbed a walkie-talkie from the charging station on the table by the door.

"Everything okay?"

"Yep." Janie went to the ATV parked out front, slid her leg across the seat, and fired the engine. Crystal followed, slipped onto the back, and wrapped her arms around Janie's waist. Janie was completely on fire now.

"Hold on." She twisted the throttle, and the ATV chugged through the snow and up the slight grade to the first section of trees. She let off the throttle, and the ATV slowed. "This section has balsam firs, which are full and a bit more fragrant than most." She pointed to another section. "Over there are Frazer firs, still fragrant, but with tiered spaces for ornaments." Then to another. "Next to that we have Noble, Douglas, and Grand." She waved her hand across the area. "All firs with great scents."

"My favorites." Crystal took in a deep breath. "I love that smell." The trees were so lush, they were the deepest green, almost black.

"Really?" Janie turned slightly, gave her a sideways glance, and smiled. "Mine too." She pointed to another area of the farm. "The other, less-fragrant trees, which shall remain nameless," she grinned, "are over there."

"Being here with you...in this beautiful place. It's almost surreal," Crystal said as she planted her chin on Janie's shoulder. "Do you bring many women here?"

"No." Janie bit her bottom lip. She had, but no one she wanted to show this to more.

"That's hard for me to believe." Crystal pulled her lips into a lopsided grin.

"Maybe a few, but you're the first one who's actually appreciated it."

Crystal took Janie's chin in her hand and guided her face toward her as she flitted her gaze from Janie's lips to her eyes and then back again. The warmth of Crystal's breath warmed Janie's lips as she moved closer, twisting for better access. The kiss was soft and tentative at first as their lips came together. Soon Crystal's tongue dipped into her mouth and began a gentle, methodical dance with Janie's, slow and sensuous as it became deeper and longer. Crystal teased and baited her to respond, which Janie did, indulging in the kiss fully. Then suddenly a shooting pain gripped Janie's leg, Pleasure and pain ripped through her. That was a whole different kissing sensation. *Fuck.* She ripped her lips away from Crystal's and hissed as she catapulted off the ATV, trying to relieve the cramp in her right thigh.

"What's wrong? Are you okay?"

"Leg cramp." She pushed her knuckles hard into her thigh. "God. ATVs are so awkward. I should've brought the UTV instead."

The look of concern in Crystal's eyes faded as she tried to stifle a laugh. "But you weren't planning to kiss me, were you?"

"No…I mean, I wanted to but didn't plan on it." She massaged her thigh as the pain faded. "You're so beautiful, and I didn't know whether you'd be interested in plain old me." She paced to relieve the cramp.

"There's nothing plain about you, Janie." Crystal got off the ATV. "And I'm definitely interested." She moved closer, touched her lips lightly to Janie's. "I've wanted to do that since you kicked ass at Hearts last night."

"So, why didn't you?"

"I don't know." Crystal shrugged, seeming insecure now. "Maybe I was worried that you wouldn't kiss me back."

"I think we've resolved that worry." Janie stepped closer, slipped her arms around Crystal's waist, and kissed her softly, sweetly, deeply. She heard static and then the whir of the chainsaw come through the walkie-talkie—Nate's signal they were ready to start. His timing was ridiculous. "We should go before they come looking for us."

Crystal backed up, bit her bottom lip. "Yeah. I guess we should."

Janie climbed onto the ATV and patted the spot in front of her. "Why don't you drive? It's just over there." Janie pointed to a section of larger trees.

Crystal's eyes lit up, and she slid onto the seat in front of Janie. "Awesome." She immediately twisted the throttle and took them quickly to the area where Nate, Janie's dad, and her grandpa were already cutting trees.

"What do we do?"

"As Nate and Dad cut the trees, we'll wrap them with netting and twine. After we're done, we'll all load together."

Crystal glanced at Grandpa standing with his hands on his hips watching Nate. "Grandpa supervises?"

Janie laughed. "Yep." She grabbed a spindle of twine. "I'll show you how to tie a trucker's knot. Unless you know how to already."

"I do not. Show away."

The hours went quicker than Janie expected as they cut, wrapped, and loaded the trees. Crystal had fit into the rhythm soon after they'd started and tied a pretty damn good knot. The whole process usually took them well into the evening, but Crystal's help and adaptability had saved them a lot of time. They were done before dark.

"We're all loaded and ready to head back. Where's Grandpa?" Nate gave his dad a head nod. "You coming with us?"

"In the house." Janie's dad gave them a backhanded wave. "You go on ahead. We're going to have a cup of coffee and rest for a minute." He turned and headed to the house. "We'll be there in a bit."

Sure. When she wanted the cab of the truck to be crowded, it wouldn't happen.

Ten minutes into the drive, Crystal was asleep, her head on Janie's shoulder.

"You sure do know how to keep a woman entertained." Nate glanced at Crystal.

"Shut up." She relaxed into her seat and let the warmth Crystal provided seep into her. Not even the bumpiness of the flatbed truck woke her. Crystal was out. "You could've let up a little today. Not worked her so hard."

"Hey. She wanted to help." Nate pointed to the floorboard. "There's hot chocolate in the thermos."

She reached for it, and Crystal slid closer. She poured some into the cap and took a sip. Her throat burned as she swallowed. "Jesus. What the hell's in this?"

"Bourbon."

She took another sip before screwing the cap on. "Kahlúa would've been better."

"Maybe so, but bourbon goes with everything."

The ride was quiet, and her thoughts drifted to the kiss she and Crystal had shared and what would come next. More kisses… then touching—lots of touching…then hot, steamy sex…then her mind spun with all the ways this scenario between them could end. Any way it played out, it ended with her and Crystal in states three thousand miles away from each other. Not a good future.

Chapter Ten

Crystal had never seen such a beautiful sight as she had today at the tree farm. So many evergreens, some so green, others flocked in snow. It was a whole different world, picturesque and untouched by the real world. She could understand the point now—why the town didn't want to bring the outside world into their serenity—why Janie's family didn't want a cell tower on the mountain in the middle of their paradise. She opened her eyes slightly as the truck slowed and the lights from the tree stand came into view. She could see the clear, white lights strung around the lot instantly from down the street. Another comforting Christmas feeling came over her as memories of similar areas from her childhood flew through her mind. Seemed she'd forgotten so many of the joys of the holiday season since she'd become a workaholic.

She continued to let the comfort of Janie's shoulder keep her warm. The day had been magical—the snow—the trees—the kiss—all of it. Her right hand was cold, but her left was warm. She glanced around the cab of the truck to get her bearings. Her hand was clasped in Janie's, being held captive on Janie's thigh. *Did Janie do that, or did I?* It seemed like Crystal was the one holding Janie's hand prisoner. She released her grip and laced their fingers together as she raised her head. Janie didn't resist. Maybe it was both of them.

Crystal covered her mouth as she yawned. "Sorry. All that fresh air got to me." The last thing she remembered was leaving the farm.

"Not to mention the work." Janie grinned as she stared into her eyes. "Nate's quite the taskmaster."

"Yeah. I haven't done hard labor in a while."

"What?" Nate's voice rose. "All I asked you girls to do was tie knots. Men should do the heavy lifting."

"Really?" Janie raised her eyebrows. "That's all you have to say?"

"All right." Nate shook his head. "Thanks for the help. We got done much sooner than usual."

Janie bumped Crystal's shoulder. "He rarely admits he needs help."

"Because I don't," he said firmly.

"Tree Man, you out there?" Janie's dad's voice blared through the ham radio on the dash.

Nate picked up the microphone. "I'm here, Papa Bear."

"We're right behind you. I'll help you unload as soon as we get there." The radio crackled as Janie's dad spoke.

"Roger that." Nate hung the microphone on the clip. He really was the perfect mountain man. Probably had women lined up, if he wasn't married already. She hadn't seen a ring, but that didn't mean he wasn't. What was his stance on Wi-Fi? Considering the ham radio on the dash, he was probably on the same side as the rest of the town. Several times today she should've brought up that subject, but she hadn't wanted to spoil the mood.

As they pulled up to the tree lot, they could see the lit fire pit. Janie's mom was sitting in one of the chairs in front of it. Crystal could understand why. The temperature had dropped a bit while they were at the farm, and snow was expected soon. She hadn't really noticed all that much while she was pressed up against Janie the whole ride home.

Nate had backed up the truck, and they began unloading the trees. The tree farm, the town, and the kiss she'd shared with Janie had been more than she'd expected when she'd arrived. She had two problems to resolve now—how to get the town to accept broadband and how to ensure Janie didn't hate her when she found out who she was and why she was here.

"Why don't you girls go grab a bite to eat." Janie's dad startled Crystal out of her thoughts. "We can handle the rest. Right, Nate?" They'd already unloaded about half of the trees.

Nate nodded. "Bring us back some burgers."

"I'll see you tomorrow." Grandpa went to the car with Janie's mom.

"Your mom's not coming with us?"

Janie shook her head "She's taking Grandpa to have dinner with Grandma at the retirement home. It's pizza night."

"You want to go? I can go back to the inn." Crystal was aching for a long, hot bath.

"No. They have a killer meatloaf at the diner." Janie glanced at Crystal. "You like meatloaf?"

"Love it." She didn't eat it much at home. Cooking meatloaf for one meant she'd be eating it for a week, and that just wasn't practical with her schedule.

They headed across the street to the diner, where they took a booth near the window that had a clear view of the tree lot. With old-fashioned lampposts and wrought-iron benches lining the streets, it really was the perfect Norman Rockwell town.

The waitress appeared immediately to take their order.

"Hey, Delta. We'll both have the meatloaf." Seemed Janie knew everyone.

"Mashed potatoes and green beans?"

They both nodded.

"Anything to drink?"

"Water," they said simultaneously. "Jinx," they both added and then laughed.

They sat across from each other in silence. Crystal needed to start talking before it got awkward. "So, does your dad or your brother own the farm?"

"Both. My dad retired a few years ago, and now my brother runs it." The booth seat crackled as she shifted. "I got Cyber Shack, and he got the farm."

"Is that what you wanted?"

"Yes and no. I mean I love the café and the farm, but I guess I never thought I'd be here in this town for the rest of my life." Janie held up her hand. "Not that I don't love it. I just never leave for anything."

"Not even a for a few days? I really thought you were kidding when you said that yesterday."

"No." Janie shook her head. "Never been out of New England."

"Can't your dad or mom handle the café for a week or two?"

"They probably could, but I don't really have any place to go. I'd hate to ask them so I could just take time without having anything planned."

"You could come see me."

"That'd be a long way to drive."

Crystal almost laughed out loud, but she could see that Janie was serious. "They have this new invention called planes, you know." She'd probably never been on one.

"I've never been to California. I guess it would be nice to visit… see you again." Janie slowly snaked her hand across the table and tapped Crystal's fingers with her own in an awkwardly shy dance. Janie's confidence seemed to disappear when it came to romance.

"You're welcome to come see me anytime." In an attempt to calm Janie's anxiety, Crystal flipped her hand and took hold of Janie's. "I'll show you all the sights." What the hell was she talking about? She didn't even live in California. How was she going to tell her she really lived in Dallas? Would Janie want to come see her at all after she found out she'd been lying to her? How far was she going to take this masquerade? She needed to stop it—now—but she couldn't bring herself to spoil the moment. "I had a wonderful time today."

"Me too." Janie glanced up from their hands, which seemed to be glued together at this point.

Delta appeared with two plates of meatloaf, mashed potatoes, and green beans. "You ladies need anything else?"

Janie glanced up. "No. I think we're good, but I need a couple of burgers and fries to go for Dad and Nate."

"The usual, coming right up."

Janie might be good, but Crystal was far from it. Everything that had happened over the past few days had her all mixed up. Maybe if she got back to business that would change. She released Janie's hand and picked up her fork. "This looks good."

"Best in town." Janie reached for her fork, broke a chunk loose with the side of it, speared it, and put it into her mouth.

She pulled her cell phone from her pocket and looked at it…A conversation starter.

"That's not going to work here," Janie said matter-of-factly.

"I forgot." Crystal set it on the table as a reminder of why she was here. "So, tell me again why you don't have broadband in Pine Grove?"

Janie stopped chewing for a moment and set her fork on her plate before she wiped her mouth with her napkin. "Because of that right there. Here we are having a nice conversation over some really good food, and you checked your phone to take you out of it—to somewhere else."

"I see your point." Looking at her phone was far from what she wanted to do right now. She wanted to bury it deep in her pocket—push her plate across the table and slide into the other side of the booth to be closer to Janie. "You're right about the food and the conversation." She took the phone from the table and dropped it into her pocket. "There's no place I'd rather be." Her mission would have to wait.

They ate quickly without much more conversation. Today's adventure had given them both an appetite. When Delta offered pie, they opted to share a slice of cherry with a small amount of whipped cream on top. She soon arrived back at the table with the bag of burgers and the check. Crystal reached for it.

"I'll get it." Janie slapped her hand on top of the paper and pulled it her way. "It's the least I can do. You worked hard today." She slid out of the booth. "Can you grab the bag?"

Crystal nodded. "Sure."

Janie went to the counter, paid, and met Crystal at the door. "We'll drop these off at the tree lot, and then I'll give you a ride home."

"I can walk."

"I'll take you." Janie pushed the door open and let Crystal walk ahead of her.

"Thank you."

Janie slipped her hand into Crystal's as they crossed the street. Seemed Janie's confidence was back and in full gear. When they got to the fire pit, Janie's dad and Nate were relaxing in front of it, a bottle of something sitting in the snow between them. There was no denying they were related. They had the same chiseled features.

"Just in time." Janie's dad reached for the bag. "Nate needs some food. I think he's getting a little drunk." He handed Nate one of the containers.

"I think you have that backward." Nate immediately grabbed the burger from the container and bit into it.

"I'm going to take Crystal home before she freezes again."

"Good night." Crystal raised her hand and gave them a slight wave. "Thanks for including me today."

"Any time," Nate said through the food in his mouth, and Janie's dad nodded as he swallowed and reached for the bottle in the snow.

Janie seemed to be inside her head as they walked to her Jeep. Crystal hoped she hadn't upset her earlier when she'd tried to dig deeper. They both went to the passenger side, and Janie pulled the door open for her. Even if she was mad, she was still chivalrous. They drove in silence the few minutes it took to get to the inn. Janie parked in the drive-through area. Was Janie intending to leave no question as to whether she would come up to her room?

"I'll walk you to the door." Janie unbuckled her seat belt and hopped out of the Jeep quickly. It seemed as though something was up with her since they'd left the diner.

As they walked to the inn entrance, Crystal wrapped her arms around herself to stifle the chill. She was cold and tired but couldn't bring herself to leave Janie without something more—another touch of her hand—another kiss—anything to keep her warm. Janie immediately removed her jacket and put it on Crystal's shoulders.

Earlier today when they'd kissed, she'd told Janie that she didn't have any worries, but that wasn't true. There were a million reasons why she hadn't kissed her last night—why she shouldn't have kissed her today—why she shouldn't kiss her again tonight. All Crystal knew for certain right now was that she didn't have the ironclad control over her mind and body she'd had in the past. Janie was doing things to her that she hadn't expected, and it scared the hell out of her. What was going to happen when Janie found out who she really was and that she'd betrayed her? That she was essentially here to convince her to bring in technology that could ruin her business?

None of that stopped her from moving closer and hoping with everything she had that Janie would kiss her good night. When Janie leaned in, Crystal didn't fight it—didn't want to anymore. She let Janie's lips capture her mouth for a long, slow, sensuous kiss. A glow of warmth swept through her, with each area their bodies touched burning hotter than the rest. She had to douse this flame somehow.

Crystal broke the kiss. "I should go in." She brushed Janie's cheek with the back of her hand. "I want you to know this is the best day I've had in a long time." She wasn't lying about that.

Janie took in a deep breath and clasped Crystal's hand in hers. "Me too. Can I see you again tomorrow? There's bingo at the retirement home."

"Sounds like fun." They'd be surrounded by lots of people, without too much pressure to move forward with whatever was happening between them. Crystal shrugged off Janie's jacket and handed it to her. "Thank you." She'd said that a lot this evening.

"I'll call you." Janie turned, tossed her jacket over her shoulder, and strutted back to her Jeep with a bounce in her step that Crystal hadn't seen before.

She watched Janie drive off, noting the writing on the tire cover. *The Black Jeep of the Family.* Had the cover come with the Jeep, or had Janie bought it herself? Either way, it provided another interesting insight into Janie. She would add it to the other tidbits she'd learned tonight.

Chapter Eleven

Even though Janie awoke early, she hadn't managed to get out of bed and was late to work this morning again. That was twice in one week. She hadn't slept well. With last night's kiss lingering on her tongue and thoughts of Crystal monopolizing her mind, she had spent a restless night. What was going on here? The woman had been captivating from the start, and yesterday's trip to the tree farm had sealed the deal. Crystal was the perfect woman. Well, maybe not perfect for everyone, but perfect for Janie.

"Good morning, Tara." She dropped the pastries she'd picked up from Sue's Sweets on the counter before she went into the small office, determined to find the tube filled with the modernization plan that she'd buried in the corner years ago.

"You okay?" Beka stood at the door watching her.

"Yeah. I'm fine." She was far from fine. Updating from this retro state she was stuck in was nagging at her again. "Bingo." She dug out the floor plan she'd created for Cyber Shack.

"You thinking about doing the remodel again?"

"Thinking about it." She slid the plan out of the tube and unrolled it on the desk. "I need coffee. You want some?"

"Sure. I'll get it." Beka held her hand up. "You sit." She came back through the door quickly with a cup of coffee for each of them. "Why the change of heart?"

"I'm just tired of fighting this battle when I don't even know if I believe in it." She stood, moved to the doorway, and glanced around the café. Almost every area was occupied. Saturday mornings were always busy. "It probably wouldn't even hurt my business. People come here to be together, not just because of the internet, right?"

Beka nodded, knowing better than to interrupt her thought rant. This wasn't their first go-round with this subject.

"They enjoy the physical and social interaction that comes along with playing games in person as well as online." Janie scanned the café again. "Don't they?"

"Of course they do." Beka seemed to be in agreement. "And my food, of course."

"Yes. That too."

"I'm going to get back to the kitchen." Beka rolled her eyes. "Let me know if you need me to tell you this is a good idea for the gazillionth time." Beka had always supported Janie in her plans for expansion—even thought broadband would help the business when Janie wasn't sure.

Janie sat at the desk and sipped her coffee as she looked over the remodel plans. She'd created them when her dad had first handed Cyber Shack over to her. He'd implied that she'd have complete control, but that hadn't been true. When she'd shown him her plans to expand and modify their connection capabilities, he'd said she could add servers to handle more load, rewire the local area network, and change anything she wanted aesthetically, but had also given her a direct order to not upgrade the connectivity to include Wi-Fi. He still wasn't ready to allow the outside world in.

Crystal slipped into Janie's thoughts again—her smile, her voice, her laugh. Man, she had it bad for this one. She growled at herself before she drank the last of her coffee, rolled up the café floor plan, and slipped it into the tube. Maybe it *was* time for another look at the renovation and a discussion about who was running the business.

❖

Janie pulled up in front of the Pine Grove Inn and put the Jeep into park. She'd been able to get away from the shack early, so she'd picked up Grandpa first. "I'll be right back, Grandpa. I need to talk to Dana for a minute." Janie got out of the car. "Don't go anywhere, okay?" On occasion, Grandpa would commandeer a vehicle when he wanted to get somewhere faster.

Grandpa crossed his arms. "Why would I go anywhere? Don't have any place to be but where you're taking me."

She opened the front door of the inn and walked over to see Dana at the front desk. "Can you let Crystal know I'm here?"

"Crystal. You have a visitor," Dana shouted over Janie's shoulder.

Janie's stomach jumped as she spun around and spotted Crystal coming down the stairs. "Hey. Sorry I'm a little early." She took a long look at Crystal, and her heart pounded. Dressed in jeans and a knee-length brown wool coat, with a bright-yellow Wolverines sweatshirt underneath, she looked pretty fantastic in Pine Grove's hometown colors.

"It's fine. I was ready." Crystal smiled, and Janie's stomach did a full-out somersault.

"Great. I swung by and picked up Grandpa first." Being alone in the car with Crystal made her anxious. She threw Dana a wave. "See you later."

"You two have fun." Dana's voice rose. Seemed she was putting them together somehow too.

Janie opened the back door of the Jeep for Crystal, and she climbed in and buckled her seat belt.

"Hi, Mr. Elliott. It's good to see you again."

"Call me Grandpa. Everyone else does."

"If you say so, but you don't look old enough to be my grandfather." Crystal grinned at him from the back seat. Seemed she knew how to flirt with the best of them.

Grandpa looked at Janie as he hooked his thumb over his shoulder. "I like this girl."

Me too, Grandpa. Me too. She took the short drive to Pine Grove Retirement Community and pulled into a parking space. "I hope you don't mind a room full of competition."

"I'm actually looking forward to it." Crystal unfastened her seat belt. "I've never played bingo before."

"Never?"

"Well, I guess not never, but I was a kid the last time, and that was only in school. Nothing like it is now."

"Well, you're in for a treat." Grandpa grinned as she climbed out of the Jeep. "Want to know how to get a bunch of women to yell fuck?"

"Grandpa. Really?" Janie's voice rose as she shook her head.

"Yell 'bingo.'" He let out a hearty laugh at his own joke.

Crystal chuckled. "That would do it for me."

They took the short walk inside and to the main room of the retirement home and found Grandma. Dressed in jeans and a green Christmas sweater with a reindeer on the front, she was waiting in line just inside the door. "It's about time." She glanced at Grandpa. "Go get the table, and I'll get the packets."

Grandpa rushed across the room while Janie and Crystal joined Grandma in line.

Grandma pulled Janie into a hug. "It's good to see you, girl." She glanced at Crystal. "Who's this young lady?"

"This is Crystal, Dana's niece."

"Oh. In for the holidays?"

"Yes. For a few more days." Crystal smiled "Pine Grove is beautiful."

Janie's stomach sank. Their time together was limited.

"It fills the bill." Grandma stepped in front of the table. "How many packets you want?"

"How many cards are in a packet?" Crystal's eyes widened at the menagerie of bingo accessories on the table.

"Six." Grandma stared at Janie as she waited for an answer.

"That's a lot to keep up with. I think I'll just watch."

"No watching in bingo. She needs a beginner's packet." Grandma handed the woman at the table a twenty. "That will get you a marker too."

Crystal pulled some cash from her pocket. "Let me get that."

Grandma pushed Crystal's hand away. "Beginners don't pay when I'm around."

The woman handed Crystal her packet. "Thank you." Crystal flipped through the cards.

Janie was sure Crystal was just as confused as she was the first time she played. "I'll help you. It's not too bad once you get used to it."

"I sure hope so." Crystal glanced around the room at all the people sitting at tables with multiple cards and markers set up in front of them.

Grandpa had already saved a table close to the caller and within sight of the board. That made it easier for Grandma to keep track of the numbers called.

Once they got settled in and had their cards arranged, the first game began. It was coming along nicely. Grandma daubed at her cards with speed as each number was called. She didn't know how, but Grandma managed to be faster at it than Janie. Crystal was still fumbling with the whole process.

"Focus, girl." Grandma daubed a square on one of Crystal's cards. "You're getting behind. You can't win if you don't keep up." Grandma took a couple of Crystal's cards and placed them in front of Janie. "Help your girl out."

Janie glanced at Crystal, who gave her a sideways smile. The back of her neck heated.

The caller took a ball from the cage and squinted before calling the number. "B-24." A woman across the room yelled "Bingo" and held up her card.

"Damn it." Grandma dropped her marker onto the table and stood. "Either of you girls want to accompany me to the ladies' room?"

"I will." Crystal stood.

"We need to hurry. They'll be playing the progressive jackpot game soon." Grandma took Crystal's arm and walked her across the room.

"We don't want to miss that." Crystal smiled as she glanced back at Janie.

Grandpa watched until they disappeared into the hallway

before he covered Janie's hand with the warmth of his own. "What's wrong? You don't seem like yourself today."

She never could hide anything from him. "I'm a little stressed out about the café. This whole broadband decision by the council is getting to me. I'm just not sure about it anymore."

"Which side are you on?" Grandpa's voice was sweet and gentle, like she remembered as a child when he was teaching her things.

"I don't know." Janie shrugged. "On one hand, I get Mason's point about keeping the small-town atmosphere, but on the other hand, I'm not sure we shouldn't move into the twenty-first century with the rest of the state." She shifted to look at him. "Can't we do both? There are so many new things I could do at Cyber Shack if we had it. We could add another gaming room to space out the groups, set up a nice patio, even have classes right here at the PGR."

Grandpa crinkled his forehead. "You know I've never been a big fan of government regulation, and that comes with Wi-Fi."

"Right. That's my other concern." Janie sighed. "Do you think customers will stop coming to the café if I add it?" She blew out a breath. "On the flip side, wireless internet provides a degree of privacy, confidentiality, and accessibility that is crucial to some people who might not be comfortable accessing certain websites at the café. Will they buy computers and start spending more time at home instead?"

"You're talking about yourself now." He smiled and relaxed in his chair. Grandpa had been the first one to catch on about her sexual orientation. He'd always suspected, and seeing her web-surfing history at the shack had solidified his hunch.

"Yes, and others like me. People I still want to see at Cyber Shack."

"Some will buy computers, but not everyone in this little town can afford one. Others will stay away because they're afraid of being tracked." He raised his hand. "Your old grandpa here is a prime example of that. It's hard to teach this dog new tricks." Grandpa never referred to himself as old, but he did sometimes admit to his stubbornness. "I think if you educate people on how it works, they'll come around once they get used to the idea." He covered her small hand with his callused palm again. A small touch of comfort Janie hadn't forgotten. "Your dad had to do that when we first put in the servers. People were afraid of *that* new-fangled technology too."

"The ghosts in the closet." Janie laughed. "I forgot about that."

Grandpa relaxed into his chair. "You're running the business now. Do what you think is right."

"Dad would never go for it."

"How about I talk to him? Help pave the way for you." He squeezed her hand and smiled.

Janie's heart pounded. The nervous teenager she'd abandoned so long ago emerged again, hoping her grandpa could help resolve her worries. "Would you do that for me, Grandpa?" Janie had thought her grandfather would be totally against it as well. She'd also thought that when he'd approached her about being gay, but he'd been the exact opposite. He was loving and accepting and had supported her when she told the rest of her family. Relief washed through her when she realized he would be the same in this situation.

"Your grandma's been showing me how to play poker online at the shack. It's helping my game with the guys."

"Really? I didn't know that."

He nodded. "I'd rather do it at home, though. Don't want any of these old guys catching me."

"Huh." Who knew a little competition would bring her grandfather around? "Thanks for your support, Grandpa. I think Dad will listen to you." She caught a glimpse of Crystal walking Grandma back from the restroom. Her yellow Wolverines sweatshirt was visible from a mile away.

Grandpa squeezed her hand again and released it. "You like this girl a lot, don't you?"

Janie nodded. "We seem to hit it off really well."

"From what I saw yesterday, she seems to be a hard worker. She sure does like the hockey team."

Janie laughed. "Seems that way." It seemed every sweatshirt she wore was fan apparel. No doubt she was borrowing some of Dana's clothes.

"She live around here?"

"No. She's from California."

"Oh." He rubbed his chin. "Well. Your dad can find someone else to run the shack." Was he actually suggesting she move to California with a woman she barely knew?

"Let's not get ahead of ourselves, Grandpa. We're not that far down that road yet."

"Just opening up the gate so you can see over the horizon. When I met your grandma, I knew right away she was the one for me. It was a feeling I'll never forget." He smiled as he stared at the ceiling like he was drifting into a memory.

"Really?" Janie knew exactly what he was talking about. "Then why did you let her move to the PGR alone?"

"I wasn't ready yet." He shook his head. "And I don't *let* your grandma do anything. She does what she wants." The love in his eyes was clear as he spotted Grandma across the room walking back to the table arm in arm with Crystal.

Janie's heart warmed at the care Crystal gave Grandma as they walked toward them. Her stomach tingled when she caught Crystal's gaze. The electricity between them was wild, and apparently everyone else could see it.

CHAPTER TWELVE

Crystal waited by the door for Janie as she made her rounds and said good-bye to the majority of people who had played bingo today. She seemed to know everyone.

"Sorry that took so long." Janie put on her coat. "You ready?"

Crystal nodded. "Where's your grandpa?" She'd thought he was coming with them. Janie seemed to be his personal taxi service.

"Grandpa's going to stay over with Grandma tonight so he can take her to the town square later for the marshmallow roast." Janie zipped her jacket and put on her knit cap. "He just needs to move in with her."

"Why doesn't he?" Crystal couldn't imagine them being apart from each other at their age.

"Says he's not ready to give up his freedom yet." Janie reached into her pockets and found her keys.

"You can't blame him for that." Crystal had always been one to do what she wanted when she wanted. Probably why she'd never been able to maintain a long-term relationship.

"He doesn't drive anymore, so he kind of already has in a way." Janie pushed the door open and held it for Crystal before she glanced back at the people still milling about in the common area. "I always have so much fun at the PGR. Everyone here is such a kick." Janie focused her attention on Crystal as she came out the door. "Did you…have fun?"

"Absolutely. Once I got the hang of it." Bingo had been stressful at first, but once Grandma gave Crystal some tips, it had become so much more enjoyable, even though she hadn't won a single game. "And your grandparents are a hoot."

"Yeah. I enjoy hanging out with them." Janie rushed in front of her to the passenger side of the Jeep and opened the door for her.

"It's a beautiful day." It was cold, but the sun felt good on Crystal's face. "Do you want to walk?"

"Sure." Janie let the door close. "It's not far. We can stop at Sue's on the way and get a cup of coffee and something sweet if you want." She shoved her hands into her coat pockets.

"I'd like that." She'd been here less than a week, but she was getting attached to this little town of Pine Grove. "Have you always been close with your grandparents?"

Janie nodded. "Since I was a kid. They've helped me work through a lot of things."

"Oh? Like what?"

"Like coming out."

"That's awesome. I wish my grandparents were like that." It wasn't that her grandparents weren't supportive. They just didn't seem to understand, which killed any conversation about her sexual orientation.

"They're pretty exceptional. Even just now, Grandpa surprised me by…" Janie seemed reluctant to talk about whatever it was.

"By what?" Crystal shook her head. "You don't have to talk about it if you don't want to."

"I've been thinking about the whole broadband ban. I've never really been totally against it, and I can see Mason's point about keeping the town atmosphere quaint. But I'm not sure I agree that Wi-Fi will spoil that anymore."

Crystal's mission seemed to have just gotten a whole lot easier. "So, what are you going to do?"

"I don't know." Janie glanced around. "I'd heard a large company was sending someone out to convince the council, but the only new person in town is you." She smiled. "And if it were you, I'd know by now. Dana wouldn't be able to keep that cat in the bag."

"Right." Crystal was surprised she hadn't tipped someone off herself. "I'm sure everyone would know. Who could keep that a secret?" She should tell Janie now—try to salvage what she could of this thing between them. "I want to—" The words stuck in her throat. She was still afraid Janie would hate her.

Janie stopped and faced Crystal. "Go with me to the marshmallow roast at the town square tonight?" Janie chewed on her bottom lip, her expression so sweet and unassuming. Like she actually thought Crystal might say no. "It's the annual holiday roasting of the mallows." She averted her eyes and continued to walk.

"Of course. I'd love to go." Crystal touched Janie's hand with her finger. "I mean...I can't think of a better way to spend a Saturday night than with you." She would hold off telling Janie who she really was and enjoy another evening with her.

As they reached the entrance to the bakery, Janie seemed nervous again. "I was thinking the same thing." She smiled as she pulled the door open to the bakery.

Sue was behind the bakery counter adding fresh pastries to the case. "What are you two all smiles about?" She glanced over the top of the case.

Janie perused the pastries in the case. "We just came from bingo at the PGR."

"Oh. I missed it again." Sue frowned. "When's the next time? I'll come with you."

"Every Saturday." Janie moved to the end of the case. "They have lunch afterward." She seemed to be looking for something. "Do you have any Kouign Amann?"

"Yesterday. You missed it. Only on Fridays."

"Man." Janie's voice rose as the whine came from her mouth. "You didn't send one in the shack's order."

"Yes. I did."

"Beka." Janie squinted. "I'm going to kill her."

"Must be good." Crystal laughed.

"It's only one of my favorite buttery, caramelized things in the world." She poked a finger at the glass. "Guess I'll have to get a cinnamon roll instead." She glanced at Sue and then at Crystal. "Extra frosting." She grinned.

"And for you?" Sue glanced at Crystal.

"I'll have the same."

"Two cinnamons with extra glaze coming up." Sue took them from the bakery case and went to the back.

Janie went behind the counter and filled two mugs with coffee. "Sue, you going to join us for a cup of coffee?"

"Sure." Sue came back out carrying two plates with heaps of what looked like nothing but frosting. A sugar high for sure.

"Plain coffee here." Janie grinned as she passed a full cup across the counter to Crystal. "You want to grab the table in the corner by the window?"

"Sure." She went across the room, and Sue and Janie followed. "This is the perfect spot." She could see all the happenings on Main Street, which was even better than the view at the inn. She glanced at Janie as she slid into the chair next to her. Warmth spread through Crystal. She could imagine spending every Saturday afternoon this way—with this woman.

"So did you win?" Sue grinned at Crystal from across the table.

"At bingo? No." The word hummed out of her mouth. "I couldn't keep up with the professionals."

"She gave it a valiant try, though." Janie tore off a piece of cinnamon roll, put it into her mouth, and began licking the remnants of frosting left on her fingers.

Zing—the back of Crystal's neck heated, and a tingle rushed through her. Everything slowed, like she was in the middle of a sci-fi movie as she watched Janie methodically suck the frosting from each digit. She unwrapped her scarf from her neck and laid it in her lap.

"Hot?" Janie raised her eyebrows and gave her a sideways smile. Seemed she knew exactly what she was doing to Crystal.

Crystal nodded and smiled back at her. "Blazing."

"Oh. Let me check the thermostat." Sue popped up and rushed behind the counter to adjust the temperature and came right back. "It should cool down in a few minutes." She didn't seem to notice anything between them.

Crystal doubted that would help, but she appreciated Sue's

effort. She licked the frosting from the top of her own cinnamon roll, then glanced sideways to see if Janie had the same reaction. Janie pulled her lip up to one side before she removed her hat and scarf. It seemed to have worked. She liked this game.

The bell rang on the door, and Sue popped up and rushed behind the counter again.

"Good, isn't it?" Janie ran her tongue over her bottom lip, sweeping up a bit of stray caramel glaze from it.

Crystal stared at Janie's lips. "Unexpectedly delightful." She could watch Janie eat all day.

Janie grinned and held up the pastry. "The roll's pretty tasty too." She seemed to be fully aware of what her actions provoked.

She nodded. "The best culinary experience I've ever had." She tore off another piece, then washed it down with a sip of coffee.

Sue came back to the table, and the rest of the hour was filled with random chitchat that Crystal had a hard time following. Janie had set all her senses on edge, and she couldn't seem to concentrate on anything but how she was going to get past the huge lie she'd been telling.

When they went outside, Janie stopped for a moment. "You okay?" She seemed to have noticed Crystal's distraction.

"Just tired. Still adjusting to the time change." The air had chilled, and the sun was hidden behind the clouds. "It's getting cold. You don't have to walk with me to the inn." It wasn't far, but she'd give Janie an out if she needed one.

"I want to." Janie slipped her hand in Crystal's "I like walking… and talking…with you."

Crystal laughed. "I like walking…and talking…with you too."

"Glad we got that settled." Janie squeezed her hand and began strolling toward the inn. "Want to meet me here around eightish, and we can walk to the town square together?"

"How about sixish, and we can have dinner first?" Janie tilted her head and smiled.

"Even better." Crystal couldn't believe how good Janie's interest made her feel.

"Okay." Janie leaned in and gave her a soft kiss on the cheek.

"See you then." She turned and bounced down the circle drive. She watched Janie walk for a few minutes before she went inside. The kiss was nice but disappointing. She'd wanted more. Perhaps tonight would bring them closer.

Dana stood at the desk. "You win anything?" The question of the day.

"Nope." Not at bingo anyway.

"Your bag was delivered earlier. I had it taken up to your room."

"Thank you." She didn't stop to chat and went straight to the stairs. She had some feelings to sort through—some decisions to make about how she planned to let this scenario play out. The more time she spent with Janie and her family, the deeper she got into the endless web of lies she'd been weaving. Soon the persona she'd been wearing was going to be shattered, and she had no idea how she would be able to piece her life back together if Janie didn't forgive her for lying.

Chapter Thirteen

The light was blinking on the phone when Crystal got to her room. She dropped onto the bed, picked up the receiver, and hit the voice-mail button. Her boss's voice came through the speaker. "You were supposed to call me with an update. I need to hear from you."

Bob was the last person she wanted to talk to right now. She ended the message, punched in a number, and flopped onto the pillow.

"Hey, sweetheart." Her mom's sweet voice came through the speaker. She heard something whirring in the background.

"Hey, Mom. What are you up to?" Baking, she suspected. Her mom's cookies were the best.

"Making your favorite cookies for the holidays." The background noise stopped. "How's the trip going?"

"It's okay. The town is nice—quaint."

"You sound down. What's up?" Her mother could always read her so easily.

"I don't know, Mom. I don't think I want to do this anymore." She let out a sigh as the heaviness in her chest magnified.

"You don't want to work for Spark?" Her mom's voice lilted.

"It's not that I don't want to work for them. It's just gotten complicated. I've been lying about who I am since I got here, and I like this town and these people. I don't know if I can keep it up any longer."

"Have you talked to your boss about it?"

"No. He's threatening to send Jack to close the deal."

"Jack the jackass?" Her mother had picked up on the nickname the first time Crystal had used it around her family, and it seemed to have stuck.

"Yes. Bob's going to get what he wants one way or the other." Another big sigh. "If I can't get it done, he'll make sure Jack does."

"Can you fix it? Tell the people who you are and work out a mutual solution with them? Maybe something that benefits the town and Spark?" Her mother was always helpful when it came to brainstorming.

"Possibly." She'd already made a list of improvements the town could benefit from. She filtered through her notes and found the page she was looking for. "Hey, Mom. Can I call you back later?"

"Sure."

"Thanks for your help, Mom. I love you."

"I love you too, honey."

She hung up the receiver and started to work on her plan.

She'd had her head down working for close to two hours and had her proposal just about finished when the phone rang.

She picked up the receiver. "Hello."

"It's about time you picked up." Bob's voice boomed through the receiver.

"I've been busy scouting the town."

"What'd you find out?"

"Not as much as I need to know." She lied. "This deal needs a bit of tweaking."

"Finally realizing that just because you have a pretty face the world doesn't fall at your feet?" The voice of Jack, her nemesis, came through the line. She hadn't realized she was on speakerphone.

"Shut up, Jack. This road needs a little paving before I let you pull your steamroller into town."

"Settle down, you two. We're a team here, remember?" Some team. Her boss was always pitting them against each other and then playing referee.

"Right." She shook her head. "Don't worry. Once I turn on the charm and give them the white-glove treatment, they'll be more receptive than you think." Now that she knew Janie might be on board, she could probably get the town council to sign within a day, but she wanted to spend more time with Janie. Get to know her better in a lot of ways.

"I need you to keep me abreast of your progress daily." Bob's micromanaging was getting even stronger, if that was possible.

"Okay." That was a ridiculous ask. She doubted he required that type of attention from Jack.

"I'm not kidding. This is a big deal."

"Got it." She flipped her pad folio closed. "I'll report in daily." She'd never been kept on such a tight leash. A lot of money must be riding on this deal.

"Good girl," Bob said, and the line went dead.

"Good girl." She mocked him, her voice filled with disdain. "Do you pat Jack on the head when he's a good boy?" She'd send him a daily email recap on her progress to keep him off her back. He hadn't said how she needed to report in.

She'd have to press Janie more this evening about why she was okay with just going along with what others wanted in regard to broadband. Was that something she did often? Did she do it to avoid conflict? Would she stand up for herself if she felt strongly about something? Crystal needed answers to so many questions. Not just because of business, but she had to know how Janie dealt with conflict in general. She couldn't date someone who just went along and didn't have an opinion. Partnerships involved mutual respect and discussion. What the hell was she thinking? They lived almost two thousand miles apart. Why was she even considering Janie as a partner?

❖

Janie stood and stared at herself in the mirror mounted on the back of the bathroom door. She'd changed her sweater four times already. She really needed to update her wardrobe. Why was she making such a big deal out of this evening? Crystal wouldn't care what she wore, would she? She pulled at the neck of the wool fabric before she tugged it over her head and tossed it onto the bed in the pile with the rest of the rejects. Definitely too itchy, and too hot for any restaurant—layers would be the best choice tonight. She tugged open her dresser drawer, found a white turtleneck, and slipped it over her head. Then she dug out a black half-zip fleece to wear over it. Not too dressy and not too casual—she would go with that. She glanced at her watch and tugged on her classic brown mid-calf Ugg boots before she rushed out the door. If she didn't leave now, she'd be late.

Janie sped through the back streets to the inn and arrived a bit early, just before six. She was nothing if not prompt. She found a space in the lot and rushed inside, hoping Crystal wasn't early and she hadn't kept her waiting.

She didn't see any sign of Crystal in the lobby when she entered, so she went straight to the desk to Dana. "Can you let Crystal know I'm here?"

"You having dinner here?" Dana asked.

Janie nodded. "Then we're going to the marshmallow roast. You want to join us?"

Dana shook her head. "Can't. Have a few more things to do before I leave. I'll see you there later. I'm working the ticket booth tonight." Dana picked up the receiver. "You two are spending an awful lot of time together." She scrutinized her as she punched in the room number.

"Just keeping her entertained while you're busy." Janie glanced at a couple exiting the restaurant. "Is that okay?" It had become more than that now, but she wasn't ready to reveal what "more" meant to Dana, since she wasn't quite sure what it meant herself.

"Right." Dana rolled her eyes. Seemed she didn't believe her. "It's about time you took an interest in someone. It's been ages since you've dated."

"Well, there aren't many single women around here. They move in and out of town quickly." Crystal would probably be no different. Was it fair that the first woman she'd clicked with in forever lived across the country?

"Your date for the evening is here." Dana spoke into the

receiver and then hung up the phone. "She'll be right down." Dana didn't miss much in this town, especially when it was right under her own roof. "You look good."

"Thanks." Janie felt a little pride in herself—that she'd done well with her clothing choice. "So how come you've never talked about Crystal before she came to visit?"

"I don't know." Dana shrugged. "She never came up."

"Yet she's here the week before Christmas for no apparent reason?"

"She's here to see me." Dana drew her eyebrows together. "Isn't that a good enough reason?"

"I suppose so." She glanced at the ceiling. "If you were my aunt, I might enjoy a visit with you."

"You're darn tootin' you would." Dana tossed her pen to the desk.

Crystal appeared on the stairs dressed in blue jeans, boots, and an ivory cable-knit sweater, her blond hair hanging in loose curls around her face and her lips dressed with a light-pink gloss. She was gorgeous.

Janie's heart pounded as she came closer. "You look really nice."

"Thank you." Crystal smiled. "You do too."

"Shall we?" Janie motioned Crystal in front of her toward the restaurant entrance.

"We have a nice salmon special tonight," Dana shouted after them. "If you're not up for seafood, the ribeye steak is always a good choice as well."

"Thanks." Janie put up her hand and waved. "I invited her along."

"You did?" Crystal's voice lilted up. Was she disappointed?

"I'm sorry. I should've asked you first."

"No." Crystal shook her head. "Not at all. That's fine."

"She declined. Has to work the marshmallow ticket booth."

"Good." Crystal gave her a sideways smile. "Not that I don't enjoy Dana's company, but I was looking forward to spending time with you tonight."

"Same." Janie laughed. "I was relieved when she said no." Janie gave her a sheepish grin, glad to have some alone time with Crystal.

The hostess led them to a table covered with a white linen cloth in the middle of the restaurant, then hesitated and, instead, seated them at a table for two in the most secluded corner of the restaurant with a small red candle holder in the middle. Janie glanced up to see Dana at the entrance giving her a thumbs-up.

Crystal chuckled as she sat. "Dana seems to be playing matchmaker." She must've seen the thumbs-up as well.

"She means well." Janie glanced at the hostess as she handed them both menus before she lit the candle between them.

"I'm okay with a little help tonight." Crystal glanced over the top of her menu and winked.

The waitress seemed to appear from nowhere, and red wine began spilling into Janie's glass. "Wait. We didn't order that."

"Compliments of the house." The waitress continued pouring.

"Would you rather have a beer?" Crystal glanced at the waitress then back to Janie. "When we were in the bar the other night, that's what you had."

"This is fine." She didn't want to refuse Dana's generosity and possibly hurt her feelings. It didn't happen all that often.

"Have you decided on your entrees?" The waitress set the bottle on the table. "Would you like to hear the specials?"

"Dana's already filled us in. Can you give us a few minutes?" Janie hadn't even thought about food. She'd been too caught up in the beautiful woman sitting across from her.

She stared into Crystal's stunning chestnut eyes as they sparkled in the candlelight. Neither of them uttered a sound as the possibilities of the evening to come crackled between them. It seemed Crystal might be caught up in Janie too. This evening might turn out to be more than Janie had expected—more than she wanted with a woman who was leaving town soon—or maybe it was exactly what she needed.

Chapter Fourteen

Crystal ate one last forkful of the death-by-chocolate cake they'd ordered to split for dessert and pushed the plate closer to Janie. "If I eat another bite, I'm going to explode."

Janie pulled the plate closer. "I, on the other hand, have a tiny spot left to fill in the upper left quadrant of my stomach."

"Oh my gosh." Crystal shifted in her chair, trying to make herself more comfortable. "I should've ordered the salmon."

"Yes. You should've. It was delicious."

"It was." Crystal widened her eyes. "Thank you for sharing a bite with me."

"Absolutely. Your steak was pretty tasty as well."

They'd shared a portion of their dinners with each other, which Crystal hadn't expected—hadn't been in the habit of doing with other women she'd dated. Dated—she rolled that thought around in her head for a few seconds. Crystal really was on a date with a woman who, in all practicality, could end up hating her when she found out why she was here. She pushed that thought from her head. Dinner had been much more relaxed than Crystal had expected. The nervousness between them seemed to have transformed into a comfortable easiness that she thoroughly enjoyed. She'd have to thank Dana tomorrow for the wine and all the extra attention she'd had their server give them.

"We should get going if we want to get a good spot near the main fire pit." Janie scanned the room. "I'll get the check, and then I need to visit the restroom before we head that way."

"I got dinner." Crystal had let the waitress know to charge it to her room when she'd gone to the restroom earlier.

"I invited you."

"I know, but you've done so much for me since I've been here. Volunteering to be my personal tour guide and all." Crystal was truly grateful for every minute of it. "I wanted to thank you somehow."

"You didn't have to do that, but thank you." Janie stood. "I'll meet you at the front desk."

"Sounds good." Crystal took a quick sip of water before she stood and followed Janie out of the restaurant into the lobby. She went straight to the check-in area to chat with Dana, who was busy working on something behind the counter. "I thought Janie said you're working at the marshmallow roast tonight?"

"I am. Just can't seem to get out of here." Dana glanced around the lobby. "My night clerk should be here soon."

"Thanks for the VIP service in the restaurant. The wine and the food were delicious."

"I'm glad to hear that. You can spread the word in your company when you get back."

Crystal's stomach knotted. She'd been ignoring her mission while she'd been enjoying Janie's company. "I'll definitely do that."

"I'm sure once you convince the town council to move forward with the Wi-Fi installation, you'll be back on a regular basis."

"Yes. Absolutely." But Crystal wouldn't be back. She'd been brought in only to make the deal happen. She wasn't the regional representative for this area. She spotted Janie on her way from the restroom. Time to get back to business. "Can you play along with me for a minute?"

Dana nodded. "Sure."

"Why is everyone in this town so against Wi-Fi?" She glanced at Janie as she approached. "Do you know how much more business you'd get if you had it here in the hotel?"

"I'm not totally against it." Dana shrugged. "It's mostly Mason and Janie who haven't bought in on the idea."

"What's the big deal?" Crystal raised her eyebrows and stared at Janie.

"It's not that simple." Janie shook her head.

"Sure it is." Crystal was starting something she knew wouldn't end well, but she had a job to do. "You of all people should embrace it within your technology at Cyber Shack."

"You've been here for only a few days. That doesn't make you an expert on the town or my café." Janie frowned.

"I'm sorry." She really was. Crystal hated putting herself at odds with Janie—hurting her in any way. "I didn't mean to hit a nerve." Crystal took her phone from her back pocket and held it up. "I've just been waiting for a call from my mom, and I'm afraid I'll miss it."

"You've given her the number at the inn, haven't you?" Janie asked.

"Yes." Crystal nodded. "But we keep missing each other."

"Dana will find you if she calls the front desk." She looked at Dana. "Right?"

"Of course. Unless I'm not here." Dana reached for Crystal's phone. "Why don't you let me hold on to that, and if she calls here while you're out, I'll leave instructions for someone to let me know at the roast, and I'll come find you." She glanced at the picture on the screen. "Your mom looks good in this picture." She held it up.

"Yes. She does." Crystal touched the screen. My mom, dad, and brother all look good." She gave Dana more information to play along.

"I've always said, you're tall like your dad, but you look like your mom." Dana flipped the phone forward. "Don't you agree, Janie?"

Janie moved closer and scrutinized the photo. "You do." She glanced at Crystal. "Nice picture. Looks recent."

"We took it at Thanksgiving. It's kind of a tradition." Crystal remembered the holiday weekend she'd spent with her family just a short time ago. That was a good day.

Dana turned it back to herself. "I guess you'll be spending Christmas with them?"

"I usually do. Yes." Crystal glanced at Janie. "Family is important to me." Crystal sucked in a deep breath to settle the weird sadness that hit her.

"As it should be." Janie smiled softly. "We should go." She turned, headed to the door, and opened it. "Don't want them to run out of marshmallows, do we?" She held out her hand.

Crystal smiled as she walked toward her. "Absolutely not." She grasped Janie's hand.

"Don't worry about me." Dana's voice rose as she shouted, "I'll catch up with you later."

They walked the circle drive to the street, where they could see the lights that lit up the square where people were gathering.

"Is this your first marshmallow roast?" Janie seemed to have reverted to small talk. Crystal blamed herself for that. She should've left the Wi-Fi subject alone.

"I have to admit it is. Well, maybe not my first, but in a small town anyway."

"Well, then you're in for a treat." Janie smiled. "They have all kinds of things to mix them with besides graham crackers and chocolate."

Crystal gave her a sideways glance. "Oh, yeah? Like what?"

"Bacon, strawberries, peanut-butter cups, even Oreos."

"You should've warned me, and I would've eaten less at dinner." Crystal rubbed her stomach.

"You didn't eat that much. Only half your meal."

Crystal had slowed her pace, tried to enjoy the food as they talked. Maybe she'd asked too many questions. "I usually eat like a bird, but recently that's changed to a very large bird…maybe even a turkey." Crystal laughed.

"The fresh air always gives me a healthy appetite." Janie breathed deeply. "Especially in the winter."

"Okay. I'll blame it on that."

They wandered through the pop-up booths that were selling various types of merchandise. Items included ornaments, handmade wooden nutcrackers, as well as gloves and scarves. It was the perfect winter village. As they ventured farther, Crystal could see the main firepit and multiple individual tables with small fire pits in the middle. There wasn't a single table that wasn't already taken by people enjoying the festival. Janie purchased some tickets for the roast and then found them a bench away from the fire pit to sit. They watched as parents helped their kids secure marshmallows on long wooden sticks.

"I love the family atmosphere here." Crystal took in the scent of the burning wood.

"Oh, yeah?" Janie smiled that beautiful smile.

Crystal nodded. "Reminds me of my childhood. My parents were really big on game nights and holiday, family adventures." She quit smiling. "I didn't realize how much I missed all that."

"You plan to do the same when you have children?"

"I guess. I hadn't really thought about it." Crystal grabbed her thighs, slid her hands to her knees and back. "That seems so far off right now."

"I get that." Janie stared at the kids. "I haven't accomplished nearly enough in my lifetime to think about having them. Most days, I still feel like a kid myself."

"But you have a business and so much responsibility. You seem to have it all together." Crystal would never be able to run her own business. She was great at closing deals, but management was completely out of her realm.

"It might look that way, but I don't. I have so many things I'd like to do with the shack but have no idea how to accomplish them."

"Maybe I can help." Crystal gave her a soft smile. "I mean, I'm pretty good at design if you want to remodel." She truly wanted to help.

"I've noticed. We're a shoo-in to win the decorating contest."

"I'm not the best with technology, but I'm sure we can find someone to help with that…I mean if you want to." *And then when you find out who I really am, you can hate me.* Crystal was digging herself in deeper.

"I'm sorry I snapped at you earlier." Janie shook her head. "I didn't mean what I said."

"It's okay. It really didn't hurt that much." Crystal was glad Janie wanted to talk about it.

"It's just that the Wi-Fi discussion is a big point of contention in this town." Janie sighed. "The truth is, I think about it a lot. I just don't know what I want anymore. Have no idea if it will hurt or help my business."

"How about we sit down tomorrow and make a list of pros and cons?" Crystal had already created that list. It was pretty standard for any town she'd worked with.

"You'd help me with that?"

"Absolutely." Crystal stood and reached out her hand. "Now, how about we get some of those marshmallows."

Janie stood, clasped her hand, and squeezed it. "Adult dipping station first."

"Sounds good to me." Crystal tugged her toward the table loaded with bowls of marshmallows and assorted liquor bottles.

When they reached the front of the line, Janie reached for a couple of sticks and handed one to Crystal. "Hey, Ron. What do you recommend we start with?" She glanced at Crystal. "By the way, this is Crystal, Dana's niece." She speared a marshmallow.

"Nice to meet you." Ron smiled.

Crystal nodded. "Nice to meet you as well."

"I usually start with the Baileys Irish Cream or the Kahlúa." He handed her a ziplock bag containing additional marshmallows and then poured a small amount of each liqueur into paper cups. "Don't add too much, or your marshmallow will literally be toast."

"Well, we don't want that." Crystal was excited to try out the new treat and to forget her earlier disagreement with Janie.

They found a place around the large fire pit and settled in. Crystal dipped hers in the Baileys Irish Cream, and the marshmallow immediately caught fire. "Whoops." She pulled it back and began blowing on it furiously. "Guess I'm bad at following directions."

"Here. Let me show you." Janie dunked part of her marshmallow in the Baileys and held it over the fire, letting the fire barely lick it as she rotated it. "You just have to be patient." It began to brown and puff out. Once it was fully browned, Janie pulled it from the stick. "Open your mouth."

Crystal did as she was instructed, and chills ran through her as Janie fed her a bite. Work was now totally off the table tonight. "That's really good."

"Right?" Janie held out the other cup. "Try the Kahlúa. It's my favorite."

Crystal dipped the marshmallow in the liqueur, paying close attention so as not to saturate it too much. Then she held it high above the flame. "Like this?"

Janie moved behind her, grasped her wrist, and lowered her arm. "Right there."

A slow tingle began low in Crystal's belly. She couldn't help but imagine how instructional Janie would be in bed. Her pulse raced, and she took in a breath, trying to still the adrenaline coursing through her. The evening had morphed into something more spectacular than she could've imagined, and she intended to ride it out for as long as it lasted.

CHAPTER FIFTEEN

Janie took in the spicy scent of Crystal's shampoo as she stood closely behind her with her chin touching Crystal's shoulder. It was unusually bold for Janie to move in and help Crystal roast the marshmallow, but she planned to enjoy her time with Crystal, even if it might be short-lived.

"Do you think it's done?" Crystal turned, and their lips were close enough to touch.

Her heart was beating so loud she could barely hear Crystal's voice. Janie released Crystal's arm, cleared her throat, and backed up. "Looks good."

Crystal hissed as she tried to pull the browned treat from the stick. Finally getting a good grip between her finger and thumb, she slid it off and took a small bite. "You were right. This is delicious." She held it out to Janie.

Janie started to take it from her, and Crystal took her hand, lacing their fingers together before she put the marshmallow to Janie's lips. She took a bite, enjoying the sweet, creamy taste, then ran her tongue across her bottom lip to capture the sticky remnants.

Crystal moved closer. "Let me help you with that." She touched the corner of Janie's mouth with her thumb before she moved in slowly and pressed her lips to Janie's, dipping her tongue inside just enough to tease a response. "This event has turned out better than I expected." Crystal smiled.

Janie tried to control the desire building within her—stop herself from making a scene right here in the town square by taking Crystal into her arms, kissing her fully, and embarrassing them both. "So far, the whole holiday season has exceeded my expectations."

"I've had enough marshmallows for tonight. Would you mind walking me back to the inn? Maybe come up for a nightcap?" Crystal squeezed her hand.

Janie stilled, looking at Crystal framed by the glow of moonlight. Beautiful, smart, and generous, she was everything Janie had been looking for. "I'd love to." It was clear they were going there sooner or later.

They'd just started out when Sue crossed their paths. "You two aren't leaving so soon, are you? I want Mason to meet Crystal." She waved him over. "Mason, this is Dana's niece, Crystal."

Mason moved quickly toward them, his long legs carrying his large frame easily. "It's nice to finally meet you. Sue's told me a lot about you."

Crystal smiled. "There can't be that much to tell."

"Says you're a decorator." He glanced at Sue. "Maybe you could help us update a few things at our house."

Crystal seemed unsure of what to say.

"I'm sure she'd love to, but she's only in town for a short time." Janie refused to let Mason monopolize Crystal for the remainder of time she was here.

"Perhaps the next time you're here?" he countered.

"Absolutely. I'd love to help you out." Crystal released Janie's hand. "Right now, I need to get back to the inn." She swiped at her thigh. "I spilled some cider on myself."

"Right. I'm going to walk with her." Seemed Crystal knew how to get out of an awkward spot when she wanted to.

"You'd better hurry, or you'll miss the caroling." Sue sung the words.

"Oh, I wouldn't want to miss that." Crystal gave Janie a sideways glance. "We won't be long." She clasped Janie's hand and walked out of the square, pulling Janie along beside her.

Janie stopped and tugged her back into her arms. "Is this what you want?"

She nodded. "It is. Now take me to my room and do something about it."

Janie quickened her pace. "I like a woman who knows what she wants and how to get it."

They'd barely made it up the stairs before Crystal turned and pressed Janie against the wall and kissed her. Each time Janie started toward the room, Crystal tugged her back and kissed her again. This…was actually happening…tonight.

Crystal rummaged through her pockets and finally found the card key to her room and slid it in and out. The lights flashed red. "Not now."

Janie took it from her. "Let me try." She slid it in and out slowly, and the lights flashed green. She turned the handle and pushed open the door.

"You have the perfect touch." Crystal stopped in the doorway to give her another scorching kiss before she rushed them through the door and toward the bed.

Janie tried to balance as Crystal pushed her onto the bed. The phone rang—Crystal groaned.

"You should get that." Janie rolled onto her side and sat on the side of the bed. "Could be your mom."

Janie sat and reached for the receiver. "Stay right there." Crystal held up a finger as she answered the phone. "Hello." She smiled. "Hi, Mom."

"I'm good." Crystal nodded. "Sure. I'll pick some up while I'm here. I can't wait to see you too."

Janie stood and raked her fingers through her hair as reality hit hard. The phone had rung in the nick of time. She was about to go all in on whatever this was between her and Crystal, and that was a bad idea. She needed to slow this down, or she was in for a whole lot of heartbreak when Crystal left town.

Crystal stared, tiny creases forming on her forehead as she watched Janie walk toward the door. "Okay. I'll see you then."

Crystal smiled again. "I love you too." She hung up the receiver and popped up from the bed. "She wants me to bring her some maple syrup."

Janie couldn't help but warm at the way Crystal spoke to her mother. Each word seemed to be filled with gentle kindness. The love for her mother was clear. "We've got the best." Janie reached toward the doorknob. "I'm going to go." She'd just received a clear reminder that Crystal was leaving town soon.

"Really?" Crystal seemed confused, and rightly so. A few minutes ago, they were headed into a night of pure bliss, but now Janie was obviously having second thoughts about getting involved—not letting her heart lead instead of her head.

Janie pulled open the door. "I think I should." She had no other words and no excuses. They'd had a wonderful time and it wasn't late, but she had to slow down whatever was happening between them. "Can I see you tomorrow?"

"Yes. Absolutely." Crystal crossed the room and stopped suddenly, fidgeting with her hands as though they'd just sprouted from her arms and she had no idea what to do with them. She gripped the edge of the door with one and let the other fall to her side. "I'd be sad if that didn't happen."

So would I. "I'll call you in the morning." Janie didn't dare kiss her again. She rushed down the hallway to the stairs, stopped, and sat at the top for a moment, remembering lips, tongues, hands battling for control on the way to Crystal's room. What the hell was she doing? She'd wanted Crystal so badly but couldn't seem to give herself to her. Why couldn't she just let herself enjoy the moment for once? Because she wanted something more with Crystal that couldn't possibly work out in the long run.

❖

Crystal rushed to the door after Janie left—held the handle tightly—forced herself not to pull the door open. She felt like she'd just been rear-ended. They'd been speeding along to a destination she'd desperately wanted to reach, and the traffic light had suddenly turned red. It seemed like fate was coming between them somehow, stopping them from doing something there was no turning back from. Janie was already going to hate her when she found out who Crystal really was and why she was here.

Earlier, when she'd stared into Janie's indigo eyes, she'd been mesmerized by the way the firelight reflected in them. The glimmer of want in them had been clear, but Janie had left for some reason. Had Janie been hurt badly before? The thought of someone hurting her made Crystal's heart squeeze.

She crossed the room and flopped onto the bed. Her mom's timing was the worst, always had been. Crystal was due at her parents' house on Christmas Eve and had only a few days with her family. Now she was torn. She wanted to see them, but she also wanted to spend more time with Janie. She shouldn't have answered the phone—should've just called her mom back tomorrow, but they'd been playing telephone tag too much over the past week. She picked up the receiver and dialed her mom's number.

Crystal's mom answered immediately. "Hi, honey. Did you forget to tell me something?"

"I feel like I rushed you off the phone. I'm sorry." Crystal's mind had been in a totally different place.

"It's okay. You probably have a lot to accomplish there." Her mom was always so understanding.

"I do, but I'm afraid I might have messed everything up."

"I doubt that. You're great at your job." Her mom had so much confidence in her.

"Thanks, Mom. I met someone here, and I really like her." Crystal fiddled with the pen on the nightstand.

"That doesn't sound like a problem."

"She's on the town council…one of the people I have to sell on Wi-Fi."

"Oh." Her mom drew the word out. "That complicates things, doesn't it?"

"More than you know." The pillow let out a whoosh as she fell back into it. "I almost slept with her tonight. Your phone call interrupted us."

"I'm so sorry, honey. I forget that it's later there. Bad timing on my part." Her mom chuckled.

"Don't apologize. You probably saved me from doing something I shouldn't have." It was amazing how easy it was to talk to her mom about her love life.

"It's okay to have a personal life. Your job isn't everything."

"It is right now. Bob has promised me a director's seat if I reel this one in."

"And then you would put in more hours? Doesn't sound like a good deal to me." Her mom was always the voice of reason. "Not that I'm not proud of you, honey, but I want you to have someone in your life who makes you happy. I know from experience that work doesn't keep you warm at night. Your dad and I had that discussion long ago."

"I remember. Dad used to work a lot of hours. How did you two hash that out?"

"I almost left him more than once." Her mom let out a sigh.

"What? I didn't know that. Why did you stay?" Crystal remembered the tension that had been obvious between them sometimes.

"He finally figured out his family was more important than a job."

"I get that. Especially now." Crystal was realizing more and more that work didn't fill her world anymore. She needed to redistribute her work-life balance.

"Then don't let her slip away." Her mom didn't beat around the bush.

"Mom, I've already told her so many lies. She doesn't even know who I really am."

"Then just tell her the truth." Her mom's voice rose. "What have you got to lose?"

"Everything." Crystal turned on her side and stared at the door.

"Well, she's going to find out one way or another. Don't you think it's better coming from you than someone else? Why don't you get some rest and talk to her tomorrow?"

"Thanks for listening, Mom."

"You're welcome, honey. You know I'm always here if you need me."

"I love you." She really had won the jackpot in the mom department.

"I love you too. Good night." The phone went dead.

Crystal didn't know if she could do as her mom advised, not yet anyway. She still had a mission to accomplish first. Telling Janie everything now would alienate her for sure. She would suppress her attraction to Janie for the time being. Judging by Janie's quick exit earlier, it seemed she was unsure of the whole interaction as well.

CHAPTER SIXTEEN

Janie tugged at the blanket as she flopped onto her side trying to get in a few last minutes of sleep. She was wound up in the covers like a mummy. It had been a restless night. She reviewed the whole evening in her head, still trying to understand why she'd left. Crystal was confident and bold about what she wanted, and Janie had been a willing participant when they'd entered the room. She'd never really been the aggressor in any interactions she'd had previously.

Considering their situation, she found it hard to suppress some second thoughts that had surfaced during the interruption. She'd had her heart broken a few times, and each experience had been brutal. It would be no different with Crystal. She probably would've stayed if Crystal had asked her to, but Crystal hadn't asked. Was that a sign? Was Crystal being cautious about what would come of whatever this was if they slept together? Was she worried about what Dana thought? She twisted under the sheets and turned on the TV to catch the weather. Sunny with a thirty percent chance of snow in the afternoon.

Today was the store-decorating-contest judging. She would see Crystal for that, but where it would go from there was uncertain. Her heart told her that she would try again—even if it meant getting hurt. Today, she wouldn't leave any doubt about what she wanted from Crystal. She'd put herself out there and risk being rejected. Everything seemed to be out of her control now. One way or another she would find out if Crystal was the woman she was meant to be with. She would worry about the details later.

She shivered as she got out of bed and headed to the shower, pushing the needle on the thermostat up before she walked into the bathroom and turned on the water. Groggy, she stared at herself in the mirror. Her dirty-blond hair was flattened on one side of her head, her summer highlights noticeably fading. Her blue eyes were more vivid than usual, encompassed by the bloodshot redness surrounding them. She pushed off from the basin, went to the phone, and punched in a number.

"Hey. What's up with my bestie?" Beka's voice sang through the receiver. The woman was never in a bad mood.

"I need some help with my hair today. Can I come over?"

"As long as you're here and gone before the sled races."

"I forgot those were today." She'd lost track of the whole town-holiday schedule since Crystal had appeared. "I'm going to jump in the shower and run by the store. Then I'll be there."

"All right. Don't hit your head on the nozzle…you know, when you're jumping."

Janie laughed. Beka never failed to cheer her up. "Okay. See you soon." She dropped the receiver into the holder and rushed to the bathroom.

❖

Janie pulled up in front of Sue's Sweets and then took a minute to people-watch before she got out of her Jeep. It was becoming more apparent to her that Pine Grove was living in the past, which in some ways she loved and others she disliked. The Norman Rockwell hometown atmosphere kept her here, but the locals' resistance to technology was beginning to weigh heavily against her desire to stay. Cyber Shack was her life's blood. Could it survive a city-wide technology upgrade? Would people still come to meet, work, and play online games if they had internet at home? She needed the answer to that question and had to decide what she wanted from her life before she got in any deeper with Crystal.

Before she could reach a conclusion on any of those issues, she needed to talk to Mason, let him know her thoughts on progress, see if he agreed.

When she entered the bakery, Mason immediately waved her behind the counter to follow him to the back-room office.

She stopped momentarily to give Sue an order. "Can I get some strudel, a few tarts, and a couple of chocolate croissants?"

"Absolutely." Sue reached up and patted Janie on the shoulder. "He's in a rare mood this morning."

She nodded, unsure of what Sue meant, but it couldn't be good if she'd felt the need to mention it.

Mason was sitting behind his desk sorting through a stack of receipts when she got to the office. "So, what's so important that you needed to talk to me now?" He glanced up and let out a sigh.

"This seems to be an inconvenient time for you." She was getting irritating vibes.

He kneaded his fingers on his forehead. "Sorry. I've been up since three. Didn't get my usual nap in."

"Understood. I'm not sure how you manage it." Janie couldn't imagine keeping a schedule like that.

"It's not so bad once you get used to it, but I've been on my feet too long today, and my shoulders, my neck…everything hurts." He hooked a hand behind his neck and moved his head from side to side. "So, what's up?"

"We need to discuss our stance on broadband and Wi-Fi."

He dropped his hand to the desk with a loud thud. "I thought we had that settled."

"I'm not so sure anymore." Janie was more nervous than she should be for this conversation. She needed to be more confident about what *she* wanted.

"That's a quick one-eighty. When did this happen?"

"I've been thinking about it for a while." She paced the office. "The future is here now, Mason, and we're ignoring it. We can't go on like this forever. The kids today aren't like us. They don't like playing outside and exploring the woods until dark. They're going to grow up and leave if we don't find ways to make them stay."

"Kids will leave anyway. New technology won't make them stay. They'll go off to college."

"But we want them to come back, don't we? If no one does, this little town of ours will slowly die." She shrugged. "Think of the customers you could bring in with online advertising."

"So, let's look at the facts." Mason shifted in his chair. "Most people won't even think about getting Wi-Fi because it's too expensive. They'll need a computer at home, and computers cost money. You already cover that expense for them at Cyber Shack. They can come and go there when they want and pay only what they can afford." He straightened a stack of receipts and clipped them together. "That's what keeps you in business." He clipped a few more stacks together and put them all into a manila envelope. "You don't want to lose your business, do you?"

"Of course not, and I don't think I will. Well, maybe a small portion."

"People in this town like their privacy. They don't want the government to monitor their comings and goings." His tone was stern.

"Come on, Mason. Less than one percent of the people across America aren't on the internet because they're concerned about privacy and online security."

"Yeah, well, that number compares to about two percent of the population who still believe the earth is flat, and I think a few of those people live here." Mason relaxed in his chair. "However credible their fears regarding privacy are, 1.75 million Americans are not using the internet because they're afraid of being tracked or don't feel secure online." He leaned forward. "That, my friend, is a fact."

Janie couldn't argue with those numbers. She'd done her research as well. Plus, she had a few customers who still rented DVDs, never touched a computer, and picked up their mail at the post office. "But I think they're mostly not interested. Almost half of the percentage of people who aren't interested in the internet are sixty-five or older. That doesn't include my grandma. She loves it.

She's teaching my grandpa to use it." Even if it was only to practice playing poker. "If they're not interested, why not let it happen? It could certainly help you with your receipts." She pointed at the envelope. "Don't you get tired of doing all that by hand? It's a huge time suck. Wouldn't you rather be baking or spending time with your family?"

"Sue does most of this."

"Well, doesn't she get tired of messing with the books? My God, you'd think her hand would cramp from it all."

Mason rotated his head and let out a sigh. "I'll think about it."

Janie smiled. "That's all I'm asking." She walked to the door. "And just for the record, if we have criminals living here, they should be tracked."

"Agreed," Mason said as she went out the door.

The bakery was empty when she got back out front, and Sue was refilling the case. "Where are you off to?"

"To Beka's. She's going to put some highlights in my hair."

"Does she always do that for you?"

Janie nodded. "Been doing my hair since we were teenagers."

"I'll have to see what she can do with mine." Sue flipped up the ends like she was modeling a new haircut. "What does she charge?"

"I bring the color and pay her in your baked goods." Janie pointed to the box of pastries she'd ordered. "I'm sure you can work out a similar deal with her."

Sue headed to the phone on the wall. "I'm going to call her right now."

Janie didn't know if Beka wanted that information getting around, but Janie was sure she'd work out some kind of barter payment with Sue.

❖

After running by the store to pick up the necessary color, Janie pulled up in Beka's driveway and parked. Beka had the door open waiting for her by the time she made it to the porch.

Janie handed her the bag from the store but held on to the bakery box.

"What's this?"

"Color and other stuff." Beka probably had most everything she needed, but Janie wanted to make sure.

"Highlights or lowlights?" Beka dropped the bag onto the table.

Janie set the bakery box next to it. "I got both." She had no idea what needed to be done. She just needed something fresh.

Beka opened the box and took out one of the chocolate croissants. "Food first." She handed one to Janie, then glanced at the rest of the contents. "Strudel. Ben will love you for this."

"I know." She'd bought several of Ben's favorites, including apple strudel and a peach tart. "I still owe him for fixing my water heater."

Beka ate quickly and got down to the business of mixing color. She already had her tools laid out on the kitchen table, along with a table-top vanity mirror standing next to it. The usual setup. She handed Janie the apron, and she wrapped it around herself, snapped it, and sat in the kitchen chair.

"Missed you at the festival last night. Did you decide to stay home?"

"No. I was there. Just spent most of my time at the adult dipping station." She didn't dare tell her what happened with Crystal last night or her hair wouldn't get done.

Beka combed through Janie's hair. "You have a gray hair up here."

Pain ripped through Janie's scalp. "Ow." She touched her head. "What the hell, Bek?"

Beka held up the strand before dropping it into the trash can. "Those are like weeds. You don't want them spreading." She separated a few clumps of hair and pinned them back. "I'm only going to add a few strands of each color." Beka handed her a stack of foils. "Tear these in half."

"I've always heard that if you pluck one gray hair, ten more show up for its funeral." She folded and ripped a couple of foils.

"That's a total myth. Only one shows up." Beka scrutinized her scalp. "You going to come watch us race today?"

"Wouldn't miss it. I have to go to the shack first for the window-decorating-contest judging."

"Oh. That's today, too?" Beka reached forward and snapped her fingers. Janie handed her a piece of foil. "I have no doubt you'll win. It looks fantastic." She painted the hair with color and wrapped it in the foil. "You and Crystal did a great job. Is she going to be there?"

"I hope so. I couldn't have done it without her." She honestly didn't know if Crystal would want to go after the way she'd left her last night.

"You've been getting to know her pretty well, eh?"

"We've spent some time together." Janie wasn't sure how much to tell Beka. If she confided in her too much, she'd become her constant wingman.

"You've got it bad for her, don't you?"

She nodded. "Why do you think I'm here? I want to look good."

"You look good all the time." Beka painted another strand of hair and wrapped it. "You want to hear my observation?"

"Would it make a difference if I didn't?"

"Nope." Beka laughed. "I think Crystal has it bad for you too."

"Really?"

"Yes." She snapped her fingers for another foil. "She watches you."

Janie stared at Beka's reflection in the mirror. "What do you mean by that?"

"Not in a weird sort of way." Beka shrugged. "In the 'I want to know everything about you' way."

Janie wanted to know everything about Crystal as well. "I'm not sure anything can come of it. She lives across the country."

"It only takes a few hours to get there by plane." Beka raised an eyebrow.

"I know, but visiting is one thing. Being in love with someone who lives three thousand miles away is another." *Whoops.* Janie closed her eyes momentarily. She hadn't planned to let that fact slip.

Beka stopped mid-foil and widened her eyes. "I didn't know we were talking about love. I thought this was just about sex."

"It's about both." Janie blew out a breath. "I've never felt like this, Bek." The attraction was front and center, constantly with her. She couldn't even explain her feelings. "She's all I think about."

"I remember that feeling when Ben and I first met." Beka pasted another foil to Janie's head. "Those little swirls you get in your stomach."

"You do?" Janie twisted in the chair. "So, this is normal?"

Beka nodded. "I wanted to be with him all the time." She separated another portion of hair. "Maybe this is your chance to be happy—to get out of this town."

"You're getting way ahead of me." Janie knew that would happen when she told Beka. "I don't want to get out of this town. I like it here, and we've only kissed a few times."

"You've kissed her." Beka rushed around in front of her, leaned over, and grabbed the arms of the chairs. "Spill."

"Once at the Christmas-tree farm and once at the marshmallow roast last night." Janie didn't dare tell her about the make-out session on the way to, and inside, Crystal's room last night.

Beka released the chair and backed up. "How was it?"

Janie closed her eyes and let the thrill run through her. "Spectacular."

"Definitely love." Beka went back to Janie's hair. "I'll make sure your hair is perfect." She snapped her fingers for another foil. "Bring her to the races. It'll be fun."

"I will." More time with Crystal was all she wanted for Christmas this year. She thought about her place in this little town and her family, the comfort they brought her. Did she want to leave? Did Crystal want to stay? She needed more time, some distance from whatever was happening between her and Crystal to figure it all out, but she couldn't stay away.

Chapter Seventeen

Crystal twisted in the sheets as the orgasm spiraled through her. Shards of brightly colored light flew into the abyss of darkness. It was much stronger this time. Janie was doing crazy things to her, and Crystal didn't want her to stop, but the incessant ringing in Crystal's head wouldn't go away. She groaned as the glorious spiral weakened. "What is that sound?"

Janie peeked out from between her legs, blue eyes dark with desire, and smiled softly. "It's reality calling."

Crystal groaned again as she forced her eyes open and focused on the phone ringing on the nightstand. When it stopped, she looked around the room, hoping to find the real Janie, but she was gone again. She'd just had another wildly erotic dream about the woman she barely knew. She slid her hand between her legs to calm the pulsing. It was weird that her orgasms in the past had required quite a bit of effort during sex, yet recently happened so easily in her sleep.

The phone began ringing again. Who the hell was calling her this early? She glanced at the clock. Not early, almost nine. Janie— it had to be Janie. She cleared the dreamy remnants of her from her mind and picked up the receiver. "Hello."

"I need an update." Bob was ridiculously persistent. If she'd had a wireless connection, she'd have known it was him and would've ignored the call.

"Good morning to you too, Bob."

"Enough with the niceties. What's going on up there?"

"I'm making progress. I think."

"You think?" His voice rose.

"I know it's hard to believe, Bob, but at least thirteen percent of the American population are just not interested or do not need to use the internet for one reason or another. No matter how much we spend on a broadband plan to provide access to the internet or how much the government subsidizes internet access, when people don't see the need or are just not interested, adoption numbers are *not* going to go up."

"You'll never convince me of that. We live and die by the internet at this company. Enough with the negativity. What happened to the ultra-connected girl I hired? I might just need to send Jack up there after all."

"No. Absolutely not. I'll get it done, but there's a whole lot more to this community than you know." The ultra-connected girl was still here. She just didn't know if she wanted to be on all the time anymore.

"I don't care about that. I didn't send you there to get involved or feel sorry for any of them. I sent you there to get that contract signed. Am I going to be able to count on you to get this done, or am I going to have to send Jack up there to seal the deal?"

Crystal let out a sigh and fought with the sheets to stand. "No. I'll get it done. It's just a little more complicated than I expected." Bob might not care about the community, but Crystal was beginning to care a whole lot more than she should. "We should use this as a rallying cry to look at uniform privacy rules across all users of the internet. So should policy makers. It doesn't matter to anyone *who* tracks them—they just don't want to be tracked at all, at any time, anywhere. Regardless of who's doing the tracking." The phone base fell off the nightstand as she paced across the room. "Do you know that Janie wipes her servers every night just to make sure her customers have privacy?"

"Good for her. Sounds like she's tech savvy."

"We need to have a better privacy option for these people. Everyone has a right not to be tracked and profiled."

"We're in the business of selling internet, not controlling it. Throw some money at them. They'll understand that. It's a universal language. Throw a lot at them." Bob seemed desperate. "Not too much, though."

"That's a pretty broad statement."

"I trust you to find ways to reel them in, but don't make promises we can't keep."

She was sure that money wasn't the issue here, and she was beginning to really love this community and understand why they liked it the way it was. "I need a little more time to do some research. I'll get back to you in a couple of days." She picked up the base of the phone and hung up without waiting for a response before she yanked the cord out of it and slammed it to the nightstand.

Bob always wanted concrete plans, and she had no idea in which direction she needed to go right now. Especially with the way she was feeling about Janie. There had to be a way to bring in broadband and wireless without disrupting the hometown culture. What could she bring them that they really needed? There had to be something, and she needed to find it. Even small, charming towns had their problems.

Crystal jotted down a few notes in her notebook. The hockey arena could use some major repair, and there wasn't any type of food bank or community center. The town didn't only need broadband. They needed support in basic social services.

She glanced at the clock again, flipped her notebook closed, and headed to the bathroom. She needed to get ready to go to Cyber Shack for the storefront-decorating contest that started at eleven o'clock.

❖

Janie paced the sidewalk in front of the inn. She'd called Crystal from Beka's house before she left, but Crystal hadn't answered, so she'd left a message that she'd be there soon. She'd checked in with Dana at the desk and let her know she'd be outside waiting. Beka had convinced her to take Crystal to the sled races after the window-decorating-contest judging. That would mean a whole new day with Crystal—a new day filled with possibilities, feelings she needed—wanted to explore with her. She could end up with a broken heart, but what if she didn't? What if Crystal felt the same and they could make a long-distance connection work somehow? She shook the idea from her head. She was getting way ahead of herself.

Janie was deep into her thoughts when Crystal appeared beside her. "What are you doing out here in the cold?"

She turned to find the most gorgeous sight in front of her. Crystal was wearing black thermal leggings that clung to her legs like the skin on a plum. Peeking out in the V where her jacket zipper stopped was a yellow turtleneck that set off her chestnut eyes perfectly. Her ears were covered with a fuzzy black-and-yellow, ear-warmer headband with a Wolverine logo in the middle. She suspected it was Dana's.

"Just walking to clear my mind." The winter air always helped Janie with that.

"You looked very caught up in your thoughts." Crystal smiled slightly. "Is something bothering you?"

Janie appreciated Crystal's concern but wasn't ready to talk about why she'd left her room last night or spill her feelings about her deepening attraction. She shifted to the other subject that had been weighing on her. "This whole keeping-the-town-small debate with the town council is maddening." Janie shook her head.

"You want to tell me about it?" Crystal gained eye contact. Her expression was soft and sincere. She really was concerned.

"I don't even know if I agree with them anymore." Janie dropped her head back and looked into the sky. "I don't know what's happened to me in the past few years. I used to be so forward thinking. I upgraded Cyber Shack and had grand plans to expand the location and the technology. Somehow, I've let Mason, my dad, and everyone else's opinion cloud that future—my future." She shook her head. "Wireless would bring so much more to this town."

"Have you talked to them about it?" Crystal laced her fingers with Janie's and stood in front of her.

"Until my voice is raspy. They're afraid *everything* will change, and it probably will. Just not in a bad way." She glanced at the inn. "Dana would be booked all the time. People would stay here for hockey games and weekend getaways rather than hours away in Stowe."

"So, what else can you do to convince them?" Crystal held tightly to Janie's hands when she tried to release them—held eye contact and wouldn't let her move away and create any distance between them.

"I don't know. I have so many ideas of how to change the café, but the council is stuck in the past. Members have archaic ideas that have been passed from one generation to the next, and that includes my own dad." She squeezed Crystal's hands before she pulled hers free. "Above all else, I don't want to be a disappointment to my family." She paced away from Crystal down the circle drive to an area of pine trees.

Crystal quickly followed her. "Would you rather be one to yourself? You've got to live your life the way you want to, or you're never going to be happy."

Janie stared down the street. "We should get to the shack. I want to be there while they're judging."

"Don't do that…" Crystal took Janie's chin and forced her to look at her. "Don't dismiss your feelings because you're worried about everyone else." She landed her hand on Janie's shoulder and let it slide down to her chest. "You are such a good soul with a huge heart. People know that and take advantage of that quality."

"Not you, though." Janie chewed on her bottom lip, more sure of her feelings for Crystal now than she had been before. "You've given me an outside view into this town…into myself." She forced herself to hold back the tears welling in her eyes as she wrapped her arms around Crystal. "The future doesn't seem so impossible now since I've talked it through with you."

Crystal pulled away slightly. "I really need to tell you some things."

"I thought you two had already left." Dana appeared on the sidewalk. "You'd better get going, or you're going to be late for your own window judging."

Crystal let out a sigh and shook her head. "Her timing is impeccable."

"Have dinner with me tonight? You can tell me everything then." Janie smiled. "We can tell each other." She'd be ready to reveal her feelings by then. "Unless you have other plans."

"No." Crystal shook her head. "No other plans that don't include you." She took her hand and tugged her down the street. "Let's go win that trophy."

The thrill that coursed through Janie almost immobilized her. She didn't care about the contest now. If Crystal had tugged her inside and up to her room instead, she'd have spent the entire day showing her how she felt.

Chapter Eighteen

The judges were lined up in front of Cyber Shack assessing the window decorations. Crystal couldn't tell by any of their flat facial expressions whether they liked them or not. A few of them jotted notes in notebooks before they huddled together and compared scores.

Dana stepped out of the huddle. "Where'd you get these decorations?"

"I've had them in the storage closet for years."

Dana narrowed her eyes and then looked at Crystal.

"It's true. I helped her carry them out."

"What's the big deal?" Crystal held out her hands. "We followed all the rules." They'd made it family-friendly, used traditional non-blinking lights, and they'd kept it all inside the store and viewable from the sidewalk.

"This contest is a big deal." Janie widened her eyes and shook her head. "People fight for this trophy."

"I still can't believe you can't include any business-related promotions as part of the display." Crystal recalled the reading of the rules. "That's so unfair. Santa would've looked awesome checking his list on a computer."

Janie smiled. "He absolutely would've."

"Sue got to display cookies in her window."

"Because they're Christmas-themed." Janie turned toward Crystal and crossed her arms. "I had no idea you were so invested in this contest."

"It's such a beautiful display." Crystal waved her hands in front of her as she spoke. "I just want you to win."

"You're right. The display is perfect, and it's ours." Janie smiled. "Thank you for helping me with it."

"You don't have to keep thanking me. I had fun doing it with you."

"Me too." Janie took her hand. "Come on. I think they're done with the questions. Let's leave them to it and go watch the sled races." She led Crystal to her Jeep and opened the passenger door for her.

"Thank you," Crystal said as she climbed in. She wasn't used to having someone open doors for her, but she had to admit that she liked it. She picked up the contest information sheet that was lying on the console and read through the prize categories. First place was one thousand Chamber Dollars, which actually equaled two thousand if you spent it at participating businesses in town. Second and third places each halved consecutively from there, so the total prizes awarded equaled thirty-five-hundred dollars. Chamber Dollars seemed to be accepted just like cash and kept the money local in the brick-and-mortar Chamber member businesses.

Janie climbed into the driver's seat and fired the engine.

"This contest really is a big deal. First place is a lot of money."

"Yeah. It would help me out around the shack for sure. I can get a lot of bakery and other items with it."

"Would you use it all at the bakery? Sue must love that."

"No. She'd kill me if I did. It's good for all the businesses in town. If we win, I'll use some of it to grant some of the Santa-letters requests from the kids. I mean, if that's okay with you."

"Of course. They put them in the box in the shack?" Crystal remembered seeing it but had forgotten to ask about it.

Janie nodded. "Some of the kids who come in don't have a whole lot at home, so I try to get them some of the specific games they want to play at the shack."

"Do you ever give them games to take home?"

"Sometimes. Noah, one of the kids, asked for a game console for home. His mom works two jobs and usually isn't home until late. He wants to play games with her at night before bedtime."

"Oh my gosh. That breaks my heart."

"Yeah. He's a good kid, helps me out around the shack in the afternoons."

"Can you find him something like that?" Crystal would gladly buy him a new one, along with a few games. "I can pitch in some money."

Janie smiled as she reached across the console and squeezed Crystal's hand. "Thank you for that, but I'll get it."

"Okay. Let me know if something happens and you need help."

"That's sweet of you, but I already found one for him on eBay. I'm keeping an eye on it. I was going to buy it either way."

Janie's generosity hit Crystal square in the chest. She wasn't all about having a successful business. She really cared for the people in this community.

When they arrived at the sledding area, Janie found a place to park in the field where all the other cars were located, then reached into the back seat and grabbed a bag. "I brought some hot chocolate to keep us warm."

It was time to let the flirting begin. "I like a woman who comes prepared."

"Preparation is the key to success."

"I think you just told me you were a Boy Scout."

Janie shook her head. "Nope. I wasn't allowed, but my brother taught me everything he learned."

"Nate's an awesome guy, but I bet you could've figured it out on your own."

"Possibly. He really is a great brother, but I'm not going to tell him you said that, or his ego will get even bigger than it already is, and I'm not sure I could stand that." Janie laughed as she tugged on the handle and pushed open her door. "I got your door." She raced around the front of the car and pulled open Crystal's door just as she was opening it. "I told you I've got it." Janie smiled widely before she leaned in and kissed her. "I've been waiting to do that all morning."

"No need to wait." Crystal's heart warmed. Chivalry wasn't dead at all. She'd never had a woman be so attentive to her needs.

Bringing hot chocolate to keep them warm, opening car doors for her, smoldering kisses. Could this woman be any more perfect?

Janie swept her arm across Crystal's back and nudged her in front of her. "We can watch from over there." She pointed to a roped-off section between a couple of stakes.

Crystal practically jumped out of her skin when Beka rushed between them from behind. "I started getting worried that you weren't going to make it."

"The judging went long." Janie rolled her eyes. "Dana kept asking questions."

Beka drew her eyebrows together. "I thought she recused herself because Crystal helped you."

"She did, but that didn't stop her from her usual scrutiny."

"Come on. We're over here." Beka led them to where Ben was standing with their sleds.

"This must be Crystal." Ben smiled and held out his hand. "I'm Ben. I belong to Beka."

Crystal shook it. "Nice to meet you, Ben." She would've loved to say that she belonged to Janie, but even though they'd become close, that wasn't quite true.

"You're both racing?"

Ben nodded. "Beka in the women's and then me in the men's." He motioned to the kids in the next section over. "We've got a little bit of a wait. The kids are up first."

"Oh, that'll be fun to watch." Crystal watched as the younger racers lined up their sleds. The energy in the crowd was amazing—charged with holiday spirit. Everyone was so happy and carefree, kids playing in the snow as their parents readied their sleds. Until coming to Pine Grove, Crystal had never imagined there was so much magic in Christmas.

"Why aren't you racing?" Ben asked Janie.

"I thought I'd just watch this year. Keep Crystal company."

"Don't feel obligated to stand here with me. You should race." Crystal motioned to the sledding area. "Go ahead." She nudged her with her shoulder. "I would." Although the hill looked pretty steep.

"Come on." Beka coaxed her with a wonky smile. "Afraid you'll lose to me again this year?"

"As I recall, I beat you last year."

"That's debatable."

"Too bad I didn't bring my sled, or I'd do it again." Janie had a competitive streak in her after all.

"No worries there." Beka grinned. "I swung by your house and grabbed it out of the garage."

Janie shook her head. "I knew it was a mistake giving you a key." She turned to Crystal. "You want to race with me?"

Crystal tingled with excitement. "Can we do that?" She hadn't been on a sled since her family had moved from upstate New York, but the rush hit her like it was only yesterday.

"Absolutely." Beka grinned. "Ben, can you get Janie's sled out of the truck?"

"On it." Ben took off toward her truck and returned a few minutes later with the sled.

Crystal watched Janie assess it for defects. The sled wasn't anything like the traditional wooden flexible flyer one with metal runners Crystal had grown up with. This one was made of fiberglass with a flat boat-like bottom that sloped up on the sides with handle grips. It wasn't small but was definitely not big either. This seat for one was going to make a cozy seat for the two of them.

Nate appeared out of nowhere behind them. "I thought you weren't racing?"

"I wasn't, but Beka said she could beat me. Seems to think she did last year."

"Well, we both know neither of those statements is true." He moved the sled to the starting line. "Get on. I'll give you the push." The family competitive streak was strong.

"Crystal's riding with me."

"Good. That'll give you more weight." Nate waved Crystal over. "You sit up front." He pointed to the middle of the sled. "Have you done this before?"

"Yes, but it's been a while."

"Remember, to steer you have to lean together. Just like on a motorcycle." Nate handed her the tow rope. "Keep this inside the sled, so it doesn't drag going down the hill."

Crystal sat on the sled, and Janie slid behind her with her knees up on each side to provide makeshift armrests for her.

"Loop your arms under my knees." Janie took Crystal's hand and looped her right arm for her. "Use them like handles to hold on. Once we get moving, we'll go pretty fast."

"All right." Crystal leaned her head back on Janie's shoulder and gazed into her eyes. "I'm totally in your control." She wasn't just talking about the race. Even though it was a chilly twenty-nine degrees outside, this proximity had set her on fire.

"I'll remind you of that later." Janie gave her a sideways smile as she shifted in her seat, bringing Crystal in closer between her legs. "Now, relax, but hold on tight. My dad lost control once with me on this hill. He fell off, and I flew straight down into a barbed-wire fence." She pointed to the bottom of the hill.

"Oh my God. That must've been horrible. Were you okay?"

"It was an absolute blast. I had just a few scratches on my face, but my mom was livid when we got back up the hill."

"Resilient little tyke, were you?"

"Still am." Janie grinned. "Don't worry, though. The fence is gone now, and they've cleared the trees to make it safer. So, no chance of that happening again." She grabbed hold of the sides of the sled as Nate gave them a push.

"Time to kick some ass," Beka shouted as Ben pushed her, and they flew off the hill side by side. The cold winter air rushed Crystal's face, and she held tight as they gained speed. They were neck and neck as they went down the hill.

When they passed the finish line, they both raised their arms and howled in victory, and the sled went out from under them as they skidded to the side to stop. Crystal landed on top of Janie, and she instinctively kissed her. She felt Janie's arms wrap around her waist, and everyone else disappeared in that moment until she heard Beka approach.

"Looks like you won two prizes today." Beka stood over them.

"I guess I did." Janie laughed as Crystal rolled to her side. "You can have the race trophy. I'm good with this prize."

"Nope. You won it fair and square." Beka reached out to help Crystal up. "Crystal can take it home with her."

"It needs to go on the shelf behind the counter at Cyber Shack."

"Where I can be reminded of it every day?" Beka shook her head. "Absolutely not."

"That's a great idea." Janie stood and wiped the snow from her legs, then felt the backside of her jeans. "I feel a draft. I think I ripped my pants."

Crystal took a look and caught a glimpse of black underwear peeking out. "You split a seam."

"Guess that's it for me today." Janie found the tow rope and began walking up the hill. "I'll drop you off at the inn and then go home to change."

"How about I go with you?" Crystal was playing with fire here, but she wanted more time with Janie. Going with her would provide more opportunity for that.

"I'd like that."

Crystal tingled with excitement of what was to come when they got there. She was hoping for more but would be happy with just hanging out and talking with Janie.

Chapter Nineteen

Janie pulled the Jeep door open for Crystal to climb in before she stowed her sled in the back. By the time they arrived at the Jeep, Janie must've spoken to a dozen people of all ages, asking how their day was going, how their kids were holding up in the cold, or just how they were in general.

"Getting colder out there. I think there's snow coming in tonight." Janie got into the Jeep and shivered before she buckled up and fired the engine. "My place isn't far. We can warm up there before I take you back to the inn." She unscrewed the top of the hot chocolate and poured some into the top, then handed it to Crystal. "This will help."

"I envy you." Crystal took the cup from her and sipped.

Janie glanced her way and tilted her head. "Not sure why. My newly acquired air-conditioning system is freezing my ass off." She tried to make light of her ripped-clothing situation. She put the Jeep into reverse and backed up.

Crystal handed Janie the cup. "You're that girl who knows everyone. The one who stands out in a crowd, who everyone likes."

"Not everyone. Plenty of people don't." Janie took a drink and set the cup in the console.

"I haven't seen anyone who doesn't since I arrived. You always look so carefree and so sure of everything, including yourself." Crystal reached across the console and put her hand on Janie's leg. "Your hair looks fabulous, by the way."

Janie warmed at the compliment. "Thank you, but don't believe everything you see." Janie looked both ways before she pulled onto the road and drove away from town. "My life used to be neat and orderly. Now it's really messy, and I can't stand it." Had she lost all her senses? Her mind was a roller coaster of insecurities. She was running straight into a disaster. "Lately, I've been working through crazy scenarios, literally throwing myself into panic attacks."

"About what?"

"The shack—the town—you." She stared out the windshield at the road ahead.

"Me? I've never thought of myself as panic-inducing."

Janie nodded. "You're something I never expected, and I'm not quite sure what to do about you." Janie's mouth got ahead of her thoughts.

"Do you have to know?" Crystal's voice softened. "Can you just take it one step at a time?"

"That's hard for me. When I know what I want, I want it now." Janie pulled up in the driveway of her house, pressed the garage-door-opener button, and watched the door rise. "I worry about scaring you away—doing too much too soon." She'd played her cards too soon in the past and had ended up alone because of it.

Crystal smiled. "Just in case you're wondering, I want you too." She leaned across the console and whispered, "So why don't we go inside, take off these clothes, and give it a whirl?"

The hot bolt of electricity that shot through Janie had her so turned on she could hardly contain herself. "I got your door." She jumped out of the Jeep and rounded it to help Crystal out.

Crystal met her with a scorching kiss that left her grasping the Jeep door for support. Her lips were soft and sweet, with just a taste of hot chocolate still left on them. Janie had no doubts now. It was clear Crystal was all in. She was surprised by the warmth of Crystal's hands as they slipped under her jacket and pulled her closer. She fought the urge to begin undressing Crystal right there in the garage as the kiss deepened and their tongues tangled gently. All of Janie's senses were topping out. She had to get Crystal inside—now.

"Let's go." Janie buzzed all over as she tugged Crystal to the door leading into the house. The pulse zapping through her was off the charts, and they'd barely touched each other. How could this woman do so much to her so quickly?

As soon as they were inside, all Janie's willpower was lost when Crystal pulled her into another steaming kiss. Their tongues moved in sync like they'd been working this magic forever. When Crystal began inching her hands up Janie's sides, she grabbed her waist and pulled her closer. She needed more contact—head to toe. She backed up momentarily, unzipped Crystal's jacket, and pushed it from her shoulders, then immediately pulled her back in for more contact.

Crystal growled as she tugged at Janie's jacket but couldn't get the zipper to release. "Take this off." She grabbed at the sides, fighting to get Janie free.

Janie yanked the zipper hard, but it went only halfway, so she pulled the jacket over her head and tossed it onto the floor, along with the flannel shirt that came with it. She pulled Crystal's turtleneck from the waistband of her pants, then swept her hands across the smooth, warm skin.

Crystal flinched but didn't move away. "Your hands are freezing." She took them in hers and rubbed the chill away before she grabbed hold of Janie's waist and tugged her closer. She snaked her hand up the back of Janie's shirt. "No bra?"

"Too confining."

"I agree." Crystal dragged her nails across Janie's ribs and cupped a breast in her hand.

"And they're not that big." Janie moaned as Crystal gave it a soft squeeze.

"They're perfect." Crystal pushed the shirt up and cupped the other one as well.

Janie took off her shirt, and Crystal let out a soft moan. Janie was even more turned on, if that was possible. Somehow, they made it to the couch, and Janie fell backward onto it, pulling Crystal on top of her. Janie felt terrifyingly exposed beneath Crystal in the lighted living room until she glanced up and was caught by Crystal's gorgeous caramel-brown eyes, watched them darken with steamy desire. This position, firmly trapped under Crystal, had her wet beyond measure, and they hadn't even created any friction.

"You're so beautiful." Crystal had become even more attractive with each day Janie got to know her.

The tiny wrinkles next to Crystal's eyes increased as she smiled. "There's that sweet-talker again." Crystal touched Janie's lips lightly before she trailed her own lips across her jaw, down her neck, and across her collarbone. Crystal continued across her chest and took a nipple into her mouth. "You taste so good. I can't wait to taste the rest of you." She weaved a path with her tongue back and forth across Janie's stomach before she stopped to unfasten the button of Janie's jeans.

Janie stopped Crystal when she slipped her fingers under the band of her underwear. "You're way overdressed."

Crystal straddled Janie's waist and pulled the turtleneck over her head. Janie shuddered at the sight of Crystal's creamy white breasts peeking over the top of her pastel-pink bra. A red-hot bolt of erotic electricity threw her into an inescapable surge of desire. She'd been waiting for this moment for days, and it was so much better than she'd imagined. Crystal popped open the clasp of her bra and let her breasts tumble out as the bra slid down her arms. Janie took a breast into each hand and brushed the nipples with her thumbs. Crystal closed her eyes and let out a moan. Every part of Janie was completely and thoroughly aroused now. It was agonizingly clear that she was about to explode right here on the couch. Crystal's mouth was suddenly on hers as tongues and hands began battling for control. Janie pulled her closer, skin-to-skin, creating the much-needed friction she craved.

She ripped her lips from Crystal's mouth. "Let's go to the bedroom."

Crystal pulled her lips into a grin. "Next round." She began working the zipper of Janie's jeans. "I want you right here." She yanked them from Janie's hips and slipped her hand inside her boy shorts and between Janie's legs. It was clear now that Crystal had control, and she wasn't going to relinquish it.

The initial touch made Janie quiver. Then when Crystal began stroking her and latched on to one of her nipples, Janie's breathing increased, and her heart pounded wildly. She thought she might orgasm right then. Crystal seemed to notice, and she immediately slid her fingers across Janie's clit and slipped one inside. Janie reached in the air for something to grab on to and found Crystal's head, then the couch cushion.

Crystal continued to swirl her nipple with her tongue as she picked up the pace with her fingers. Janie couldn't help the cry that ripped from her throat as she sailed over the edge into a surging orgasm. When Janie's muscles relaxed and the spasms began to slow, Crystal slid her fingers free before she took one last gentle suck of Janie's nipple, moved up next to Janie, and kissed her softly. "You're *very* responsive."

"Well, both those things at once will make that happen. Most people aren't that coordinated."

"It's an art, I know. Like the whole rub-your-belly-and-pat-your-head-at-the-same-time thing." She circled her finger around Janie's nipple. "You just have to concentrate on the more difficult of the two motions."

"So, which was harder?"

"The hardest part was not replacing my fingers with my mouth."

"Oh. Well, feel free to do that anytime."

"You're very agreeable. You know that?"

"Not usually, but with you I seem to be." In fact, Janie was bad about taking control during sex. She knew what turned her on and how it had to be done, but Crystal had managed to push her over the edge without any directions.

"I like that."

"I can show you a whole lot more you'll like in my bedroom." Crystal slid off Janie, stood, and held out her hand. "Let's go."

Janie took her hand and led her to the bedroom. The comfortable ease between them that had been there from the beginning remained and had only become clearer now that they were becoming intimate with each other. Janie had never thought she'd fall in love—not like this—with someone who lived so far away. It had been only a few days since they'd met. Never had she ever felt this way about someone so quickly. She couldn't go back from this.

CHAPTER TWENTY

Crystal had never been more grateful for leggings as she was when Janie went to her knees, slid her fingers under the waistband, and tugged them off, taking her panties along with them. Movement stopped, and Crystal glanced up to see Janie staring down at her as though she were taking in every inch of her. This woman could melt her with one look.

Crystal sat up, took Janie's face in her hands, and kissed her hard, sending another steaming shot of arousal through her. Janie took her into her arms and laid her gently onto the bed, then sucked a nipple into her mouth and rolled it around on her tongue before she snaked her hand between Crystal's legs. As soon as Crystal felt Janie's fingers skim the wet heat of her center and then push into her, they both groaned.

Janie sucked a nipple into her mouth and let it pop out. "I'm not going to fight the hard battle." Janie repositioned, slipped her arms under Crystal's knees, and pulled her to the edge of the bed. "I'm going to ravish you." She sank her mouth into Crystal's center.

Glorious heat filled Crystal. Then the first light swipe of Janie's tongue had her on the verge of combustion, and she grabbed a fistful of sheet. She wanted to savor every moment of pleasure in all its intensity as it happened. Janie took another swipe, just barely gliding her tongue through the slickness, and let out a moan. "You taste incredible."

With that, another jolt flew through Crystal. She pressed her shoulders to the mattress and lifted her hips higher. She felt a bit of déjà vu from her dreams as Janie came in stronger. There was no slow incline to this orgasm. This was happening...Now. She lost all control and let out a scream as she spiraled into a blissful pool of ecstasy. Janie's tongue created a magical experience—one that Crystal rarely felt—ever let herself feel. Tremors rolled through her, and she twitched with every stroke of Janie's tongue as she came down from the cloud that had taken her. When the aftershocks finally subsided, she reached for Janie and urged her up next to her.

"You're good at that."

"I try to always give it my best." Janie gathered Crystal into the crook of her arm and pulled the sheet and blanket on top of them.

"Overachiever." Crystal laughed. "I've been dreaming about this since I first met you."

Janie quirked her lips into a half smile. "Really?"

Crystal nodded. "Literally."

"I have to admit, it's been front and center in my mind as well." Janie smiled as she shook her head. "I'm really glad I split my pants."

"Me too." Crystal laughed, then took in a deep breath. "After last night...when you left, I was worried."

"I wasn't sure about it all—about this."

"And now?"

"I'm sure. I want to spend every minute with you." Janie closed her eyes briefly as though she was trying to gain composure. "Until you go home."

Until you go home. That phrase sounded so final. "Every second of every minute." Crystal's gut clenched. She'd been fearing the day she'd have to leave—have to tell Janie who she really was, and why she was really here. Should she do it now? No. That would ruin everything they'd just shared. Could she just escape without telling her anything?

"You okay?" Janie's forehead creased.

Crystal wasn't, but she couldn't bring herself to tell Janie why. "I'm not very good at intimacy. I'm pretty insecure about it."

"I would never allow you to feel insecure with me."

Crystal brushed a hank of hair from Janie's face. "No. I don't believe you would." She kissed her before she settled into the crook of Janie's shoulder. This, right here, was something Crystal could do forever. The whole glorious time would be cemented in Crystal's mind for eternity. The breathtakingly gorgeous woman lying next to her was seeping her way into her heart.

❖

"You awake?" Janie's voice came through the fog in Crystal's brain.

She wasn't dreaming again, was she? She struggled to open her eyes, and when she did, the room was darker, lit only by an amber glow. "What time is it?"

"A little after six. It gets dark really early here."

"You wore me out." Crystal stretched and gazed up at Janie.

"Same. We both kinda zonked out." Janie kissed the top of her head. "I was going to take you to dinner tonight. Remember? A nice fancy place away from Pine Grove. You still want to go?" She ran her fingers lightly over Crystal's hip.

"Not if I have to put on clothes and leave this cozy spot right here."

"That's what I was hoping your answer would be." Janie smiled. "I'll order pizza. What kind do you like?"

"I'm good with just about anything."

"I'm a fan of supremes."

"That's my favorite too."

"Fancy that." Janie chuckled as she plucked the receiver from its cradle and punched in a number. "Hey, Johnny. Can you send the usual?" She was silent for a moment. "That's fine." She hung up the phone. "It'll be about forty-five minutes. They're busy. I can probably find us a snack if you're starving."

"Nope. That gives me just enough time for me to explore you a bit more." Crystal lifted the covers and peeked underneath. "Ooh. I didn't see this freckle before." She gave Janie's belly a light kiss and laughed when she flinched. The quiver beneath Crystal's lips intensified as she trailed them across Janie's stomach. The move made all kinds of senses come to life. Having Janie's soft, warm body beneath her was absolute bliss. She continued farther down Janie's belly and glided her hand over the soft patch of hair that led to the entrance of Janie's legs, letting it tickle her palm. She glanced up to catch Janie watching her intently. With her hair all mussed around her face, she looked raw, pure, and wildly attractive. Crystal nestled herself between Janie's legs and skimmed her clit with her lips. Janie opened her legs wider, allowing more access, and Crystal took her cue. She made one swipe, then another, and watched Janie's stomach bounce with each subtle touch she made. Unable to stand it any longer, she buried herself between Janie's legs and let the tangy taste take over her mouth. She was going to explore every inch of Janie while she had the chance.

Chapter Twenty-One

Janie flipped the bacon as memories of the night before floated through her mind. Their first kiss had been sweet, and tentative, like a light snowfall spread across the countryside by a soft breeze on a winter's day. The second was borderline scorching, something that the most torrential blizzard couldn't douse. She'd been involved with women before, but nothing had burned so hot, so quickly as it was with Crystal. Janie was going to get hurt badly this time, and she didn't even care. She intended to ride this one out to its fullest, not planning to back away to save her heart as she had in previous relationships.

"Thanks for letting me shower." Crystal emerged from the bedroom, sat on the couch, and pulled on her boots. "I can't believe we slept until noon."

Janie was thankful the water heater made it through them both showering this morning. "I can't believe you kept me up all night. I haven't done that since I was…well, a lot younger." Janie reached into the refrigerator and took out the eggs and a bowl of blueberries.

"I believe it was *you* who kept *me* up all night." Crystal looked around the place. "Where's your tree?"

"Don't have one."

"Your family owns a tree farm, and you don't have a tree?" Crystal popped up from the couch, came into the kitchen, and gave Janie a soft kiss before she nestled herself in the corner between the stove and the sink.

It only took one kiss from Crystal to warm Janie all over. "I have the one at the shack. I spend more time there than I do here." It was sad but true. She didn't have much to come home to these days.

"I get that. I'm kinda the same way, but I still put up a tree. I like to get up early in the morning and stare at it while I drink my coffee." Crystal smiled like she was remembering doing just that. "It starts my day off in the right direction."

"What do you stare at when it's not the holiday season?"

"A rubber-tree plant with a string of lights on it."

"Sounds nice."

Crystal closed her eyes like she was going there right now. "It is. The house is quiet and serene, the best time to meditate."

"You meditate?"

"I try. I can't always say that I'm successful." Crystal plucked a blueberry from the bowl and popped it into her mouth. "These are good. They taste fresh."

"Frozen, actually. Picked fresh throughout the season. I freeze them in batches, so I can have them during the winter."

"You're very resourceful."

"Kind of have to be when you live in a small town. Everything isn't available year-round." Janie took the bacon from the pan and laid it on a paper-towel-lined plate. "Can you hand me a fork from that drawer behind you?"

Crystal spun and pulled open one of the drawers. "You have an iPad?" She held it up.

Janie nodded. "I use a router to connect to the satellite dish on the roof." She pointed to the box next to the TV. "The silverware is in the next drawer over."

"Seriously. After all the opposition you spout about Wi-Fi in the town?" The silverware rattled as Crystal pulled open the drawer and took out a fork.

Janie stopped mid-bacon turn and set down the tongs. Again with the Wi-Fi. Why did Crystal care so much about her stance on it? "You must spend a lot of time online at home."

"Truth be told, I do. I work a lot from home and don't have much of a social life."

Janie understood that. There were times she'd rather be at

home working than at the shack. "The decorating business must be booming in California."

"More than you can possibly imagine." Crystal glanced at the iPad in her hand. "Can you do metrics or inventory on this?"

Janie shook her head. "I only use it to check the security cameras at the store."

"Really? I wouldn't think a town like Pine Grove had a lot of crime."

"We don't generally, but last year a couple of teenagers got blasted and decided to break in and play games." She cracked an egg into a bowl. "Scrambled okay?"

"Sure. That's awful. Did you press charges?"

"No." Janie shook her head as she cracked a few more eggs into the bowl. "The kids were harmless. I know them, so I arranged to have them do some community service. I had to replace the back door and put in a deadbolt, which wasn't cheap."

"That was sweet of you." Crystal slid the iPad back into the drawer. "You really care about this community, don't you?"

"It's where I grew up." She whisked the eggs. "I understand the challenges these teenagers face. Small towns are hard on them. The only activities are sports and sex. At the shack, I try to provide another outlet for some of their time." She poured the eggs into the pan and brushed up against Crystal as she set the empty bowl in the sink.

"Sex, huh. I don't think that's limited to small towns." Crystal quirked her lips into a half smile.

Janie planted a hand on each side of the counter around Crystal. "You talking from experience?" She kissed her quickly before taking the bread from the counter and dropping two slices into the toaster.

"Not me, but my friends were pretty active in that area." Crystal opened a few cabinets, found the plates, set them next to the stove, and added a few pieces of bacon to each. "I covered for them a lot." The toast popped up. She hissed as she took the slices from the toaster and buttered them before adding a piece to each plate as well.

Janie laughed. "You and I have way too much in common."

She pointed to the refrigerator. "I have strawberry jam, if you're interested."

"I am." Crystal crossed the kitchen and tugged open the refrigerator door. "I like a little sweet with my savory. How about you?"

Janie nodded as she stirred the eggs. "Absolutely."

Crystal added a spoonful of jam to each piece of toast and spread it before placing one on each plate. Janie scooped half of the eggs onto each and carried them to the table, which she'd set earlier after she put the bacon on.

Janie sat in her usual spot, and Crystal took the chair adjacent to her. The closer the better as far as Janie was concerned.

"So, what's on the agenda for today?"

"I have to pick up cupcakes and deliver them to Grandma at the retirement home. They're having their annual Christmas party. You want to come with me?" She pushed her eggs around on her plate, worried that Crystal might say no.

"Do you even have to ask?" Crystal bit off a piece of bacon and chewed.

"I didn't want to assume." She shoveled a forkful of eggs into her mouth.

Bacon scattered across Crystal's plate as she dropped it. She pinched the napkin between her fingers before she covered Janie's hand with hers. "From now on, you can assume that I want to spend every minute of my time with you while I'm here."

It was a bittersweet moment for Janie. Happiness exploded inside her, along with trepidation. Crystal was going to leave soon, but Janie planned to make the best of their time together while she was in town. That was more than she'd been hoping for. She needed to stop being so self-conscious about everything between them and just let their connection happen naturally.

❖

When they reached the Pine Grove Retirement Home, Crystal took one box of cupcakes, and Janie took the other from the back of the Jeep. The parking lot and walkways had all been cleared. Thankfully, they'd received only a couple of inches of snow, not the huge amount that Dana had mentioned when she arrived. As they walked the short distance to the entrance, Crystal could see everyone milling about getting ready for their annual Christmas party. They seemed to have already finished lunch and were setting desserts out on the buffet table. Crystal hadn't realized that Janie's grandma had invited them to lunch until they had already finished breakfast.

"Janie." Grandma's face lit as she rushed across the room. "Did you bring the cupcakes?" She pulled her into a hug.

"Got 'em right here." Janie held out the boxes in her hands.

"Put them here on the table." Grandma pointed to the cake stand on the table between the bowls of spice drops and candy canes. "You brought your friend along." She turned, gave Crystal a hug, and whispered, "I'm glad she's socializing more. I worry about her."

"I'm right here, Grandma. I can hear you." Janie plated the first box of cupcakes before she picked up a spice drop and popped it into her mouth. "I'm plenty social. I have lots of friends."

"You know what I mean." Grandma took Crystal's hand and led her to the coat rack in the great room. "Take your coats off. You girls are just in time. We're practicing for the ball." She motioned them to the center of the room, where everyone was forming a circle. "We're just about to do the circle-waltz mixer. You can slip in next to me and your grandpa."

Crystal widened her eyes as they were brought into the circle. "I have no idea how to do this." She'd never learned any kinds of traditional dances, skipped out of that session during her PE class in high school. Even though she hadn't officially come out until after she graduated, the awkwardness of being paired with a boy was front and center for her back then.

Janie stood to her right and took her hand. "It's easy. Just follow my lead."

The group moved in and then out, and then Janie took Crystal's hand, and she glided to her right. They moved in and out again, and Crystal went to the next person. This happened one more time before she was paired with Grandpa, who took both her hands and glided her to the middle and back again, while everyone else did the same. She glanced over his shoulder to see Janie give her a grin and a wink. They went through the whole process several more times until she was paired with Janie.

"You're really good at this."

"I fill in when they need me. It's kinda fun."

"It really is." Just another plus on the list of all things Janie. She was a dream come true. Why did she have to live so far away? "What other dances do they practice?"

"The polka, foxtrot, the swing."

"You can do all those?"

Janie nodded. "Grandma taught me." She moved her around the floor and pulled her in closer as the music changed to a slower tune. "Grandpa's not always available."

"And what is this dance called?"

"It's the breather." Janie tucked her face next to Crystal's. "Gives the single guys a chance to make the ladies they paired up with swoon." She planted her hand on Crystal's back and pulled her closer.

"Oh, really?" Crystal's heart pounded wildly. "I'm feeling a little swoony myself." The giddy feeling was beginning to take over her life lately. How long would it last? Would she lose it when she got back to Dallas—when she didn't have Janie to make it happen?

"Works every time." Janie kissed her on the cheek before she released Crystal and pushed her out into a twirl. An older gentleman immediately snapped her up and took her into a foxtrot before the music changed and he traded her off to another man, who bounced her across the floor in a polka. Finally, Janie slipped in for the next dance and took her off the floor.

Crystal heaved out a breath. "Keeping up with these guys is hard work."

"Right? They can barely walk down the block, but they can sure cut a rug." Janie grinned. "Especially when a pretty young girl is in the house."

"You should know." Crystal bumped her shoulder. "You must be their favorite dance partner."

Beka came out of the kitchen with a tray of glasses. "It's time for some bubbly."

Everyone raced from the middle of the room to surround Beka.

"They don't get booze often either." Janie chuckled. "Come on. Let's sit while we have the chance." She led Crystal to the couch and sank into it.

"Your grandparents have some nice friends." Between bingo and dancing, she was beginning to get to know quite a few of them.

"Yeah. I really enjoy them." Janie glanced at the lot of them enjoying their champagne. "I get so many history lessons here."

"I bet that's interesting. I used to love hearing stories from my grandparents. Especially about all the antics my parents were up to when they were young."

Janie turned slightly and rested her arm on the couch behind Crystal. "Like what?"

"You know, the normal stuff you keep from your kids. The first time you snuck in late, snuck out after they were asleep, your first drink."

"You're quite the rebel."

Crystal laughed loudly. "If only. That's more like my brother. He was always getting caught, though."

"What's he like now?"

"He's calmed down a lot. He volunteers as a youth pastor. Pretty ironic, I know."

"Well, at least he's putting the lessons he learned to good use."

"He's married now, with three girls." Crystal grinned.

Janie raised her glass. "To karma."

"Exactly." Crystal tapped her glass to Janie's before she sipped. "All three of them have different personalities too. The youngest is just like him, though. Challenges him all the time."

"I get along really well with Grandpa." Janie glanced across the room at him. "My dad and I always butted heads. Still do on occasion."

"You seem to be close with your whole family."

"Yeah. They're good to me. Don't know what I'd do without them." Janie smiled as she watched her grandparents interact with the rest of the PGR residents.

Not the first clue Crystal had picked up. Janie was happy in Pine Grove, which meant she wasn't likely to leave. She needed to readjust her expectations of this romance. Nothing could come of an affair with someone who lived so far away unless Crystal was willing to make some pretty large sacrifices.

Chapter Twenty-Two

Crystal couldn't believe it was already Wednesday. She'd been so wrapped up in Janie that she'd lost a day somewhere. She'd put the fact that she was leaving in a few days out of her mind. As she and Janie entered Cyber Shack, Crystal noticed the sign on the counter.

Early Bird Special $.99 Coffee & free console games
(Xbox One & PS4) 6 AM – 10 AM

She didn't recall seeing it before. Was she so wrapped up in Janie that she'd missed part of her marketing? "Has that always been there?"

"No. Business is usually slow during the mornings with the kids in school, so I decided to put out a leader to bring some of the older generations in."

"That's a great idea."

"Beka's not a fan. It means she has to be here early, along with Tara, to open and get the kitchen going earlier."

"She helps you out a lot."

"She's a good friend, and I pay her a lot to handle things when I'm *otherwise* occupied." Janie grinned and winked.

"I'll have to thank her for that." Crystal glanced around, checking the various rooms. "I would expect more kids to be here earlier while they're on winter break."

"Nothing really beats sleep for them." Janie opened the *Letters to Santa* box near the door and fished out the newest additions.

"So, what do you do with all those wishes?" There seemed to be quite a few.

"I do my best to fulfill them here in the store, some at home if I can." Janie handed Crystal the stack of letters as she went behind the counter. "You want a latte this morning?"

"Just coffee. Please." She would save the sugar high for later.

"Good morning," Janie said as she maneuvered around Tara—who was busy making an espresso—to get to the coffeemaker.

Crystal found a table away from others eating pastries and enjoying their coffee and opened the letter on the top of the stack. Janie joined her with two full steaming mugs of coffee.

"This one says she'll hide some cookies for you this year, since her dad ate them all last year." Crystal set it on the table and picked up her mug.

"That must be from Aria."

"How'd you know?" The coffee burned Crystal's tongue as she sipped and then set it down to cool.

"She's trying to butter me up." Janie sorted through the letters. "Wants me to buy *Call of Duty* so she can play it."

"That's kind of an adult game, isn't it?" Crystal had heard about it before. "My brother plays it with his friends. My sister-in-law isn't too keen on him doing it around the kids."

Janie shifted in her chair and leaned her elbows on the table. "Your brother who has the girls?"

"Yes. I have only one brother. He and his wife want a big family. Probably won't stop until they have five or six." A thought popped into Crystal's head. Did Janie want kids?

"Your sister-in-law must love being a mother."

"She lives for her kids, and she's great at it. Makes it look so easy." The way Shannon interacted with her kids made Crystal want to be a mom.

"I remember you saying your brother volunteered as a youth pastor. What does he do for a living?"

"He's an architect. Designs huge structures in San Francisco."

That wasn't even a lie. Austen had dreamed of creating structures since he was a kid. Crystal wished she'd been that decisive about her career. Maybe if she had, then she'd be in the business of helping people instead of hounding them.

"Sounds impressive."

"He is…at work, but still just my brother at home." Crystal cupped her mug and rolled it between her hands. "What about Nate? Do you think he'll ever have kids?"

"He talks about it. Needs to find the right girl first." Janie grinned. "Could our brothers be any more different?" She picked up another letter and glanced at it. "Do you plan to have children?"

There it was—the million-dollar question that was knocking around in Crystal's head as well but she was reluctant to ask. "I think so. Probably not five or six, but one or two someday, when my job isn't so busy." She kept eye contact. "You?"

"Absolutely." Janie added the letter in her hand to the pile to her right and picked up another. "I'm going to need a couple to help me out with this place someday. You know, sweeping, mopping, bussing tables." She laughed. "If it's still around."

"I have no doubt it will be." Cyber Shack seemed to be popular with young people and adults alike. Crystal didn't think that would change even if Janie brought in Wi-Fi.

"So, what in the interior-design world would prevent you from having kids sooner rather than later? Don't you get to set your own schedule?" Janie seemed genuinely interested.

Crystal had to think about that question for a minute because she'd forgotten she'd told Janie she was a designer. "I guess nothing, but I just hadn't thought about making space in my life for them yet." Or even for someone to co-parent, in fact. Crystal grabbed another letter. Time to move away from this subject. "This one says, 'Kyle is picking on me at school. Can you make him stop? He's starting to pick on my friends too, and I don't like it.'" Crystal held up the letter? "Do you know Kyle?"

Janie nodded. "He comes in here. Tries to pull the same crap."

"What do you do about it?" Bullies affected most people in one way or another, and Crystal was no exception. She'd had her fair share of torment in high school, enough so that she hadn't cared to attend any of the planned reunions.

"I threaten to erase his saved-game progress from the shack's server, and he shapes right up." Janie took the letter and set it in a separate pile. "I know his parents. I'll mention it to them."

"Listen to this one from Sammy. 'I want a little sister for Christmas. The sooner the better.' You'd better alert his mom and dad to that just in case they aren't already trying."

"I'll tell her, and I think they're already expecting."

"Whew." Crystal swiped her hand across her forehead. "I wouldn't want Santa not to be able to deliver." She picked up another letter. "This one knows he's on the naughty list, but he wants a big-boy bike anyway."

Janie glanced at the scribbled signature. "He's getting one."

Crystal dropped her hands to her sides and let out a breath. "Do you know everyone around here?"

Janie nodded. "It's a small town. Went to school with half of their parents."

Crystal tossed it into the stack and opened another one and read it out loud. "'Can you bring a Camaro for my dad? He really wants one, and my mom said no.'" She laughed. "You certainly get the feel for the dynamics of some families."

"More than you will ever know." Janie shook her head. "Too much information isn't better."

Crystal's eyes widened. "Ooh, listen to this one. 'I know you've been watching me, so you can see I have been being nicer to my little brother even though he's always getting into my stuff. I don't want a lot this year. Just one thing. A dirt bike to ride the trails behind my house. You know, like all the other kids have. I'll leave a beer instead of milk like I did last year, unless you want whiskey. Okay. I'll leave both.'"

"I bet that's a little drinking tidbit you didn't know."

Janie winked. "Not for certain anyway."

"Nothing surprises you, huh?" Crystal could never keep up with all of this intel.

"Not really. Been doing this a long time."

Crystal read another. "'Can you take the Elf on the Shelf with you this year? He's creepy.'" Crystal widened her eyes. "My sister-in-law got one, and I think he's creepy too."

"Is that Mary?" Janie glanced at the letter.

Crystal nodded. "She wants Santa to wake her up this year so she can pet the reindeer."

"She can't have animals because her sister's allergic, so they have no pets."

"Not even a barn cat?"

Janie shook her head. "They'd have to have a barn for that."

Crystal laughed. "She'd probably like Santa to take her sister too."

"No doubt." Janie giggled. "Bring all the animals and take my sister. She gets in the way of everything."

Crystal laughed along with her, and they both couldn't stop. These letters were hilarious, and she thoroughly enjoyed reading through them with Janie. She'd grant every one of their wishes if she could.

Janie opened another one, and her laughter faded. "Not sure how we're going to fulfill this one, though. We can give them food for the holidays, but what happens for the other three hundred and sixty-four days a year?" She handed it to Crystal, and she read it. It was from Susie, a child asking only for food for Christmas. Her parents don't want anyone to know, but her dad was out of work, and they didn't have any food in the house.

"This is heartbreaking." Now Crystal really wished she'd gone another way with her career. Maybe she could use her current position to leverage some benefit for the community. Seemed a new hockey arena wasn't the only thing Pine Grove needed. "Can we set up a fund to help them?"

"We could, but they wouldn't publicly accept it. Her dad has too much pride."

"So, how will you provide them food for Christmas?"

"I'll have my dad dress up like Santa and take some gifts to their house." Janie glanced at the letter she was holding. "We'll send a turkey, maybe a ham, and some other items so they can have a nice

Christmas." She folded the letter and put it in her pocket. "Outside of the holidays we just leave it on the porch to avoid an awkward encounter. It's what we do for people in the community."

Pine Grove was such a cute, quaint town, she hadn't thought about the usual hardships that came with any community. "I'd like to pitch in, if you'll let me." All she did was work, so she had plenty of money to help. She donated to the food bank at home on a regular basis.

"You don't have to do that. I've got it covered."

"I want to help. We can double the amount of food. Get them some canned goods, rice, beans." Crystal lifted her shoulders. "And lots of other pantry items to tide them over for a while until their dad finds work."

"That's very generous of you." Janie smiled softly as she patted the pocket containing the letter. "We can pick up a few things for them today."

Crystal would put a community center and food bank at the top of her list of items for Spark Wireless to provide for the town. Those would be a needed and well-received incentive they could offer, along with updating the hockey arena. She just had to get her boss to agree.

❖

Janie backed her Jeep into the first vacant space in front of the grocery store. That would make it easier to load when they were finished. Crystal hopped out before Janie could get around to open the door for her, a habit she wished Crystal would stop. Apparently, she didn't like to be pampered all the time.

Her energy heightened as they passed through the automatic double doors at the entrance to the store. Doing good things for people always gave her a great feeling.

"I'll grab a cart." Crystal bounced ahead of her. Apparently, it did the same for her.

"You want to start to our left and work our way over to the produce?" Crystal pointed and then motioned across the store.

Janie snagged another cart. "I'm right behind you." She'd let Crystal lead the way. They'd end up hitting every aisle whichever way they started. "Maybe we should've made a list?"

"I got it." Crystal pointed to her head. "I've volunteered at the food bank at home and have a good idea of what is needed. Peanut butter, canned soup, fruit, vegetables. Stew, fish, and beans. Some SpaghettiOs for the kiddos." Crystal turned around and walked backward. "Ha! I made a rhyme." She winked and spun back forward. "Spam." She glanced over her shoulder. "Do you like Spam? I do."

Janie let go of the cart, held her palms up, and shrugged. "Ham in a can. What's not to like?" She'd never seen someone so excited about grocery shopping and was thoroughly enjoying it. Everything Crystal did seemed to be fun—she was the glass-half-full girl Janie had always imagined herself with.

"Right? Everyone talks a good game when it comes to eating healthy, but when it's actually time to walk the walk, they still eat their childhood favorites." Crystal talked as she zipped down the next aisle.

"Anything that comes in a can that can be heated in a microwave." There was always plenty of that on the shelves at Janie's house when she was growing up.

Crystal stood back and looked at the variety of Spam. "Who knew there were so many choices."

"Let's just stick with the classics." Janie grabbed a case and added it to the cart.

"They have turkey. Let's get that too." Crystal grinned as she put another case in the cart. "It's healthy...ish."

Janie pulled her lips into a half smile. "If that makes you feel better, but it's still canned meat."

When they arrived in the meat department, Janie sorted through all the frozen turkeys to find the biggest one. She held up the huge bird. "This twenty-two pounder should give them plenty of leftovers."

Crystal's mouth dropped open. "Would you mind if I kiss you right here in the meat department?"

"Not at all." She added the turkey to the second cart. "In fact, I'd recommend it." She moved around the cart and opened her arms.

Crystal took her face into her hands and kissed her softly. "You're generous to a fault, aren't you?"

"Well, I hate seeing people suffer. So, if I can do anything to help, I do." Janie took control of her cart. "Now on to stuffing—and pasta—and rice. Let's try to get some whole-grain pasta and brown rice to offset the healthyish items we got."

"Stop. You know you love white rice."

Janie chuckled. "I do. With lots of butter. We'll get some of that too." She had no idea how Crystal read her so well, but she liked it.

By the time they got to the checkout counter, they had two full baskets of food.

The manager came over to help with bagging. "What's the occasion?"

"Just buying food for some people in need."

"That's a noble thing to do." He held up a finger. "Excuse me a minute." He glanced at the baskets before he went to the service desk and picked up the phone.

"Looks like you scared him off." Crystal handed Janie several items to put on the conveyor belt.

He came back soon after. "I just talked to the owner. We're going to give you a ten percent discount on your purchase, and we can also donate a few cases of canned goods."

"That's very thoughtful." Janie's heart warmed. The generosity of the Pine Grove business community always amazed her. "Thank you, *and* the owner." Since this store was only one of several in the area, she didn't know the owner personally. An exception to the rule.

Once they finished checking out, the manager insisted on helping them load everything into the back of the Jeep. They almost couldn't get the back closed, and the back seat was full, so Crystal had to ride with her feet on a couple of cases of canned goods stacked in the footwell of the passenger seat.

After the discount on their purchase plus the additional food for free, they'd been able to get many more groceries than they'd planned. They would be able to fulfill Susie's wish and have a good supply to assist them until her father was able to find work. The storage room at Cyber Shack was equipped with shelves and had plenty of room to store the food for now. Janie would have an extra supply if she discovered anyone else in need during the rest of the holidays and into the new year. All in all it was a productive afternoon.

Chapter Twenty-Three

Crystal bolted up in bed when she heard the phone ring. She picked up the receiver, and Bob's anxious voice spewed through the speaker and smashed against her ear. "Where are we at on this? Do you have signatures yet?"

"No. Not yet. I'll pick up the syrup before I leave." She held the receiver to her chest, then turned and whispered to Janie, "It's my mom."

Janie sat up and kissed her bare shoulder before she got out of bed and headed into the bathroom as she made hand movements of scrubbing her hair and back. Crystal grinned and covered the phone as she attempted to hold back a laugh. Janie pointed to her and then made a washing motion on her boobs.

"Save those for me," Crystal said softly.

"What the hell? I don't want any syrup. I want a signed contract."

She waited for the water to click on, then pulled the sheet up around her and sat back against the headboard. Speaking to her boss in this state of undress was disturbing. "I have a plan. This community has several needs, not the least of which is an upgraded hockey arena. The town absolutely adores hockey." The biggest need, though, was actually a new community center that included a food pantry, but she was starting with sports because Bob understood that language.

"They're all about hockey, eh? I think we can rustle up some funding for that."

"While you're doing that, find some money for a community center with a work program and a food pantry. These people are very proud and don't like asking for help." Even after all the food she and Janie had acquired yesterday for the family of the little girl who had written the letter, the community clearly needed something in place to continue helping needy families throughout the year.

"What makes you think they'll take kindly to someone giving them a community center?"

"They need it, Bob. The kids need somewhere to play other indoor sports besides hockey."

"Can't play football inside."

"But you can give them internet." She was tired of his siloed thoughts, but she still had to play to them. "There's so much more to life than internet and football."

"When are you going to present your proposal to the council?"

Janie peeked her head through the opening to the bathroom, held up a finger, and beckoned her inside.

"I have to go. I'll call you later." She hung up the phone quickly and raced to the bathroom without giving Bob a chance to grill her on the rest of her plan, which she really didn't have yet anyway.

"We'll pick some up today." Janie scooted back to allow Crystal to immerse herself in the water.

"Some what?" Crystal found the bar of soap on the ledge and created a lather between her hands.

"Syrup for your mom. I know just the right place to get it." Janie took the soap from her and began washing Crystal's shoulders. "There's a small local place that bottles it. I'll call and have them bring some by the store later."

Could this woman be any more perfect? Janie not only met her every need in bed, but she was going to fulfill her fictitious maple-syrup order without Crystal even asking.

❖

Crystal bounced down the stairs with Janie right behind her. They'd spent the night in Crystal's room at the inn exploring each other for the third night in a row. Crystal could get used to this—in fact she had already. She was dreading the day she had to leave.

"Where are you two heading off to today?"

"We're going to the tree lot to help Grandpa. Nate and Dad ran to the farm to pick up more trees." Janie stepped in front of Crystal as they moved toward the door.

"Wait." Dana looked down at the area in front of her behind the counter. "You got a message from someone named Marie." She handed Crystal a piece of paper. "There's her number."

Apparently, her ex, Marie, hadn't made the trip to St. Croix after all. Crystal took the note from Dana and stuffed it into her pocket. Dana had probably insisted on getting Marie's phone number. She already had it and was doing her best to forget it. "Work associate. Thanks. I'll call her back later." Marie had probably already filled her voice mail with messages that weren't being delivered, messages that Crystal had no interest in hearing.

"She sounded a little put out that she couldn't reach you. Said something about you spending the holidays with her family."

Janie immediately stopped walking. "Wait. Did I hear that right? You're spending the holidays with another woman and her family?"

Heat burned Crystal's neck. "No. I'm not."

"Then why would she think that?" Janie's expression changed instantly, the warmth that usually spilled out through her smile gone. "Are you involved with someone else?"

"No. I mean yes. I was." Crystal shook her head. "None of this is coming out right. We broke up recently."

Janie stiffened. "But she still thinks you're coming to her family's house for Christmas?" She was confused and had every right to be. Crystal was pretty confused right now as well.

"No." Crystal shook her head again. "I told her that wasn't happening before I came here." She moved closer, hoping Janie would understand, and the knot in her stomach would vanish. "Before I met you."

"I need some air." Janie rushed out the front door.

Dana scrutinized Crystal. "You sure there's not more to it than that?"

"Absolutely certain. I'm spending Christmas with *my family* in California." Marie was the one who'd broken things off with Crystal.

"But there's history there." Dana narrowed her eyes.

Crystal nodded. She couldn't deny that. "It's exactly that. History." She wasn't about to open that door again and walk into that turbulent space of emotional uncertainty. Especially not now that she'd found something so much different with Janie.

"Doesn't sound like Marie knows that."

"You'll just have to take my word for it." She didn't have to explain herself to Dana.

"Okay." Dana narrowed her eyes. "Just remember, Janie is my friend. If you hurt her, I won't be happy."

"I would never hurt Janie." Crystal's stomach dropped. She was, in fact, going to cause her a lot of pain at some point, and she couldn't do a thing about it. "Not purposely, but she's going to be upset when she finds out why I'm really here."

"That's a smaller hurdle to jump than having a girlfriend would be."

Crystal wasn't sure she agreed with that. "I don't have a girlfriend." She really didn't have anyone...except Janie, and any future for that relationship was still up in the air. "Please don't lead Janie to believe that."

"I don't have any plans to do that." She picked up a pen and jotted something down. "I also don't have any reason not to believe you, so I'll take you at your word."

"Thank you."

"Don't thank me." Dana glanced up. "You still have to get yourself out of that other tub of hot water. I can't help you there."

"I'm fully aware of that fact. Thanks for your confidence."

"Don't get me wrong. Janie's stuck on you like a honeybee is on a daffodil. I think you can pull it off. You just have to yank that Band-Aid off quickly so she doesn't know what's happened and then immediately beg her for forgiveness."

"Not sure it's going to be that simple. She's going to know

exactly what happened as soon as I tell her." The longer she waited, the more it was going to sting. For now, she needed to figure out how to fix the current problem. "I need to go." She hightailed it out of the inn and toward the tree lot.

Chapter Twenty-Four

Janie flopped back onto the small bed in the tree-lot trailer and stared at the metallic ceiling as she fought for breath. She'd run almost the whole way there. Never in her life had she been the other woman, and now it seemed she was exactly that. How could she be so stupid? Now that she thought more about their interactions, it was clear why Crystal had been reluctant to give details of her life. Janie was just a holiday fling. She'd let it happen—gotten caught up in the magic of it all. Just the thought of Crystal made her stomach twist. Man, she had it bad for this one, and it seemed someone else did as well.

She contemplated her next step. Should she believe what Crystal told her about Marie? That they had broken up before she arrived in Pine Grove? She really wanted to, but she'd been fooled before and didn't relish the thought of getting hurt any more than she already was. She didn't like losing her heart or her pride.

The knock on the trailer door was slight, immediately followed by the sound of the door being pulled open. Janie bolted up, but by the time she got to the front of the trailer, Crystal was already inside. "Guess I should've locked that." She clenched her fists as she paced the aisle of the trailer. "I told myself not to get involved with you, and then I did it anyway. If I'd known you had a girlfriend, I wouldn't have—"

Crystal bolted forward and blocked her path. "Slept with me. I know." She put her hands on Janie's chest.

"Don't touch me." She felt used and ridiculously guilty, and she didn't even know Marie. "You should've told me." She walked farther down the aisle to where the bed was located.

Crystal followed, cornering her. "Janie, I've done a lot of shitty things in my life, but not this one. I *do not* have a girlfriend. I would've never started anything with you if I had." She reached for her free hand. "The *only* woman I'm involved with is you."

"Doesn't seem like Marie knows that."

"She doesn't know about you, but she does know we're done. She's the one who broke it off."

That tidbit wasn't good to hear either. It was killing Janie to say this, but it had to be said. "I don't want to be in the middle of your unfinished business or be a rebound. If you still have feelings for her, I can't continue with"—she spun, trying to find a way out of the trap she'd made for herself—"whatever this is." All she could do was clench the top of the threshold into the sleep area for balance as she tried to hold back the tears welling in her eyes.

"I don't know what this is either." Crystal moved closer and put her arms around Janie's waist. "But I know it's not a rebound. It's something very special. Something better than I've had with anyone in a very long time."

Janie felt Crystal's heat radiating against her back—couldn't stop the warmth from seeping into her heart. When she let loose of the threshold and turned around, Crystal hooked her hand around Janie's neck, pulled her closer, and locked her lips with hers. Janie lost herself in the sweetness of Crystal's mouth, the familiar taste she'd come to crave. She took Crystal's face in her hands and slid her tongue into her mouth, indulged in the buzzing shiver that rushed her as Crystal's tongue danced along with hers in a seamless waltz as though they'd been dancing together forever. She didn't want to be in the middle of something messy, but she didn't want to lose this feeling either. Her willpower puddled, and she relaxed and let Crystal seep back into her heart to seal all the small cracks that had begun to surface earlier.

❖

Standing at the stove in the trailer, Crystal watched Janie through the window as she warmed milk on the stove for a new batch of hot chocolate. She couldn't believe how desperate she'd felt thinking she'd almost lost her. How was she going to prevent that from happening when she found out the truth about why she was really here in Pine Grove? Crystal had been having so much fun that she'd almost forgotten her mission—shoved the real reason to the back of her mind and ignored it for as long as she could.

She had to find a way out of this mess she'd gotten herself into. She rummaged through the drawers in the trailer, found a pad of paper and pen, and began jotting down some notes. She made two columns—one for Janie, one for the town. She tapped her lips with the pen as she thought about all things Janie. She cared about the community, her family, and her business. The town needed a new hockey arena, a community center, and a food pantry. She could go to Mason and discuss giving the town all the items she'd listed in exchange for a contract with Spark.

She traced a heart around Janie's name. None of that would guarantee that Janie wouldn't hate her when it was all said and done. She ripped off the top page of the tablet, folded it, and shoved it into her pocket. There was no way out of this sinking hole of lies. Sooner or later, she was going to lose Janie. It wouldn't hurt any less if it happened long-distance, but as it stood now, she preferred later.

Crystal's heart pounded when she glanced out the window and spotted Jack crossing the street to the lot. She raced out of the trailer past Janie, who luckily was already helping someone with a tree, to intercept him.

"What the hell are you doing here?"

"Looking for you." Jack gave her an idiotic grin. "We just got in."

"I told Bob I had everything handled."

"Doesn't sound that way. I just left him and the head of the council, Mason something or other. He seems very receptive to the updated hockey arena, as well as the new community center and food bank." They must have been already on their way when Bob called her this morning.

"You took my hand and played it? Does Mason know I work for Spark?" Bob really hadn't trusted her at all, and it turned out that he had a good reason.

"Don't get your panties in a wad. We've got it covered without revealing who you really are. Your friend Dana at the Pine Grove Inn explained to us how you've been making progress, in more ways than one, with the owner of Cyber Shack." Jack raised an eyebrow. "Bravo, by the way. I wouldn't have thought to get in on the ground floor by sleeping with her."

"I didn't sleep with her for business." Jack would never let her live this one down.

"Then even better." He glanced at Janie, who was finishing up with her customer. "She looks like quite a catch."

"When are you leaving?" She wanted him out of her business— now.

"Not until Sunday. Bob wants to spend a couple of days. You know, get a feel for the town." He glanced around the lot.

"You need any help over there?" Janie's voice floated through the air.

"Nope. I got it." Crystal grabbed a bag of mistletoe from the peg on the post and handed it to Jack. "Give me ten bucks. Now."

"What am I going to do with that?" He took out his wallet and opened it.

"Throw it in the trash for all I care. Just give me the ten." Crystal reached in and plucked out a bill. "Now get out of here. Janie can't know that we work together, or the whole deal will explode." She moved him toward the street. "And stay away from Cyber Shack."

"We can't have our mole be discovered now that I'll be getting half the commission." He was saying that to get a rise out of her, but Crystal didn't even care about the money or the executive position now. She didn't particularly care to be described as a subterranean, grub-eating rodent, but that label seemed completely accurate.

"Tell Bob to keep his mouth shut as well."

"I won't put it that way, but I'll ask him nicely to keep it to himself." He tucked the bag of mistletoe under his arm. "You need to learn to suck up better."

"I bet you could give me lots of advice on that, huh?"

"Better be nice, missy." He waggled his finger at her. "You have a whole lot to lose if your profession becomes public."

"I know. Thanks for getting the agreement wrapped up." Letting Jack take the credit gave her the out she was looking for. Maybe she didn't have to tell Janie why she was there after all.

"My pleasure."

Janie showed up behind her. "Everything all right over here?" She must have noticed the tension between her and Jack.

"Everything's fine. This gentleman is staying at the inn and just wanted something to brighten up his room."

"I thought they had the whole place decorated for the holidays."

"Apparently not in the cheap suites." Jack glanced at Crystal. "Thank you for your help." He smiled and held up the bag of mistletoe before he spun and walked away.

"That was interesting."

"Yeah. I guess he's in town for a few days with his boyfriend." Bob was going to love that story when he heard it, but Crystal really didn't care anymore. "Can we stay at your place tonight? Build a nice fire and do lots of fun things in front of it." She tugged on the collar of Janie's jacket to pull her closer.

Janie's smile widened. "Absolutely." She kissed her.

Crystal planned to keep Janie as far away from Bob and Jack as she could for the next couple of days.

❖

Crystal had managed to occupy Janie in a multitude of pleasurable ways since she'd found out Bob and Jack were in town. Although Janie needed to be at Cyber Shack to open and do the banking, Crystal had managed to convince her to take some time off and show her more of the countryside. Yesterday, while Janie was busy handling the details at the shack, Crystal had walked to the inn, changed, and gotten back to the shack in record time. This morning had been more of a challenge because Janie had insisted on dropping her off. Bob and Jack were in the restaurant having breakfast and apparently had seen them drive up. Before she knew it, Jack was at the entrance waving to her. She'd shrugged it off as him recognizing her from the tree lot the day before and then quickly raced inside and up the stairs. She'd waited at the top for several minutes until she knew Janie had left before she went down the stairs and into the restaurant.

"Hey. Look who's here." Bob stood as Crystal approached their table. "Sit. Have some breakfast with us." He pulled out the adjacent chair for her and motioned for the waitress.

"Nothing for me, thanks." Crystal smiled at the waitress. She'd already had pancakes at Janie's house. "How did your meeting with Mason go?"

"I have to admit, I was worried, but you did some great research here." Bob glanced at Jack. "Right, Jack?"

He nodded as he swallowed a bite of scrambled eggs. "Mason likes your idea for the new hockey arena."

"What about the community center and food bank?" That was what the town really needed. It was what Janie would appreciate and what Crystal now realized meant something to her.

"I thought that whole package was a little much." Jack took another bite and washed it down with his coffee.

"Mason was on the fence until I mentioned those ideas." Bob eyed Jack. "Sometimes you have to give a little more to get what you want."

"Good." Crystal took a deep breath. "I need a favor. Could you both steer clear of me until I tell Janie who I am?"

"Haven't done that yet, huh?" Jack grinned. "She's not going to take it well."

"I know that, Jack." She gritted her teeth as she spoke. "But I can't have you blabbing to everyone who I am and why I'm here. That will only make it worse."

Bob touched her shoulder. "Calm down. We'll keep our distance. We don't want any of this to go south on Spark or you." He glanced at Jack, and the crease between his eyes deepened. He must be due for another round of Botox. "Won't we, Jack?"

"I suppose your girlfriend could kill the whole deal for us."

Jack pushed his plate away and relaxed into his chair. "Don't want to do that."

"You know, you're still the same asshole you've always been."

"Thank you." Jack grinned and picked up his coffee.

"Let's stop the squabbling, you two." Bob shifted in his chair. "Crystal did an awesome job bringing this one in, and we're going to close it."

Crystal stood. "I'll see you when I get back to Dallas."

Bob nodded. "Have a nice Christmas with your family."

She glanced around the restaurant to make sure no one she knew had seen her at the table, then headed out of the restaurant and up to her room. Now that she'd settled that situation with Bob and Jack, tonight was her last night with Janie, and she planned to enjoy it.

Chapter Twenty-Five

Janie walked silently alongside Crystal to the town square. The soft winter breeze floated through Crystal's hair, carrying her sweet, familiar, scent into the air, igniting all Janie's senses again. The memory of Crystal's touch filled her head. She'd woken early this morning and spent an hour watching Crystal's chest rise and fall as she slept, memorizing the curve of her nose, the line of her jaw, every tiny line of her beautiful face. How could she have developed such deep feelings for Crystal in less than two weeks? Janie had considered how she felt about this whole whirlwind affair, what it would be like to live in California, and wake up every day next to Crystal. How she would make a living if she left Pine Grove—whether Crystal would even want her there. Janie had only just drifted off to sleep when she was awakened by Crystal's lips on her neck, her hand drifting lightly across her stomach, her fingers gliding across her clit and inside, pushing her into another pulsing orgasm.

They'd spent another blissful morning tangled in the sheets together. She hadn't wanted it to end, but today was the day they would find out the winner of the window-decorating contest, and Crystal had forced her out of bed and into the shower early. She'd of course bribed her with the washing of body parts as they bathed—the only reason she'd agreed to get up.

"Nervous?" Crystal asked as she slid her hand into Janie's.

"Nah." Janie shook her head "You?" In the past Sue had always been a shoo-in, but Janie was sure it would be close this year. Each and every time she entered the store, she admired the window. Janie was proud of what she and Crystal had created and hoped the judges recognized the essence of the winter wonderland it portrayed.

"Maybe a little." Crystal rocked her head from side to side as they crossed the street to the gazebo centered in the middle of the town square. "I've never taken part in a Christmas contest before."

"Well, you're about to take part in another one after the judges announce the winner." Janie pointed to the sign that said *Snowman Building Contest at 1:00 p.m.*

"I love creating snowmen." Crystal squealed. "It was one of my favorite winter activities when I lived in upstate New York."

"Well, if we win the window contest, you can bet Sue and Mason will be coming in strong with a snowman."

"I'm always game for some good competition."

"I bet you are." Janie chuckled and squeezed her hand.

Crystal glanced around. "What about Beka and Ben? Will they enter as well?"

"Always do." Janie nodded. "They have it down to a science by practicing with the kids in the front yard whenever there's a good snow."

"That doesn't sound quite fair. Maybe we should've been practicing instead of doing other things."

"Absolutely not." Janie grinned. "I'd forfeit any contest that required giving up *other things*."

"Duly noted." Crystal smiled widely.

When they arrived at the gazebo, all the judges were waiting, as were the other store owners. Three tripods held posters, each covered by a piece of black cloth with the town seal printed on it as usual.

"I wish they'd hurry up. The suspense is killing me." Crystal was squeezing Janie's hand so tight she thought it might go numb at any minute.

"Me too." Janie glanced around and gave Sue and Mason a nod. She liked to keep the competition friendly. Personally, she wouldn't be disappointed if their display lost, but she wanted the win for Crystal. She'd done all the design and deserved the recognition.

Dana stepped out in front of the tripods holding the traditional award envelopes in her hand. "All right. Everyone gather 'round." She thumbed through the envelopes and held one up. "Third place goes to Rod's Liquor Barrel." Everyone clapped as one of the judges removed the cloth from the first poster.

"Woohoo!" Rod shouted as he rushed up to receive his prize from Dana.

Dana moved to the next tripod and held up another envelope. "Second place goes to..." She glanced at Crystal, and Janie's stomach dropped. Then she flipped her glance to Sue and Mason. "Sue's Sweets." The judge yanked the cloth from the second poster.

Sue grinned as she hurried up to accept her prize envelope. She gave Janie and Crystal a thumbs-up as she walked back to Mason. Sue was a good friend.

They either won or didn't place entirely. Janie hoped for the win.

Crystal squeezed Janie's hand tighter. "Cross your fingers."

"I can't. You've killed them." She chuckled.

"Use your other hand." Crystal grinned and loosened her grip.

Dana held up the last envelope. "First place in the Pine Grove Christmas Window Decorating contest goes to"—Dana turned to look at the poster—"Cyber Shack." She shouted as the judge pulled the cloth from the poster.

"You did it." Crystal threw her arms around Janie and bounced with happiness. "Go get your prize."

"No. We did it." Janie took her hand and tugged her into the gazebo.

"Congratulations. Great job." Dana pulled them each into a hug. "Now Crystal will have to come back and defend your title next year."

Crystal looked at Janie and smiled gently. "I guess I will."

Dana immediately held her arms in the air like she was directing an airplane to the runway. "Now everyone who's entered the snowman-building contest, get over there. It's about to begin."

The crowd moved that way, but Janie needed a moment to take in the win, and how excited Crystal was about it. "We can split this."

She held up the envelope. "I really couldn't have done this without you."

"Use my half on the kids." Crystal didn't blink an eye.

"You sure?" It was a generous gift and would really go a long way in helping grant wishes.

"Absolutely sure." Crystal smiled. "I want them to have it."

"You're really something, you know that?" Janie tugged her close and gave her a quick kiss. "You up for a little snowman building?"

"Absolutely." Crystal snaked her arm around Janie's waist and tucked herself under Janie's arm. "Lead the way."

The announcer read the rules to the entrants. "All entrants are given three sections of the snowman, but you can make them as unique as you want. You don't have to stick with a traditional snowman. You can also build animals, people, or famous characters. However, you must build your snowman in your own designated area between one and three p.m. and use only the items given in the teams' common area. As usual, you'll have hats, scarves, branches, carrots, rocks, and many other items to accessorize a snowman appropriately." He held up a starter gun and looked at his watch. "Five, four, three, two, one." He fired the gun, and everyone scrambled toward the common area.

Crystal stopped and read the sign at the entrance. "All entries must be appropriate for public display." She widened her eyes. "I just wish I knew the story behind the need for this to be posted."

Janie laughed. "It's a doozy. I'll tell you later." She grabbed several branches and a handful of rocks. "I'll leave the hat, scarf, and nose picking to you." She grinned, knowing Crystal would get the corny pun.

"I prefer to do my nose picking in private, thank you." Crystal pilfered through the hats and scarves, some of which she remembered seeing at Ann's Vintage Mall when she'd been shopping earlier in the week.

"Grab some Twizzlers too." Janie shot over her shoulder. "They make great lips."

"What if I want to eat them?" Crystal grabbed a package, opened it, and put one in her mouth.

"Just save a couple for the snowman, babe." Janie was already working on the buttons.

Babe. Crystal had never really been fond of that term of endearment, but it didn't sound so bad coming from Janie. She dropped the rest of the accessories onto the ground next to the snowman.

Janie glanced over at the pile. "Did you bring a vest, by any chance?"

"I didn't see one."

"Damn it. They usually only have a few of them. Sue and Beka must have gotten to them first."

Crystal stood back and stared at the snowballs.

"What are you thinking?" Janie stared at Crystal as she seemed to be working an idea in her head.

"Do you think we can split the large snowball in half and use it for a table?" She sorted through a couple of the branches and created a square on the ground with a couple of sides sticking up.

"I see what you're getting at. A computer table with the snowman plucking the keyboard." Janie had never been that inventive.

"Exactly." She ran back to the common area and returned with a black, loosely knitted scarf and pressed it into the flat area of the snowball. "Looks like a keyboard, right?"

"It does." Janie fished around in the branches and found a couple of thicker pieces, broke them into somewhat equal sizes, and lined them up behind the scarf. "Laptop complete." She held her hand up for a high-five, and Crystal slapped it.

They quickly assembled the shortened snowman, and Crystal began accessorizing it with a scarf and earmuffs that looked like headphones, while Janie created the face with rocks for eyes, a carrot for the nose, and Twizzlers for the mouth.

Janie wandered over to Sue and Mason's snowman, and Crystal followed. "Ah, heck. They're going to win for sure."

"Don't give up yet. I think we really have a shot." Crystal flipped her gaze from one snowman to the other.

"Look at that. It's great." Janie pointed to Sue and Mason's entry. They'd created the perfect snowman, wearing a chef's hat and coat. Somehow, they'd been able to fasten a plastic bowl on a makeshift hip, with one spindly arm holding it and the other holding a spoon in the bowl.

Crystal leaned into Janie. "It is kind of awesome, but so is ours." She snaked her arm around Janie's waist. "Even if they do win this one, *you* got the trophy for the window contest, and that prize is way better."

"Right." Janie rolled her eyes at herself. "Can't be too greedy, can we?"

"Well, I didn't say that. We absolutely can." Crystal cupped her mouth with her hand and lowered her voice. "We just can't be sore losers in public."

Janie couldn't hold back her laughter. Crystal was the sweetest, but she seemed to have an evil streak that Janie really liked.

The judges went from section to section taking notes as they walked. They got all the way to Sue and Mason's, then backtracked to hers and Crystal's.

"Looks like it's going to be a close call." Crystal grinned and started squeezing the life out of Janie's hand again.

Janie gave Crystal a sideways smile. "I might not be able to use those fingers later if you don't stop that."

Crystal loosened her grip. "Well, we don't want that."

The judges tore off the top page from their small pad and handed it to Dana, who read each one of them. "Third place goes to Janie and Crystal."

"Third. What the heck?" Crystal whispered before she strolled up to get the prize envelope.

"There's a gift certificate for a nice dinner at the Pine Grove Diner in there." Dana handed Crystal the envelope. "You and Janie can use it before you head home tomorrow."

"Thanks." Crystal's stomach twisted. Dana had given her a realistic reminder of how impermanent their union was.

"Second place goes to Sue and Mason." She held out the envelope to Sue as she approached.

Crystal seemed confused. "If we're second and third, who's first?"

Janie pointed to the intricately sculpted panda in the square adjacent to the baker. "Practice makes perfect, and everyone loves pandas."

Dana held up the last envelope. "First place goes to the reigning champs, Beka and Ben."

Beka grinned as she rushed up to get her prize, then walked quickly over to Janie and Crystal. "We all know who the champs are, but really great job on yours." She spun and headed to Ben, waving the envelope in the air.

"What's first prize?"

"Dinner and a night at the inn." Janie bit her bottom lip. "Hope she doesn't expect me to babysit." She laughed. "Speaking of that, let's get you back there, so you can rest before the ball tonight." She laced her fingers with Crystal's and walked across the street.

"I need a nice long bath to help me warm up." Crystal bumped up against her. "Want to join me?"

"I wish I could. I have to check in at the shack before I head home, shower, and make myself look dapper enough to escort the most beautiful woman at the ball."

"You don't have to do that. You're already gorgeous."

The heat rose in Janie's cheeks. No matter how many times Crystal complimented her, she still wasn't accustomed to it.

CHAPTER TWENTY-SIX

Janie had tried on at least a half dozen pairs of pants. She'd gained a few pounds over the past year and hadn't realized how tight everything was going to fit. She finally pulled the last suit from the back of her closet and wiped the dust from the shoulders. It wasn't stylish or modern, like Crystal dressed, but it would have to do. It was charcoal gray with a subtle crosshatch pattern that she'd forgotten about. Once she had it on, it felt pretty good. She debated whether to wear anything around her neck, tried on a few ties, including her traditional candy-cane-striped favorite, but decided to go with a mock-collared cream-colored formal button-down. She fished out her black wingtip shoes from the bottom of the closet and put them on before she assessed herself in the mirror that was attached to the back of the bedroom door. She didn't look half bad after all.

Just in case Crystal was in the mood for a nightcap after the ball, she grabbed a bottle of red wine from the rack in the kitchen and slipped it into her overnight bag. She reached into the refrigerator and took out the vase of flowers she'd picked up on the way home. It had been difficult to get them since Crystal had been with her pretty much all the time, but she'd managed to phone Dana this morning when she'd snuck out of bed to make coffee. Dana had been happy to order the flowers for her and advised her to go with a mixture of red and white roses, with just a touch of baby's breath. She stood back and looked at them. Dana was right; they were beautiful.

She locked the door as she left and loaded everything into the back seat of the Jeep, being careful to stabilize the vase on the floorboard. It was a short drive, but she wanted everything to be perfect tonight. Parking was sparse when she arrived at the Pine Grove Inn. Clearly she'd taken too much time trying to figure out what to wear. She drove around the back to the small connecting lot. The sign at the entrance said *Employees Only*. Dana usually had no problem with Janie parking in the employee lot if there was an open spot. She killed the engine, got out of the Jeep, and checked her suit before she leaned down and looked in the side mirror. This was as good as it was going to get. She pulled open the back door, gathered her things before she collected the flowers, and went in the back entrance. The lobby was busy, so it was easy to slip behind one of the large columns and up the stairs before Dana could see her and pull her into a conversation.

With the vase in one hand and her overnight bag in the other, Janie tried to settle herself before she knocked on Crystal's door. She was more nervous tonight than she had ever been before, probably because Crystal was flying home tomorrow, and this was possibly their last night together. She didn't know how to make a long-distance relationship work or even if it would, but she was willing to try. She planned to tell Crystal about that decision tonight.

When Crystal opened the door, Janie had to catch her breath. Dressed in a form-fitting, long-sleeve dark green scoop-neck velvet dress, Crystal was stunning with her blond hair pinned up elegantly and just a few curly strands hanging down on each side. The contrasting, creamy skin covering her collarbone made memories of kissing her way across it fill Janie's mind. She shook the thought from her head and tried to calm herself as she stood in the doorway. "You look positively radiant tonight."

"You look pretty dashing yourself." Crystal's gaze roamed her from head to toe.

"Well, thank you." Janie entered the room.

"These are beautiful." Crystal took the vase and set it on the dresser. "I'll just be a few more minutes." The sexy, sideways glance Crystal gave her as she turned toward the bathroom sent a jolt directly between her legs that practically knocked her off her feet. This was going to be the longest event ever.

Janie watched the slow sway of Crystal's hips as she walked across the room, then dropped her overnight bag next to the bed.

Crystal returned to the room and crossed it quickly to Janie. "Just one more thing before we head downstairs." Crystal slipped her hands under Janie's suit coat and tugged her closer. Crystal's lips captured her mouth, and she swept her tongue gently across the inside of Janie's lip before diving inside, mingling with hers—touching, baiting, and making Janie want to abandon the ball altogether. Janie didn't think it was possible to want Crystal more than she already did, but Crystal was slowly and methodically proving her wrong.

"I think we should be late." Janie held Crystal's hips against her.

"I think we should be on time and leave early. Once I have you in that bed, I won't want to leave it."

"Maybe we should skip the ball altogether."

"Your grandma's been practicing all week for this. She would never forgive you."

Janie blew out a breath as she dropped her head back and stared at the ceiling. "You're so right. She'd come looking for us."

Crystal covered her mouth when a huge laugh escaped her lips. "I bet she would."

Janie moved aside and placed her hand on the small of Crystal's back. "Wouldn't that be awkward?" She reached forward and opened the door.

Crystal assessed her again. "Not that you don't look perfect, but I kind of expected you to add some sort of Christmas accessory."

Janie held out her foot and pulled at her pant leg to allow the red and white to show. "Santa socks."

"Nice." Crystal gave her a sexy smile. "Do they match your underwear?"

"You'll have to find that out for yourself later."

"I can't wait." Crystal took her hand and squeezed. "Now let's get downstairs and make an entrance."

No problem there. At this point, Janie would follow Crystal just about anywhere.

Chapter Twenty-Seven

Crystal was amazed when they entered the Pine Grove Inn banquet room. It was decorated in the most beautiful holiday style—like something straight out of a Christmas movie. The ballroom had been transitioned from a traditional columned, white-walled space with framed windows and wrought-iron chandeliers into something spectacular. Crystal had peered into the space earlier in the week and found it to be plain and vast. Now, with nearly the full room wrapped in luxurious white sheers, the texture and movement in the space resembled that of a winter wonderland. The whole transformation was amazing.

Blue up-lighting set the icy tone from floor to ceiling, with white snowflake projections reflecting on the sheers creating the perfect snowfall effect. The shining white dance floor centered the room and was surrounded by the glow of white-linen-dressed round tables set around it. Tables of different heights topped with red tablecloths and small tea lights added layers to break up the room. Cocktail-height, mirror-topped mingle tables centered with miniature poinsettia plants were a delightful focal point in the corners of the space. The red leaves of the plants added just enough color to make the corners pop.

A white-paneled glow bar, at the opposite end from the dance floor, fit in perfectly with the icy-white rope lighting that lined the edges of the wall. The whole combination of elements set the perfect holiday mood, as the sheers took in the luminescent effects of their surroundings and grabbed the light.

Crystal scanned the room, her gaze skidding to a stop on Jack, who was already at the bar having a drink with Bob. Most likely celebrating the fruits of her efforts. She had been avoiding contact since she'd snuck away to meet with them briefly yesterday and didn't realize they would be coming to the ball as well.

"Shall we get a drink?" Janie was always very attentive.

"How about we find a table first?" Crystal squeezed Janie's arm and led her to one of the corner tables away from the bar. "Somewhere away from the crowd."

"I'll get us something. Porter or wine for you?"

Crystal nodded, barely taking her gaze from her boss and coworker as they mingled.

"Which one?" Janie seemed to notice her staring. "You sure you don't want to come with me?"

"Sorry. White wine tonight." She would have one glass and switch to water. She planned to stay as far away from the bar as possible.

"Okay. I'll be right back."

Crystal watched Mason intercept Janie on the way, talking as they walked together. Once at the bar, he seemed to be introducing her to Bob and Jack. A rush of heat hit her neck, and she fanned herself with her clutch. She continued to watch them interact—all of them. Their interchange seemed friendly. Hands were shaken and smiles exchanged as they interacted.

After a few minutes of conversation, Janie came across the room with their drinks and took the seat adjacent to Crystal. "Well, that was a surprise."

"What?" Crystal snapped her gaze to Janie, hoping they hadn't said anything about her.

"Apparently Mason is on board with all the technology now. You know the guy you were talking to yesterday?"

She tilted her head and squinted, trying not to let on that she knew him.

"The one who bought the mistletoe?"

"Oh, yeah. Right."

"They work for Spark Broadband and Wireless."

"Really? So, what made Mason change his mind?"

"They've promised to provide funding for the hockey team—skates, pads, helmets, sticks, jerseys—and to do a major renovation on the stadium."

"That's awesome." She knew it was wrong, but she just played along like she had no knowledge of the pitch and promises they'd made to the council.

"That's not even the best part. They offered to build a community center *and* put in a food bank."

"Everything we've talked about is coming true."

"Seems so." Crystal sipped her wine. Apparently, Jack was playing his part well—acting as though he were the one sent out to make the deal.

"I wish I'd had a chance to sit in on the meeting, but it sounds like they got it all wrapped up." Janie stared across the room at the group at the bar.

"Does the council have to vote on it?" Crystal needed to know if it was a done deal.

"That's only a formality. Mason's calling an emergency meeting tomorrow morning at the bakery before Jack and Bob leave, so they can present all the facts."

Crystal was taking a chance just playing along like she didn't know them—acting like she had no inkling about the deal. She wanted one more blissful night with Janie before she found out—before Janie hated her. She should've gone along with Janie when she'd suggested skipping the ball entirely.

Dana rushed across the room and sat at the table. "I saw you at the bar with Mason and the two broadband fellows." Dana glanced from Crystal to Janie. "I'm glad to see that you two are still getting along really well."

Shit. Crystal had been waiting for the other shoe to come careening across the room and drop in her lap. Dana was about to let it fly.

"We sure are." Janie covered Crystal's hand with hers.

"I'd have thought you'd have had issues with Crystal after you found out she worked for Spark." Dana was either oblivious to what she was doing or couldn't stop herself from being in the middle of everyone's business.

"You work for Spark?" Janie's smile faded. "With Jack and Bob?"

Dana's eyes went wide. "You haven't told her yet?"

Janie slid her hand from Crystal's and shifted in her chair. "You've been here all this time trying to convince me to follow my own dreams, and it's all been about sealing a deal for broadband?"

"Janie. No." Crystal's heart pounded and leapt to her throat. "Not at all. It might have started that way, but all that changed when I met you."

"Spark is in Texas. Do you even live in California?" Janie had done her research.

"I did before I moved to Dallas. My family still lives there." She watched Janie's eyes widen as she veered her gaze to Dana. "Don't look at her." She reached for Janie's hand, but she slid it farther away. "It's not Dana's fault. I asked her to go along with my story—all of it." Dana had blown it for her, but she wasn't the one who'd started the lies.

"You knew why she's here? Is she even your niece?" Janie's voice rose.

"She's not my aunt. When I checked in at the inn and told her why I was here, she offered to help." Crystal had done this—all of it.

Dana shook her head. "I'm sorry, Janie. I didn't think you were going to get all involved with her." She seemed to realize she wasn't an innocent party.

"Thanks for being such a great friend." Janie stood and took off across the dance floor.

"Hey," Dana called after her. "It wasn't even about that. I just wanted better internet and Wi-Fi." She looked at Crystal. "You'd think I just told her I ran into her Jeep without insurance."

"I'm afraid it's much worse than that." Crystal stood, rushed after her, and caught up with her in the lobby. "Janie. Wait."

"You just don't get it, do you?" Janie stopped and turned. "It's not about the money. It's about the community."

"But you said yourself you didn't agree with the council's

decision." Crystal reached for her. "Don't you see? Dana wants it too. She believes broadband internet and Wi-Fi can help her compete with inns of the same caliber in nearby towns who already have it."

"I don't care what she or anyone else wants. You lied to me from the first moment we met."

"I had to. I didn't know anything about you. I thought you were my opposition...I had no idea we wanted the same things." Crystal couldn't stand that she'd hurt Janie. "Would you have talked to me at all if you'd known I'd come here to announce that my company intended to build and operate a Wi-Fi broadband network? To put up a tower on your family's land? To offer broadband service to residents of Pine Grove that might shut down Cyber Shack?" Everything was out in the open now.

"You know I wouldn't have." The pain was clear in Janie's eyes.

"Then I would've never gotten to know this town and the people the way I did. Even worse, I would've never gotten to know you."

"I should've never trusted you—and definitely shouldn't have slept with you."

"Don't say that. That would've been the worst mistake of my life."

"Instead, letting you in is the worst mistake of *my* life."

"All I can do is stand here and hope that you believe me. I'm just so very sorry that we didn't meet under different circumstances."

"And now I wish we'd never met at all."

Janie rushed out the door. She was gone, and it was Crystal's fault that she wasn't coming back. She grabbed hold of the wall, the pain in her heart more than she could take. She'd never felt so strongly for anyone before, and she'd ruined it all.

Chapter Twenty-Eight

Janie slid into the driver's seat, fired the engine, and pressed her head to the steering wheel. She shook as sobs spilled out of her as she tried to catch her breath. She couldn't drive—she couldn't do anything except cry at this very moment. She'd known she would have to say good-bye to Crystal because she lived so far away. But she had no clue that Crystal had been lying to her since she got to town—lied to her about everything. She wiped her face with her palms, put the car into gear, and drove.

By the time Janie reached the tree farm, the crying had stopped, but her head was spinning with the newly discovered information about Crystal, not to mention that it was the only reason she'd come to Pine Grove. She thought about the phone message from Marie that Crystal had received the day before. Had Crystal lied about having a girlfriend as well? Was anything she'd ever told her true? She had no idea who the real Crystal was—who she'd actually fallen in love with.

Her jaw clenched as she knocked on the door to the cabin and waited. Nate wasn't one to dance, so he didn't usually attend the Santa Ball unless the girl he was dating at the time roped him into it. Since he was single at the moment, she hoped he was home and not out at a bar somewhere.

The door swung open, and Nate stood before her in gray sweats and a white T-shirt. "What are you doing here? I thought you'd be at the ball with that new sweetheart of yours."

"I was, but then her boss showed up." Janie brushed past him into the cabin.

"Her boss?" Nate scrunched his eyebrows together, clearly confused at her deliberate vagueness. "Her boss is here from California?"

"From Texas. She's been lying to me since she got here."

"About what?" He gave the door a shove and let it swing closed.

"Her hidden agenda." Janie raked her fingers through her hair. "She works for Spark Wireless."

"Holy shit. Really?" Nate was just as surprised as Janie had been. "I don't remember her mentioning wireless at all when I was around her."

"She did to me. A couple of times, but just casually." She flopped onto the couch. "She told me she was an interior designer." She shook her head. "I'm such an idiot."

"You had no reason not to believe her." He went to the refrigerator and took out a couple of beers.

"As far as I knew she was in town visiting Dana." She bolted to her feet and took off her suit jacket. "That's another thing. They're not related at all. She convinced Dana to go along with her when she first got here."

Nate handed her a beer. "Huh. The woman's got some mad imposter skills. I thought she was legit."

"Yeah. Me too. Here I was trying to figure out how I can see more of her, only to find out she's probably going to ghost me as soon as she leaves town."

"You still want to see her, though, don't you?" Nate could always read her.

Janie nodded. "This thing between us has all been a crazy fantasy." She took a long pull on her beer.

"You gonna talk to her before she leaves?"

"I don't know if I can right now. I'm too angry." And hurt— so hurt. She set her beer on the coffee table and laced her fingers together. "She weaved herself into my life to find out all about the town and the people who live here. She fed all that information to her boss, and they've got Mason ready to vote in favor of changing the ordinance to allow broadband and Wi-Fi. He's called an emergency meeting for tomorrow morning."

"I know you're not pissed about the technology. You've been back and forth on that issue for a long time. So, it's just about Crystal."

"I guess it is." No matter how mad she was at Crystal for lying, she was still in love with her.

"You can have the bedroom. I'll take the couch." Nate flopped onto the couch next to her, turned on the TV, clicked through the channels, and landed on *Die Hard*, his favorite Christmas movie. Totally appropriate for the way she was feeling.

❖

As Bob and Jack gave their spiel to the council, Crystal stared out the window, watching for Janie. They were halfway into the discussion, so it was clear she wasn't coming, wasn't going to talk to Crystal before she got on the plane in a couple of hours. She'd planned on one last romantic night with Janie after the ball, but everything had blown up in her face—and it was her own fault.

After the meeting ended, Bob sat beside Crystal and held out a cup of coffee to her. "I like this little town. I think I'll come back soon." He sipped his coffee. "You came up with a good plan, and I'm happy to invest in it." He bumped her shoulder. "I'm ready to invest in you as well. Congratulations on becoming the new director of East Coast Sales."

That news did nothing for her. Her heart was still in her throat, and it probably would be for quite some time. "I'm going to head back to the inn and grab my stuff." She stood. "I'll meet you at the airport."

"Our flight's not until later." Bob relaxed in his chair. "Take the week and enjoy your family in California. I'll see you in the office after that." He winked. "You did a great job here."

"Thanks." Not that she could enjoy anything right now, but time with her family would help her. She needed some unconditional love.

When Crystal got to her room, she sat at the desk and wrote a letter to Janie. It was clear that was the only way she could communicate with her.

Janie,

I'm so sorry for all the pain I've caused you. It was clear to me from the start how much you love the Pine Grove community, and how much you love your family. I never intended to hurt you. I never intended to fall in love with you either. If you believe nothing else, please know all of that was real. I hope you can forgive me someday.

All my love, Crystal

She stopped at the front desk. "Can you spare an envelope?"

"Sure." Dana opened a drawer, took one out, and handed it to her.

Crystal slid the folded letter into the envelope and sealed it before she wrote Janie's name on the front and slipped it into Janie's overnight bag, which she'd left in Crystal's room. Her stomach clenched when she saw a bottle of wine. Apparently, Janie had planned a much different evening last night as well. She set the bag on the counter. "Can you give this to Janie?" She rummaged around in her purse and found the diner gift certificate they had won at the snowman contest. "This as well." She handed it to Dana.

"Sure." Dana took the bag and the certificate and set them behind the counter. "Listen. I'm sorry about last night. You know, blowing everything for you."

"Not your fault. I should've been more transparent from the beginning." She wrote her cell number on the pad sitting on the counter and pushed it to Dana. "That's my number. In case you…or anyone else wants to call."

"I'll let her know." Dana smiled. "It was good getting to know you, kid. I'm sorry it turned out the way it did with Janie." She walked her to the door. "Give her some time. She'll come around."

"I doubt that will happen, but thanks for the encouragement."

Crystal hoped but didn't plan to see Janie any time in the future. She'd burned that thread through completely.

"Either way, come back and see us sometime." Dana pulled her into a hug. "You can have a night on me. Give me some advance notice, though. We might be booked, considering we could have Wi-Fi by then."

"Will do." Crystal went out the door to the Uber she'd called for earlier. The driver was the same guy who'd brought her to town.

He loaded her luggage in the back before he got in and fired the engine. "How was your stay?"

"It turned out much differently than I'd thought it would." She'd never imagined finding the perfect woman and losing her all in the same trip.

"Glad to hear it." He glanced in the rearview mirror. "Be sure to tell your friends about us."

"Don't worry. I'll spread the word."

The ride was short and the conversation sparse. Crystal was mentally exhausted. She thanked the driver for taking her bags inside and passing them off to his twin behind the counter before she found a seat.

Crystal's heart felt heavy as she sat at the tiny little airport waiting for the tiny little plane to take her away from this tiny little town. She hadn't followed Janie last night when she'd left her standing in the doorway. She hadn't tried to call. She'd done absolutely nothing to try to convince Janie that she wasn't a complete shit because she wasn't convinced herself. She'd had plenty of chances to come clean and tell Janie why she'd come to town, and she hadn't. In her book, that was the exact definition of a complete shit.

CHAPTER TWENTY-NINE

Janie sifted through the letters from Santa and matched the inventory she'd received last week to each request. She'd been able to grant all their wishes except for the Camaro for a dad, which she didn't have the inclination or funds to grant. At the last minute she'd also secured an older game deck for Noah to play games at home with his mom late at night after work. She'd had to outbid someone several times.

The fact that she'd been able to provide food for a family in need warmed her heart. She remembered how much fun she'd had with Crystal shopping, then stocking the storeroom with all the extra supplies they'd received. It had taken them longer than she anticipated due to their multiple kissing breaks. She'd never be able to enter the storeroom again without feeling that bliss. She would send in Beka or Tara until she was able to wipe it from her mind, but she didn't know if she was ready to forget it yet.

She moved to the coffee bar, poured herself a cup, and took a swig. Her tongue burned, but she didn't care. She needed the caffeine today.

Sue came through the door with a box of pastries. "You forgot to pick these up this morning."

"Yeah. I saw the bakery was full." Janie had pulled into a slot in front of the shack before she'd gotten out and walked slowly down the street to the bakery, where the emergency council meeting was being held. Her pace became slower as she neared. She'd been only one store away before she turned and went back to the shack. She couldn't talk to Crystal—she wasn't ready. Didn't know if she'd ever be ready. Her heart was shattered, and that was going to take a lot of time to heal.

"You missed the council meeting." Sue's tone lowered.

Janie opened the pastry box and began placing her selections in the case. "You didn't need me there." Mason had called and told her the council had taken the vote without her, and it had passed unanimously. She would've given them her support anyway.

"We could've used the vote. Earl gave Mason an earful, but that was the only opposition." Sue pulled her gloves from her fingers and dropped them onto the counter. "Probably afraid Darlene will leave him for someone she meets online."

"You might be right. Can I get you something hot for the walk back?"

"Give me one of those lattes Crystal always ordered. I kind of like them." Sue planted her elbows on the counter. "They're going to do a lot for the town." Sue covered Janie's hand with hers. "You know that's because of Crystal, right?"

"Right." Janie turned and prepared the latte.

"I think she had good intentions."

"Whatever her intentions were, a whole lot of lying was involved." Janie pushed the latte across the counter.

"I know." Sue patted her hand. "I think you're forgetting about your recent change of heart surrounding Wi-Fi. You'd been kind of uncertain for a while. Crystal might not have been truthful about her job, but I think she honestly cares for you." She turned and headed out the door. On her way out, she glanced at the clock on the wall. "She might still be at the airport. You could probably catch her if you wanted to."

That wasn't going to happen. She wasn't up for more turmoil this holiday season. As it was, everything she did reminded her of Crystal now. Janie had let her life completely revolve around her for the past week and a half. She took a deep breath to hold the tears at bay. Life would go on. Was Sue right, though? Would she have held out if the time she'd spent with Crystal hadn't softened her? If Crystal hadn't learned about the community's needs from Janie and brought them to the negotiating table? That she would never know.

CHAPTER THIRTY

As the sun took its brightness away, Crystal sat in the darkness on the couch at her parents' house and stared at the multicolored lights dressing the gorgeous nine-foot Christmas tree. The joy Crystal usually got from spending Christmas with her family just wasn't there. She'd had breakups before the holidays in the past, but the yearning for something more had never impacted her mood like this. Spending time with her family and the Christmas holiday in all its spectacular glory was always able to bring her out of her sadness. She'd been able to push whatever was haunting her aside and just be in the moment to enjoy the few days she had with everyone.

"Are you going to tell me what's bothering you?" Her mother stood in the entrance from the kitchen, her silhouette perfectly outlined by the kitchen backlighting.

"I hurt someone, Mom."

"Marie?"

"How did you know about Marie?" She'd never shared that relationship with her family because she hadn't thought of it as permanent.

"She called here several times last week looking for you." Her mother crossed the room and sat on the couch next to her.

"She broke it off with me. I'm just not willing to try with her again." The stability she'd felt with Janie in only a couple of weeks far outweighed the tumultuous months she'd spent with Marie. "I guess I hurt her too." She hadn't taken any responsibility for her part in that.

"Then who? The woman you met in Vermont?"

Crystal nodded. "I went for work, and I met the perfect woman. Only problem was that she was one of the holdouts."

"But something must've changed, or you wouldn't have gotten close to her."

"I lied to her, Mom. From the first moment I met her, everything I said to her, told her about myself, was a total lie, and I hate myself for it." Crystal couldn't suppress the tears that began streaming down her face.

"Oh, honey." The cardboard box rattled as her mom plucked a few tissues from it, then daubed Crystal's cheeks with them. "Did you lie about your feelings for her?"

Crystal shook her head. "No. I never lied about that. Everything that happened between us was real."

"Do you think it was real for her as well?"

"It felt like it. We had an amazing time together. I ignored all the facts about what I'd done because I didn't want it to end."

"Then why are you here, and not back in Vermont telling her this?"

"She found out the truth about me from someone else before I told her. I tried to explain, but she was so angry, she wouldn't listen. Now she won't talk to me." Crystal swiped the remaining tears away with her palms. She'd called the shack several times, but Janie wasn't answering and wouldn't come to the phone.

"I'm sure that anger was fueled by hurt." Warmth spread through Crystal as her mom put her arm around her and tucked her in close. "She probably feels about the same way you do right now."

"Maybe." Crystal relaxed against her mom's shoulder. "But I can't fix it if she won't listen to me."

"You can't fix it, honey. It's out of your control now. She's going to have to decide if she can forgive you and move past it." Her mom's voice was soft.

"I don't know how I was going to make it work anyway. She lives two thousand miles away from where I do."

"Yet, knowing that, you still let yourself fall in love with her."

"I did. I was living in some kind of Norman Rockwell fantasy. Dreaming of living in a small town, knowing everyone in the community." She sat up and shifted toward her mom. "Janie knows everyone in Pine Grove and treats them like they're her family. Once I got to know them too, I found things Spark can do to help the town—fix their hockey arena, build a community center that can provide food for the less-privileged. Bob agreed to do it all if they signed the contract, and they did."

"Sounds like you did some good for Pine Grove." Her mom smiled.

"I think I did." Crystal shrugged. "Bob promoted me to Director of East Coast Sales. I've wanted that position for so long, Mom, but having it doesn't feel good at all."

Her mom patted her on the leg. "So, once you get this worked out with Janie, I'll fly to Dallas and help you pack your stuff for the move to Vermont."

That thought sent a tingle through her before the sinking feeling took her again. "I can't do that. My job is in Dallas."

"Is that really the job you want?" Her mom brushed her thumb across Crystal's cheek before she tucked a strand of hair behind Crystal's ear with her fingers. "You just told me a very different story."

"I don't know." Crystal let her head fall back and stared at the Christmas lights reflecting off the ceiling. "But moving to Vermont is a big deal. It's so far away from you and Dad."

"What's the difference between there and Dallas?" Her mom shrugged. "It's not like you live close enough to come over for coffee. You still have to get on a plane. Are you glued to a life in Texas?"

"No. Not really. I mean, I have some friends, but I've neglected them enough lately that they probably wouldn't even care if I moved." Crystal had been too focused on work to socialize.

"They'd probably care, but that's not the point." Her mom brushed the hair from Crystal's face. "You're not going to stay just because your friends want you to. You need to make a life with someone, and if Janie is the one you want to do it with, you should tell her that. *Then* if she wants the same, you can both look at the options of being together."

"How do you do that?" Everything made so much more sense now. Her mom had a way of sifting through all the crap.

"What?"

"Make everything sound so simple."

"Because it is. When it comes down to it, your happiness is what's most important." Her mom shook her head. "Not a job, a house, or friends."

"I'm afraid she hates me, though." That was her biggest worry—that Janie wouldn't be able to get past the huge lie she'd told her.

"You'll never know until you tell her how you feel."

"You think I should go now?" Did she really have a chance with Janie? "Austen will be upset."

"I'll take care of your brother. Maybe you can convince her to come back here and spend New Year's Eve with us."

Crystal bolted off the couch. "Cross your fingers for me." Energy coursed through her as a smidge of hope sparked in her heart.

Her mom held up both hands with crossed fingers. "Now get yourself a plane ticket and go get that girl."

She ran up the stairs to her bedroom and turned on her laptop. A ticket was probably going to cost a fortune, but she didn't care. Janie was worth it.

Chapter Thirty-One

Janie helped Beka set up the buffet table in the dining area of the Pine Grove Retirement Home. She'd been up early to pick up both Grandpa and Grandma, take them to her parents' house for Christmas morning breakfast and presents, then deliver them back to the PGR for the midday holiday lunch. Most residents would have family members here, yet some people had none. Other families always brought them into their fold to celebrate. Janie loved this event and would participate, even though it felt different this year.

Beka glanced at the front door. "I'm gonna finish getting the turkey onto the platter in the kitchen."

"Nobody'll be here for another hour."

"I just want to be prepared." Beka rushed past her. "Check the door, will you? I saw someone coming up the walk."

"What? Can't you get it on your way?"

Beka was already in the kitchen. Janie blew out a breath and headed to the door and pulled it open. Standing in front of her was the most beautiful vision—one she thought she'd never see again. "You came back." Janie's heart felt as though it might launch out of her chest.

Crystal smiled softly as she nodded. "I can't leave things between us the way they are."

"You left a pretty long path of destruction." Janie went back to setting up the buffet table. She needed some distance.

"I'd like to fix that, if I can." Crystal stepped inside but didn't follow Janie. "I'm sure by now you know that Bob is my boss."

"Yep. I figured as much. Mason told me about the donation." No matter how mixed up Janie was about Crystal, she was thankful for what she'd secured for the community.

"He's offered me a director position."

"I guess that'll be a good promotion from your interior-designer position." Janie couldn't help saying that. The lie Crystal had told her still stung.

"I deserved that." Crystal nodded slowly. "But I truly feel that wireless doesn't have to push people apart." She shrugged. "You can use it to bring people together." She stepped forward. "Cyber Shack could be so much bigger. You know that." She reached into her bag and took out a long, rolled-up piece of paper. "With the donated money from Spark you can turn the shack into part of the community center, with a food bank branching off next door, and still keep the café to feed those who can and can't pay." She unrolled the paper onto an empty section of the buffet table. "The community center and food bank will provide plenty of new jobs for the people of Pine Grove to fill. You can accomplish so much for everyone in this community."

"Looks like you have it all worked out." Janie's heart was ready to explode as she looked at the plan Crystal had mocked up. Crystal really was a good person—her person.

Crystal's eyes welled with tears. "You might never forgive me, but I wouldn't forgive myself if I didn't tell you how much you mean to me…how much the time we've spent together has changed me." She shook her head slowly. "I used to be so driven by my career, money, and all the things I could buy. Once I came to Pine Grove and met you, I realized none of that really matters." Tears filled her eyes. "I was happy just being with you."

When Janie didn't react right away, she could see the disappointment in Crystal's eyes. "You have something wrong." Janie couldn't let Crystal suffer any longer. She rounded the corner of the table and took Crystal into her arms. "Any changes I might make to the shack would be our accomplishment. I can't do it without you—I don't want to."

"I'm so glad to hear you say that." Tears streamed from Crystal's eyes. "Because I declined the director position in Dallas."

Janie pushed back and stared into Crystal's eyes. "You did?"

Crystal nodded. "I did. I'm going to be the sales rep for this region, so I can get the community center and food bank up and running." She smiled softly. "I'll be staying here in town for the foreseeable future, if that's okay with you?"

"It's absolutely okay. It's perfect." She held Crystal close, couldn't believe this was happening. All her dreams were coming true, and the biggest one of all was having someone to love who loved her enough to see what was really important to her.

"Yay. Looks like you two got it all worked out." Beka's voice boomed through the room. "Now let's get this food on the table before the hungry visitors arrive and eat us alive."

"Can I help?" Crystal wiped the tears from her cheeks.

"Of course. Grandma will be glad to see you." Janie kissed her softly. She didn't want to do anything without Crystal ever again.

EPILOGUE

Crystal watched Janie put the finishing touches on the new sign to display in the window of Cyber Spark and Sprinkles, the new name for the café that fit the space well. They had a floor plan similar to the previous one for Cyber Shack, only the coffee bar had been moved to the back, and they had a larger eating area for general food orders. New doors led to each adjacent space, with the community center on one side and the food pantry on the other. Spark Wireless had funded the year-long renovation as promised, and it turned out to be well worth the time and cost. The name change was due in part to the agreement to include the company name in some way and the new bakery case containing a variety of goods from Sue's Sweets. There was also a small byline below the title that gave Spark credit for the donation.

Everyone ordered food at the counter now, and a roll-top window opened between the café and the community center, so people could order from both areas. Janie had hired at least a dozen new employees just to handle the café alone. She couldn't run the business with just Beka and Tara any longer.

Everything had been completed for the community center yesterday, but they'd been up late into the night putting the finishing touches on the new café. The ribbon was draped across the front of the door for the cutting ceremony. The grand opening of the new café would be happening in less than thirty minutes.

Janie went behind the counter and prepared Crystal her favorite latte. "I have a surprise for you before we go outside." She slid the latte across the counter.

"You know that's not really a surprise anymore. You fix it for me every day."

"Well, that's not the surprise." Janie reached behind her and removed a piece of paper covering the last item on the new menu they'd created. "I added one more thing to the menu. Crystal's Indulgence. Two shots of espresso, a splash of nonfat milk, and a big squirt of caramel."

"My favorite." Crystal warmed inside. "And I'll never have to explain it again."

"Exactly." Janie rounded the counter and gave Crystal a scorching kiss. "I say we go home early and celebrate in our own way tonight."

Crystal shrugged. "Who am I to argue with the boss, but just to be clear, how early is early?"

"As soon as this crowd disperses, we're out of here." Janie held up the new sign and read it aloud. "*Cyber Spark and Sprinkles will now be known as a safe space for those in need. Free coffee, food, and console games for all who don't have money to pay. Donations accepted from those who can afford to contribute.*" She secured it to the window. "Ready?" She held out her hand.

Crystal took Janie's hand and pulled her into her arms. "Thank you for giving me a second chance." It was the only thing she'd wished for last Christmas.

"Thank you for coming back. None of this would've happened if you hadn't." Janie pressed her forehead to Crystal's. "We make a great team."

"Indeed we do." Crystal tugged her toward the door, and out they went to a new beginning for the two of them and the town of Pine Grove. The new additions to the town were destined to make a difference in everyone's lives. But the best part of the whole deal was that they'd done it together.

About the Author

Dena Blake grew up in a small town just north of San Francisco where she learned to play softball, ride motorcycles, and grow vegetables. She eventually moved with her family to the Southwest, where she began creating vivid characters in her mind and bringing them to life on paper.

Dena currently lives in the Southwest with her partner and is constantly amazed at what she learns from her two children. She is a would-be chef, tech nerd, and occasional auto mechanic who has a weakness for dark chocolate and a good cup of coffee.

Books Available From Bold Strokes Books

A Haven for the Wanderer by Jenny Frame. When Griffin Harris comes to Rosebrook village, the love she finds with Bronte de Lacey creates a safe haven and she finally finds her place in the world. But will she run again when their love is tested? (978-1-63679-291-0)

A Spark in the Air by Dena Blake. Internet executive Crystal Tucker is sure Wi-Fi could really help small-town residents, even if it means putting an internet café out of business, but her instant attraction to the owner's daughter, Janie Elliott, makes moving ahead with her plans complicated. (978-1-63679-293-4)

Between Takes by CJ Birch. Simone Lavoie is convinced her new job as an intimacy coordinator will give her a fresh perspective. Instead, problems on set and her growing attraction to actress Evelyn Harper only add to her worries. (978-1-63679-309-2)

Camp Lost and Found by Georgia Beers. Nobody knows better than Cassidy and Frankie that life doesn't always give you what you want. But sometimes, if you're lucky, life gives you exactly what you need. (978-1-63679-263-7)

Fire, Water, and Rock by Alaina Erdell. As Jess and Clare reveal more about themselves, and their hot summer fling tips over into true love, they must confront their pasts before they can contemplate a future together. (978-1-63679-274-3)

Lines of Love by Brey Willows. When even the Muse of Love doesn't believe in forever, we're all in trouble. (978-1-63555-458-8)

Only This Summer by Radclyffe. A fling with Lily promises to be exactly what Chase is looking for—short-term, hot as a forest fire, and one Chase can extinguish whenever she wants. After all, it's only one summer. (978-1-63679-390-0)

Picture-Perfect Christmas by Charlotte Greene. Two former rivals compete to capture the essence of their small mountain town at Christmas, all the while fighting old and new feelings. (978-1-63679-311-5)

Playing Love's Refrain by Lesley Davis. Drew Dawes had shied away from the world of music until Wren Banderas gave her a reason to play their love's refrain. (978-1-63679-286-6)

Profile by Jackie D. The scales of justice are weighted against FBI agents Cassidy Wolf and Alex Derby. Loyalty and love may be the only advantage they have. (978-1-63679-282-8)

Almost Perfect by Tagan Shepard. A shared love of queer TV brings Olivia and Riley together, but can they keep their real-life love as picture perfect as their on-screen counterparts? (978-1-63679-322-1)

The Amaranthine Law by Gun Brooke. Tristan Kelly is being hunted for who she is and her incomprehensible past, and despite her overwhelming feelings for Olivia Bryce, she has to reject her to keep her safe. (978-1-63679-235-4)

Craving Cassie by Skye Rowan. Siobhan Carney and Cassie Townsend share an instant attraction, but are they brave enough to give up everything they have ever known to be together? (978-1-63679-062-6)

Drifting by Lyn Hemphill. When Tess jumps into the ocean after Jet, she thinks she's saving her life. Of course, she can't possibly know Jet is actually a mermaid desperate to fix her mistake before she causes her clan's demise. (978-1-63679-242-2)

Enigma by Suzie Clarke. Polly has taken an oath to protect and serve her country, but when the spy she's tasked with hunting becomes the love of her life, will she be the one to betray her country? (978-1-63555-999-6)

Finding Fault by Annie McDonald. Can environmental activist Dr. Evie O'Halloran and government investigator Merritt Shepherd set aside their conflicting ideas about saving the planet and risk their hearts enough to save their love? (978-1-63679-257-6)

The Forever Factor by Melissa Brayden. When Bethany and Reid confront their past, they give new meaning to letting go, forgiveness, and a future worth fighting for. (978-1-63679-357-3)

The Frenemy Zone by Yolanda Wallace. Ollie Smith-Nakamura thinks relocating from San Francisco to her dad's rural hometown is the worst idea in the world, but after she meets her new classmate Ariel Hall, she might have a change of heart. (978-1-63679-249-1)

Hot Keys by R.E. Ward. In 1920s New York City, Betty May Dewitt and her best friend, Jack Norval, are determined to make their Tin Pan Alley dreams come true and discover they will have to fight—not only for their hearts and dreams, but for their lives. (978-1-63679-259-0)

Securing Ava by Anne Shade. Private investigator Paige Richards takes a case to locate and bring back runaway heiress Ava Prescott. But ignoring her attraction may prove impossible when their hearts and lives are at stake. (978-1-63679-297-2)

A Cutting Deceit by Cathy Dunnell. Undercover cop Athena takes a job at Valeria's hair salon to gather evidence to prove her husband's connections to organized crime. What starts as a tentative friendship quickly turns into a dangerous affair. (978-1-63679-208-8)

As Seen on TV! by CF Frizzell. Despite their objections, TV hosts Ronnie Sharp, a laid-back chef, and paranormal investigator Peyton Stanford have to work together. The public is watching. But joining forces is risky, contemptuous, unnerving, provocative—and ridiculously perfect. (978-1-63679-272-9)

Blood Memory by Sandra Barret. Can vampire Jade Murphy protect her friend from a human stalker and keep her dates with the gorgeous Beth Jenssen without revealing her secrets? (978-1-63679-307-8)

Foolproof by Leigh Hays. For Martine Roberts and Elliot Tillman, friends with benefits isn't a foolproof way to hide from the truth at the heart of an affair. (978-1-63679-184-5)

Glass and Stone by Renee Roman. Jordan must accept that she can't control everything that happens in life, and that includes her wayward heart. (978-1-63679-162-3)

Hard Pressed by Aurora Rey. When rivals Mira Lavigne and Dylan Miller are tapped to co-chair Finger Lakes Cider Week, competition gives way to compromise. But will their sexual chemistry lead to love? (978-1-63679-210-1)